HANNAH BLOOM
DREAM JUGGLER

JACQUIE HERZ

Black Rose Writing | Texas

ISBN: 978-1-68513-680-2
LIBRARY OF CONGRESS CONTROL NUMBER: 2025939710
PUBLISHED BY BLACK ROSE WRITING
www.blackrosewriting.com

Printed in the United States of America
Suggested Retail Price (SRP) $22.95

Hannah Bloom: Dream Juggler is printed in Chaparral Pro

*As a planet-friendly publisher, Black Rose Writing does its best to eliminate unnecessary waste to reduce paper usage and energy costs, while never compromising the reading experience. As a result, the final word count vs. page count may not meet common expectations.

Praise for
Hannah Bloom: Dream Juggler

"An engaging novel on many levels --the plot lines are interesting, the female narrator is very likeable and believable, especially as she struggles to balance her many roles. The details about running a company and the complications that inevitably occur are relatable to anyone in business."
–Evelyn Wajcer, Professor of Literature (Retired) and Business Owner

"A multi-layered novel, Herz does a great job of taking us into Hannah's head and heart and also exploring the complicated nature of both familial and business relationships. A sensitive and timely read!"
–Meryl Ain, Ed.D. Author, *Shadows We Carry* and *The Takeaway Men* and Host, *People of the Book Podcast*

"Ms. Herz describes and develops all her characters in depth and, accordingly, they feel so very real. She integrates a palpable sense of ongoing self-exploration, wondering, questioning, struggling, `dream juggling.' Loved this second work and looking forward to the next!"
–Ellie Aronowitz-Witkes

"I particularly appreciated Hannah's journey and quest for meaning while living a very full meaningful life. Excellent."
–Cindy Pinkus

"What is the subject of our thought? Experience! Nothing else! And if we lose the ground of experience then we get into all kinds of theories."
– Hannah Arendt

HANNAH BLOOM

DREAM JUGGLER

Time after time after time. . .

Buried and forgotten, the nameless rise up from sleep's deepest
gravity and settle into the dusty corners of my muddled wakefulness.
Why do you come? I ask. Is it to help sweep away those strange
feelings and disbeliefs that remain as confusing and mysterious
to me as when I first travelled on the train from Berlin to Prague
and saw a forest of tree trunks all awash in ghostly white, and
hardly even wide enough for the smallest child to hide behind?

Filled with shattered promises and painful
longings, the nameless conjure up fantasies from
long lost sun-drenched afternoons, where springtime
leaves shivered in gentle breezes and the soft blue
shallow pointillist waves licked at sandy shores; but
is this scene, so reminiscent of Seurat's
La Grande Jatte, forever and only bound to his day?

And now that I'm here, in this past's future, I want to
thrash out the old forewarnings, unbury the straw-
covered earth, hunt for the broken, the perished, the
forgotten, and find those worn-out souls traipsing
through mud, while their eyes—sunk deep into
gaunt faces—peer with hope between the twisted
bands of barbed wire.

Always remember us, my ghosts cry out in the dead of
night. *Never again,* they plead in shrill voices. But these
words remain unheeded in a world incapable of reimagining
its past. And here I am, next in line, and frightened by the ugly
rumors portending thunderous times ahead, while my ghosts
remain helpless and locked up in their own era; as if their
damaging world had never even existed.

Never again: A promise. A dream. A fantasy, where
deep in sleep, I dig to unearth the jewels of recollected
memory, wishing to display them for everyone to see, as
I might, an array of twisty-shaped seashells gleaned from the
water's edge: and it's here I discover a forgotten, a raw emptiness,
where once upon a time, a gold bead lay gleaming, but then. . .

. . .the summons of a newborn's cry ruptures my dream.

—Hannah Bloom: Dream Juggler

Chapter One

The clock radio alarm clicks on.

". . . at first, you know, I just heard a wailing . . ." A man's deep, lilting voice booms into the stillness of Hannah and Jake's bedroom. ". . . and when I passed through the platform gate," the voice continues, "I noticed a white Seagram's liquor box sitting in a corner and there, inside it, was a baby, all swaddled up in nothing but yesterday's *Newsday*. God knows for how many hours the poor creature had been there, its face beet-red from hollering its tiny head off."

What a way to come into this life, Hannah thinks, as she turns toward Jake, taps him on the shoulder, and whispers, "Ten more minutes?" She feels him reach out for the snooze button and, thankful for the sudden silence, closes her eyes against the shards of sunlight beginning to sneak in through the narrow gaps in the blinds. Then, what seems like only seconds later, the radio announcer drifts back into her consciousness. "It's going to be a hot one on this twenty-eighth day of July . . ."

And now completely out of the fog of a short sleep, she hears, "Temps are expected to reach the upper eighties by this afternoon, with a potential threat of a thunder shower or two."

She can only groan now as her sleepy, rambling thoughts become suddenly fixed on the contents of the FedEx envelope that had arrived unexpectedly late yesterday afternoon: A poisonous missile from Artie's lawyer's office to Jake and Hannah's. Seeing their full names printed in such an officious manner made the whole situation feel unreal but daunting at the same time, as if the packet of legal papers – *the Answer to the Counterclaims* – were pieces of muddled fiction she had to read over and over, just to make some sense of it all.

The United States District Court, Eastern District of New York

Playful Promotions and Arthur Grossman
Plaintiffs,

-against-

Bloom & Co., and Hannah Bloom and Jacob Bloom
Defendants.

"There's been a crash," she hears, and at once envisions a pile-up of cars, trucks, and SUVs. "So, it's best to avoid the Cross Bronx Expressway if you're heading into Manhattan."

And that's exactly what she'll be doing on this blistering, sultry morning; heading into Manhattan for her mother's seventy-fifth birthday.

•   •   •

The westbound train rattles into the Stamford station. Hannah steps into the first car, finds a row of vacant seats and, after settling into the one by the window, retrieves her battered copy of Hannah Arendt's *Eichmann in Jerusalem* from the bottom of her straw Kenya bag. As she flips through the book to find her place, the photograph of her two young daughters, taken at sleep-away camp, slips out from between the pages – a souvenir for parents on visiting day. She studies their faces. Sighs. And opening her hand, she presses it up against her belly, where her third, barely the size of a peanut, is steadily growing inside her.

Now she frets. Jake insisted he will manage simply fine without her today when he talks to their attorneys about the claims in the lawsuit. Besides, he said, he can always call her if he needs to ask her something.

Trying to redirect her focus back to Arendt's book – her Bic pen poised to write notes to herself as well as to underline strings of words she feels compelled to come back to – she becomes sidetracked again when she hears one of the two young girls in the seat behind her, chatting too loudly about her boyfriend and their breakup. Half amused and very thankful those days are over for her, Hannah turns to look at the all-too-familiar scenery outside her window. First come the winding, leafy side streets, the manicured backyards, and the masses of blossoming pink and blue hydrangeas that barely hide the in-ground swimming pools and wooden swing sets. Then strings of small shops and a little farther on down the line – and here she is still unable to pull herself away from the view rushing by – a park of corporate headquarters housed in all-glass, high-rise office buildings. Luckily for her younger self, she thinks, stifling a small smile of satisfaction, she never had to work in corporate America. Looking back at the younger person she once was, she is positive she would never have made it.

The train conductor is suddenly at her side. She fumbles in her wallet for her ticket, hands it over and turns back to the window. But now she barely pays any attention to what is outside. Memories from her youth have their insistent way. They barge in on her like too-chatty, uninvited guests.

Determined to ignore all those old, unwished-for memories, she props up an elbow on the narrow window ledge, rests her chin on her clenched fist, and looks back down at the page she has been trying to read. As she struggles to concentrate on the words, a sudden glint of sunshine crosses her face and, once again, she is brought back to the window. Through the murky glass, she gazes out at the fleeting view of Long Island Sound, a picture of watery crystals, bobbing up and down in the sunlight and sees herself not all that differently – sometimes in the light, other times out of it – but always bobbing up and down.

The misty trace of an old dream drifts by. Weightless. More like a feather tickling at the barriers of her consciousness. And while she can't stop listening to the break-up chatter from the girls behind her, she also can't stop her twenty-year-old self from hijacking her thoughts. Half a lifetime ago and it's almost, but not completely, impossible for her to recognize who she was then. Floundering? For sure. Scared of where her life was headed? Always. Worried she had screwed up so badly, her path back would be lost to her forever? Luckily and thankfully, it never was. And as crazy as it sounds, even to herself, she believes there has always been a strange force in her life – plain old lady luck, perhaps? – to keep her on track.

As she contemplates the hardships and heartaches of growing up, the train unexpectedly picks up speed and she's jerked forward in her seat, almost dropping her book. She catches it just before it slides off her lap. Her pen, though, clatters to the floor and rolls away beneath her seat.

Never mind, she tells herself, as she digs into her bag for another, then forces herself back to the text. Although the going is painfully slow, and for reasons she can't altogether grasp, she nonetheless feels compelled to incorporate Arendt's words into her own identity, her origins, and to help her find and cement those jagged edges; that incomprehensible legacy passed down to her.

Her life. Ha! What legacy will she have to pass on to her own children? What has the world taught her?

Dropped from college for her failing grades at the end of her sophomore year, she went to work at the main branch of the New York Public Library, the one on the corner of Forty-Second Street and Fifth Avenue. Fortunately for her, the photocopying division – where she spent her days Xeroxing Russian chemical abstracts for American pharmaceutical companies – had proven to be a very forgiving place to work, filled as it was, with college dropouts like herself, all in varying stages of their education and all trying to find themselves among the books, the dust, and the bright green bars of light, faithfully rolling back and forth under the glass tops of the Xerox machines, as they spewed out those valued copies of the pages taken from the many different volumes, all crammed with the symbols of an indecipherable language.

She remembers the many days when, for no true reason at all, she would call in sick. Most often, it was after nine o'clock, after she was due at work, after she was already on the subway on her way into Manhattan from where she lived in Queens. Standing in the overcrowded car, barely able to hang onto the strap above her head, she would feel the summer heat wrap around her like a straitjacket. And with no room to move, there always seemed to be a strange man standing too close behind her, rubbing his front up against her backside, in time to the jerky movement of the subway. Or else she'd become overwhelmed and sickened at the stink of garlic, from the previous evening's dinner, blowing in her face. In either case, by the time the train screeched to a halt at the Roosevelt Avenue station, the last express stop in Queens, she'd feel so overheated, dizzy, and nauseated, all she could think to do was bolt from the subway car, march the few steps across the platform and wait for her homebound train; tremendous relief overriding her spineless guilt.

Squealing to a stop at 125th Street, the doors slide open and four or five people get off, briefcases in hand. As she watches them rush away, she likes to imagine what jobs await them. Then she thinks of her own at the company she shares with Jake. Is being a boss of this destiny of theirs, with all its irregularities, missed paychecks, long hours and uncertainty, worth it? Yes. Absolutely yes. At least that is what she believed the day before yesterday, the day before the FedEx envelope arrived at their door. But not today, no, not *now*. Although, she must admit, right at this *very* moment – with her two children away at sleep-away camp in the Adirondacks, her third growing inside her, and the freedom that allows her this day-dreaming window seat on the 10:55 to Manhattan – all their hard work and her worry has made it worthwhile. But, like a sudden flip of the switch, a different reality shines its too-bright light in her head and an image of Artie stares at her; his dyed-dark hair slicked back off his forehead, the phone piece forever sticking out of his ear, and his all-too-ready tearing eyes. She looks out of the window again, the landscape industrial now. Concrete buildings house the small factories they pass. Their names and addresses, in desperate need of fresh coats of paint, are peeling off the whitewashed walls. She wonders how they deal with their problems.

The train enters the tunnel under Park Avenue and the girls' chatter behind her becomes even louder, as if the darkness outside the windows has impeded their hearing as well. Not so for Hannah's memory, though. Unimpeded now, it brings her away from the current problems with Artie and clicks back through her mind's eye, like a sped-up slide show. Of course, she knew all about those same, sad, unavoidable dramas as the one she is overhearing from the seat behind her. But oddly enough, it's not her own story that immediately comes to mind, but one from the new girlfriend of an ex-boyfriend of hers. She smiles at the memory. And looking up, is suddenly surprised by her own reflection in the blackness of the train's window. Eyes hollowed out and cheeks like dents in her face stare back at her, ghostlike. As her memory unfolds, she wonders if she ever knew why her ex's new girlfriend had come to see her in the first place. She can only remember the darkness of the evening enveloping the parked car they sat in, the passing headlights shining too brightly in her eyes, and this new girlfriend who, with tears welling up in her eyes and through a stuffy nose, told Hannah that she was pregnant. And Catholic, she'd added, as though news of the pregnancy itself wasn't bad enough. Hannah remembers feeling sorry for this new girlfriend and, at the same time, relieved for herself, as though she had just walked out into the wide-open air from the underside of a narrow escape. It could have been her sitting in the driver's seat, fists hitting the steering wheel, tears streaming down her face, nose running, and a future already made up for her before she was anywhere near ready to take it on.

In the tunnel outside her window the single bulbs, placed yards apart and barely illuminating the part of the walls they shine from, tell her they are close to Grand Central. But she can't pull herself away from the blackness outside her window. In its darkness she imagines the Seagram's liquor box in a corner, the newborn wrapped up in the blanket of newsprint inside it, and even the sound of its wailing. But can she imagine the raw desperation its mother must have felt?

Curling around her like a wisp of smoke, that old memory, stealing into her consciousness, continues. She's standing next to a crib, *oohing* and *aahing* at the baby. Its mother, proud and happy, lifts the baby out of its crib. But the baby's father, hobbling from one foot to the next, darts poisonous dark looks at Hannah, as if she were somehow responsible for this new life and had purposefully arranged it for him. Had he forgotten that it was he who did the breaking up? He, who did the cheating, the hurting? He, who had found a new girlfriend? How strange and unnerving to be thinking of all this ancient history now.

Hannah's hands flatten again to the small mound of her stomach, a new habit she has acquired, she realizes. It's almost as if her hands spread wide on the outside can protect the growth of her unborn baby on the inside. When she delivered the news of her pregnancy to Jake, he was so stunned at first; he was speechless. "Aren't two children the absolute perfect number?" he'd asked, when his words finally came back to him. "One for each of our hands to hold on to. One for you and one for me. Yes, two is the perfect number. Besides," he'd continued on a roll now, "aren't you about to turn forty, for God's sake?" As if this was news to her. "And to top it all off," he concluded, as though she alone had created this little being, "how will you manage?" You. Not we. But the question suddenly became a moot point when three or four days later, she began to bleed. Every day a little more. And poor Jake worried he had jinxed her pregnancy by questioning whether he'd even wanted it.

Was it the uncertainty that had propelled and then instilled in her an even stronger urge for this child to live – to bring back that sensation of a new life growing within her and to feel that mysterious wateriness stirring inside her?

By the time the bleeding had stopped, Jake felt he had been granted a reprieve. Their baby would be born.

She shakes her head at the memory, looks down at the open book, *Eichmann in Jerusalem*, and reads: *It was as though in those last minutes he was summing up the lesson that this long course in human wickedness had taught us—the lesson of the fearsome, word-and-thought-defying banality of evil.* Hannah reads the sentence again, and again, the words bobbing in her mind like the daggers of sunlight on the water. *The Banality of Evil.* Are those the words that had infuriated the world's Jewish community?

Although she feels guilty about the slow progress she's made, she refolds the corner of the page she's been trying to read, re-attaches her pen to the cover, puts the book back into her bag and gets up to wait by the door for the train to arrive at the station. Looking out into the darkness of the underground railway passage, she's brought back again to the abandoned baby. Hannah can't imagine going to term, giving birth, and afterward deserting her newborn. Yet can she guarantee to herself, right now, that there might never be a condition – lifesaving, perhaps – under which she would have to leave her baby to a chance upbringing?

As soon as the doors slide open and she steps onto the platform at Grand Central, a blanket of heat presses down on her and another thought takes hold in her mind. She has lived a protected and lucky life so far. And as that thought settles, another crashes into her. Nebulous and unformed, except for a sudden queasy sensation, it rises like jitters from the pit of her stomach, up through her chest and into her throat. *The banality of evil* is one thing to consider, but what about the banality of life? Is she guilty of that? Of accepting her own life, not for what she wants out of it, but rather as it comes to her, willy-nilly? Without direction? Of believing herself ordinary? Does the desire for this third child, by necessity, cause her to push away those answers to her questions, to let them slide back behind her conscious thought, as easily as shuffling the queen of hearts behind a knave of diamonds in a card game? Yes, her answer must be yes, at least for the near future. Because her life's priority is the well-being of her two children and now, with the third coming, she knows this will prolong the finding of her answers even further into her future. Her poetry will wait. It will gestate and grow inside her mind as surely as the baby will mature and grow inside her womb.

Out on the street, she hoists her Kenya bag onto her shoulder, reaches for the sunglasses propped on top of her head and brings them down to shade her eyes. As she hurries uptown on Lexington Avenue, dodging the lunchtime crowd, she keeps an eye out for a Korean grocery where she will buy her mother a bunch of fresh flowers for her birthday. Why, she wonders, is she always so useless at choosing presents?

Chapter Two

"Hot enough for you?"

Hannah finds her mother standing in the shade under the covered entrance to Bloomingdale's. She's fanning her face with a postcard-size ad for one of those miracle face creams – *guaranteed to smooth away all your wrinkles* – that a hawker must have pressed into her hand on her way downtown.

Hannah kisses her hello, first on one damp cheek, then on the other. "Happy birthday," she says, handing her mother the mixed bouquet of purple dahlias, pink roses, and daisies, with a smattering of baby's breath. "How's your day been so far?"

"Way more perfect, now that you're here," her mother says, holding the flowers up to her nose. "Leo's been such a sweetheart. He even brought me breakfast in bed this morning."

"Wow," Hannah says, trying her best not to conjure up the image of her mother's boyfriend, Leo, in pajamas or worse yet, without them, setting the breakfast tray down on her lap, then sliding into the bed next to her. "And afterward? I mean, after you'd had your breakfast and gotten up."

Her mother turns toward Hannah. She smiles, like she knows exactly what Hannah's been thinking, and says, "I went up to the pool, swam my few laps, came back to the apartment, showered, dressed, and well . . . here I am." She shrugs, seems to be at a loss for more to say until, looking down at the bouquet, as if for the first time, she adds, "These . . . they're beautiful, you really didn't have to."

"Sure, I did," Hannah says and, laughing, she puts her arm through her mother's and guides her in the direction of their favorite restaurant. As they pass by Bloomingdale's, where the windows are currently being spruced up for the latest fall fashion, Hannah tries hard not to look but doesn't quite succeed.

"I have a surprise I'll let you in on when we sit down for lunch," her mother says, slowing their walk to a saunter, which exasperates the people behind them, in a rush and anxious to keep moving.

"A surprise? What sort of surprise?"

"Patience, my dear, patience. I'll tell you all about it just as soon as . . ." But the rest of her words are lost when the sidewalk on Lexington becomes narrower, and they walk in single file under an enclosed temporary shelter of steel pipes and wooden boards that have been set up to protect the pedestrians from the construction work on the building above. As she strides to stay right behind her mother, Hannah's curious to know what her mother will say about her own little surprise.

"Everything's good, then?" Hannah says, catching up to her mother as the sidewalk opens and they're able to walk side by side again.

"Yes, yes," she says, edginess seeping into her voice. "It's just that I don't want to tell you in the street like this. We need to be sitting down, a glass of wine in our hands . . ."

"Ah, so you've got good news to tell me," Hannah says, feeling relieved she won't have anything more on her plate to worry about.

"Of course, but now it's your turn to fill me in." Her mother stops them mid-stride and, pulling Hannah in to face her, says, "How are the girls doing at camp? They must be loving it."

"Ugh! I wish," she says, directing her mother to keep going.

"What do you mean?" Hannah feels her mother's pull to stop her walking again.

"I get these terrible, pitiful letters from them every day. 'I love you, Mom. If you love me, you won't leave me here in this terrible place. I miss you. Do you miss me? I have no friends here. I hate it.'"

"How horrible for them."

"No, not for them . . . for *me*."

Her mother laughs as they resume their walk uptown.

"Reading their letters, you'd think I'd sent them to some god-awful prison camp up in the wilds of Siberia," Hannah goes on, trying to ignore the idea that her mother thinks this funny. "Not to an expensive, posh children's summer camp, nestled beside a gorgeous lake in the beautiful Adirondack Mountains."

"What a shame."

"But even worse than their letters . . ."

"What could possibly be worse?"

"Visiting day."

"Oy! What happened?" Her mother stops again, this time an expression of shock and worry on her face.

"It was the absolute worst."

"Someone get hurt?"

"God, no, nothing like that." Hannah is about to move her mother forward and continue with her story when a fire engine, its lights flashing and sirens blaring, roars noisily past them. Distracted, they stand in place, their eyes following the bright red engine as it disappears downtown.

"Tell me already," her mother says as they turn to resume their walk.

"At the end of visiting weekend, when it was time for us to leave, Ella – my sweet angel Ella – grabbed ahold of my legs and wouldn't let go."

"Your legs?"

"Yes. Here was my beautiful nine-year-old child, her knees planted on the graveled driveway, her back up against the car door, and both arms wrapped in a tight, tight, bear hug around my legs, with her fingers poking deep into my calves, and sobbing, 'Don't go, don't go.'"

"Oh no, the poor thing."

"You can't imagine how incredibly horrible it was. And . . . painful."

"Painful?"

"Her fingernails were sharp; they felt like little mini forks digging into my skin. They must have needed a good cutting."

"So, what did you do?"

"I sat myself down on the ground next to her, took her in my arms, and held her close. I told her how much I loved her, that I was depending on her to be my big, brave girl, and that I really needed her to stay in camp for me because she was the only one there who would do the best job of watching out for her big sister."

"And that worked?"

"Yes, after a little while, she loosened her grip. But let me tell you, I felt like I was the shittiest, the absolute worst mother-torturer of all mother-torturers."

If Hannah had thought about it, when they brought Miri and Ella to the rendezvous at the Cross County Center in Westchester, she might have changed her mind about sending them off, right then. But Hannah was too fascinated by the other parents and thrilled to be standing alongside them, watching them wave and blow kisses at their children on the bus, to think about anything else. And those kids, the ones who had done all this before, were hanging out of the windows, shouting last-minute directives to their parents, while laughing and pushing each other out of their way. Hannah, meanwhile, walked along the length of the bus on her toes, craning her neck to catch sight of her girls. She hoped they would come to the window too, looking happy, and blowing kisses at her. But, instead, when she did catch a glimpse of them, they were quiet, sitting still in their seats, their unsmiling eyes facing forward. And now, as she thinks about it, she wonders how she could have expected anything different when she, herself, felt so out of place, so obviously from another world – in her long peasant skirt, her thick, brown, curly hair, hanging most of the way down her back, and Jake in jeans and sandals – to be waving alongside those other mothers, in their diamonds and tennis whites, and fathers, in their lawyer suits and designer silk ties.

"You weren't thinking of bringing them home on visiting day, were you?" her mother says, a tone of slight disdain to her voice.

"No." Hannah shakes her head. "God, no. I mean, what would that teach them?"

"You're right. They need to learn to stick things out."

At the corner of 63rd, they wait in silence for the light to change. Hannah sneaks a peek at her mother. Is she serious or is she mocking her about the need to learn to stick things out? She can't tell.

"What about you?" her mother asks, as they cross the street. "Have you been able to take advantage of this free time for yourself? It would be a terrible pity to waste it, no?"

Talk about sticking things out. Sometimes Hannah can't figure out why she still does. What keeps her coming back to the desk in her little room by the kitchen, for those few extra spare minutes she finds for herself? To turn her words backward and forward, to shake them up and toss them out, as if their landed sequence were no more than a roll of the dice? And now, with Artie gone, and the arrival of the lawsuit against them, what time, what energy, what peace of mind will she have?

●   ●   ●

At Marigold's, they're seated at an outside table, her mother facing the street and Hannah, her own reflection in the restaurant's window. She is curious about her mother's blind encouragement now, especially since she has hardly an inkling as to what Hannah's been working on. And then, if the little bit of encouragement coming this late in her life is still better than none. As hard as she tries, she isn't always able to deafen her ears to the old words she was used to hearing as a young child. *Why aren't you more like . . . ?* Who, I wondered? The skinny girl? The quick-moving girl? The pretty girl? Or the girl who never daydreamed away her days? There are other times, though, when Hannah is so drawn to her mother, she feels she could tell her anything, spill it all out – her dreams, her fears, her founded and unfounded anxieties – and be the true half of a real mother—daughter relationship, the half that lets herself be enveloped by her, caressed, and cared for. Will her own girls feel this way about her as they grow up? Will they, when they eventually sit in her seat, wonder about her, their mother, as she does about hers? Whether it's the turn of her mother's face or the gazing, enquiring look in her eyes as she leans in and consciously unrumples the wrinkled furrows on her forehead, or the movement of her hands as she talks that will suddenly and inexplicably turn Hannah's heart into a stone-cold fortress and her skin raw to her mother's touch.

"Are you going to tell me your surprise?" Hannah says, after their server has brought them each a glass of water and menus.

"Well, my darling, I'm thinking of moving."

"Oh, my God, how exciting," Hannah says. And for a very few rosy seconds, as she props her elbows on the table, rests her head in her hands, she pictures her mother giving up her Manhattan apartment to move near her, maybe even down the street or only a short walk away. She can't stop the trajectory of her imagination; it gallops along at full speed ahead. Her mother would be there for her. There to help with the new baby, with Miri, with Ella and . . .

"To Basel," her mother says.

"Basel? Switzerland?" Hannah slouches back in her chair as she slams on the brake to her runaway imagination. "Basel, Switzerland? But why?"

"My friend, Leo. You do remember him, don't you?" her mother says, her tone slightly sarcastic as she gives Hannah a sly look. Then she smiles, picks up her water glass, and puts it to her lips, almost draining it before putting it back down again.

"Just like that, you'd pick up and move in with him?" Hannah says.

"Well, no, it's not quite like that, but . . ."

A young man, his tie loosened with his suit jacket slung over his shoulder, hovers over them waiting for her mother to pull in her chair so he can get to the table next to theirs.

"But what?" Hannah says in a screechy whisper as she leans in toward her mother again, while stealing a quick peek at the young woman who passes around her and sits in the chair across from the young man.

"Look, I'm not getting any younger."

"But why would you ever want to go back to Europe to live?"

"You think it's that marvelous here?" she says.

Hannah lets out a long, deep sigh as she sinks back into her chair, the burning sun strong on her back and her arms, the restaurant's awning not quite long or wide enough to shade her fully. The young man and woman are holding hands across the table. Hannah looks away; feels by observing them, she's intruding. She tries to sit up a little straighter and forces herself to focus back on her mother.

"What about his family? I seem to remember . . ."

"He's a widower and has two married daughters." Then, looking up and past Hannah, she adds, "I'm going over to meet them."

"Over? Why? Where do they live?"

"Basel, of course."

"Yes, of course." Hannah's attention strays from her mother and, like a magnet, is drawn back to the young couple sitting at the next table. They are studying their menus, their arms still extended, their hands still entwined. "When are you planning to go?" she says, turning back to her mother.

"Probably sometime in late September."

"That's quick."

"No time to lose, as the saying goes." And she smiles.

Hannah rolls her eyes.

"Wait 'til you get to be as old as me. You'll see."

But her mother is seventy-five and looks young for her age. What is her rush? Why is she in such a hurry to leave Hannah and her family behind, as well as her life here in New York?

"Is he Jewish?" The words slip out without thinking.

"What difference?" comes the snapped retort.

"Just curious," she says in a whisper to herself as she shakes her head. Why did she even ask the question? She uncrosses her legs, stuck together now from the heat, and holds her thick, curly hair up from the nape of her neck. Whatever little air circulates around her feels good. She closes her eyes for a moment.

"Hannah, you should be happy for me. Why are you so angry?"

"I'm not. I mean, I'm happy for you, not angry." She lets go of her hair, picks up her water glass, takes a long drink, and as she puts it back down on the table, adds, "I mean it, I am truly very happy for you."

"Look, nothing's cast in stone. His daughters might nix the whole idea and, for all I know, will hate me."

"They aren't going to hate you. Honestly . . . I can't imagine any reason they wouldn't absolutely love the idea of you living with him. You would be there for their father . . ."

"Not ever as a nursemaid, I can assure you." Obviously irritated, her mother reaches down by the side of her chair, retrieves her large bag from the floor, and settling it on her lap, begins rummaging around in it.

"No?" Hannah says, waiting for her mother to raise her head. But her mother fixes her eyes on the bag in her lap as if, Hannah thinks, to hide her face or perhaps to avoid the expression she imagines might be on Hannah's.

"No, absolutely not." Her mother's voice sounds thick, as if she were coming up from a deep place for air. Then, exhaling loudly to mask her anger, she pulls out the case holding her eyeglasses and puts her bag back down on the floor by the side of her chair.

"Okay," Hannah says, though unable to dispel the image forming in her mind of her mother, at some time in her future, sitting beside Leo's bed in the possible, though unwelcome, role of wifely caregiver. "Anyway, how old is he? Do you even know?"

"Of course I do." Now the words spit out of her in sudden exasperation. She takes her eyeglasses out of their case, puts them on, and concentrates on her menu. "Anyway, age doesn't matter to me at all right now." She says this quietly, lifting her gaze up to Hannah's, her eyeglasses magnifying the defiance in her eyes.

"That's fine, I guess."

"Right. So, what do you say we order lunch? And then let's hear what's new with you."

"Trying to change the subject, are we?" Hannah can't help but smile.

"Yes, well, maybe I am. And I'm sure you must think of me, like an ostrich, hiding my head in the sand, but I just can't envision my life, my future, like that. A nursemaid, for God's sake."

"Well, mom, if you're happy, I'm happy too. Let's have a toast. Here's to your birthday." Hannah raises her water glass.

"But we have nothing to drink. Where is the server?"

"And to having all your dreams come true, even if it means you moving away from your loving family."

"Thank you, my darling. But don't worry, I'll only agree to go if I can come back to New York, say, twice a year, at least."

Twice a year? Hannah measures the time by her unborn baby's growth, six months, a year, as good as a lifetime. She groans inside herself.

"I also have something to . . ." Hannah says, but the words come out too timidly. Her mother hasn't heard her. The server is at their table. Her mother hems and haws about whether she is in the mood for a cheeseburger or a roast beef sandwich, while still checking out the menu through her oversized tortoise-shell eyeglasses.

"What do you feel like?" she asks. "A Caesar salad?"

Hannah laughs at her mother's predictability, as if she would ever deviate from her usual. The server leaves and Hannah leans in over the table.

"Since you're such an old hand at birthdays," she begins.

"Gee, thanks a bunch. Old hand. I may not be the youngest, but I am certainly not that old either. Am I?"

"Obviously not too old to beguile." Hannah chuckles.

"Don't be ridiculous," her mother says and gives Hannah a look.

"But, seriously, which of all your birthdays was your favorite? Do you remember?"

"Certainly, none as a kid, that's for sure. By the end of July, all my school friends were away on summer holidays, so I never had birthday parties."

"Well, truthfully, you didn't miss much," Hannah says. "They were such a drag."

How she had hated them as a child. Hated the black patents, hard on her feet, the white ankle socks that invariably slipped down under her heels, the tartan bow in her curly, dark hair, the black-and-white checkered party dress in shiny taffeta with the bright red smocking across the chest and the stiff white petticoat beneath it. Everyone singing, *London bridge is falling down, falling down, falling down*. And she was always at the end of the line, waiting and watching. Then it was her turn. *Oranges and lemons say the bells of St. Clements*. Scurrying under four little arms. Hands clasped together, an arch stretching high one moment, swinging low the next. Everyone is running. Hurry, hurry. *Here comes a candle to light you to bed*. Shoving, pushing, shouting. *Here comes a chopper to chop off your head*. And the fright and the thrill as those little arms would come crashing down in sudden rough entrapment. *Off with your head*. And afterward the boredom of having to sit on the side waiting for the game to be over, the crème-filled cake to be served, and the consolation prize – the requisite six-color tin paint box or the four-page Mother Goose coloring book – to be handed out.

"I didn't know you were *that* averse to birthday parties. Or did I?" A puzzled frown on her face, she looks up at Hannah.

"You might remember my fourth birthday. Or was it my fifth? You'd set up a long trestle table upstairs in my bedroom. We had just moved into the house. Ring a bell?"

Her mother nods and smiles. "Yes, I remember," she says, and momentarily distracted by the people walking in the street, looks away from Hannah, as if that would help her bring the afternoon, from all those years ago, into sharper focus.

Hannah crosses her arms at her chest and goes on, unable to stop both the rush of memories and the telling of them. "And there I was, the birthday girl, the paper crown still on my head, sitting all by myself at the top of the table with only a mess of crumpled streamers, plates of leftover mushed sponge cake, sprinkled with chocolate icing, and half-filled glasses of Ribena to keep me company. I felt . . . well . . . abandoned."

"Oh, you poor thing, you," her mother says and laughs.

"It wasn't funny then."

"Yes, I know, sweetheart."

"And you were so mad at me," Hannah says.

"I was? Why?"

"For staying at the table while all the other kids were downstairs playing games."

"No, no. That wasn't it. Now I remember why I was mad. When you finally did come downstairs, you sat on the sidelines in a sulk and refused to join in any of the games. I was utterly embarrassed."

Hannah shrugs her shoulders and smiles at her mother. "Sorry," she says and thinks it odd – or is it discomforting? – to know how, all these years later, she can still summon those thick walls of stubbornness to rise all around her, as if she were a toy boat being pulled down into a rough, high sea. Why can't she ever let herself go? Float up to the lightness in the air, where she can be carefree and sunny? Why couldn't she have been a happy-go-lucky kid?

"Now, you've got me thinking," her mother says, biting her lower lip. "There was no way for you to have known it back then, but those children's birthday parties were most probably more meaningful and heartfelt to us, your parents, and your grandparents, than to you, our children. And not only because those times had deprived us of having them; no, our childhoods had been lost, anyway, stolen from us, forever. But because those parties for you, our children, were the celebration, the affirmation of life continued, so to speak. But best of all, we had survived against all odds, despite what Hitler and his henchmen were planning for us."

Hannah doesn't know what to say. She turns her face up to the sky, closes her eyes, lets the sun beat down on her.

"How silly, how spoiled I must've seemed," she finally says, bringing her face back in line with her mother's.

"Yes." And laughing now, her mother shakes her head. "What an impossible child you were, sometimes."

"Thank God neither one of my kids have taken after me, although I do see some of myself in Ella and . . ."

The server brings out a basket of bread for them. As Hannah watches her go back inside the restaurant, she realizes how underneath it all, and despite her almost forty years, she must still seem to be that impossible child.

"What were you about to say?" Her mother takes off her glasses, puts them back in their case and into her bag.

"Oh, I was just wondering if you'd heard about the abandoned baby at Grand Central." Images of the baby, swaddled in sheets of newspaper and tucked inside the Seagram's liquor box, float once again to the forefront of Hannah's mind. Put away, hidden in the remotest corner of the station's darkest platform, as if it were merely a doll, outgrown or simply broken and no longer of any use to its owner. She imagines hearing the newborn's cry – oh, how she never could bear the sound of her own babies' cries – that the mother had to have blocked from her consciousness to walk away from those terribly urgent, high-pitched wails.

"Hard to miss," her mother says. "It was all over the news this morning. The poor little creature. And his mother. I feel for her too. Think how desperate she must have been to leave her baby like that."

"Yes, but I still can't get over the fact that she *abandoned* it. I mean, you would think she could've found . . ."

"Desperation makes you do all sorts of things you mightn't do otherwise. Just think about Nazi times," her mother says, a defiant tone underscoring her words as they are pushed out from that other place usually well hidden inside her. Leaning in now, she plants her elbows on the table, clasps her hands together, laces her fingers, and stares, unblinking, at Hannah. "What about all those desperate parents giving up their babies to complete strangers? Or leaving them on the steps of an orphanage or a convent or a church, all in the hopes of saving them from the gas chambers?"

"Those situations are completely different," Hannah says.

"Yes. This is nowhere near as dire; I'll grant you that. But in any case, none of us has any idea what hardship this baby's mother has been facing. Things aren't always so black and white, you know."

"I'm sure you're right. I simply can't imagine it. I mean, leaving your own baby to chance, never to know who would adopt it, how it would grow up, and who or what it might become."

Hannah wishes this talk about the abandoned baby would stop. The truth of it – dawning on her now, as her hands automatically settle down to their newly accustomed place, with her too-warm fingers spreading wide over her abdomen – is that these thoughts of abandonment are making her feel jittery and scared. "Yes," she repeats. "I know nothing's ever quite simply black and white." Her hands press even harder into her belly.

"Anyway, the story is such an old one," her mother says. "A mother's desperation for her child's life goes back eons, even to Moses."

"Moses?"

"Yes, don't you remember it was his sister, Miriam, who put him in a basket of reeds and cast him out onto the river?"

"But he was going to a palace."

"Ah, but a gamble, nevertheless. Supposing the princess never discovered him, or a Hebrew hater got to him first or the basket tipped over in the river and he drowned."

Their lunches arrive. Her mother asks for another glass of wine, Hannah more ice for her water.

"And then," her mother continues, as she unfolds her napkin and drapes it over her lap, "just the other day, I happened to read about something called the Baby Moses Law. Have you ever heard of it?"

Hannah shakes her head.

"It's where parents unable to take care of their newborn can drop it off anonymously at a designated safe place, such as a hospital or a police or fire station, to receive emergency care and afterward . . ."

"It gets put up for adoption?"

"Yes," her mother says.

"Sounds like an animal shelter."

As Hannah picks up her knife and fork, thoughts of the deserted baby she can't seem to let go of, keep whirring around in her thoughts, a frenzy of confusion. She wonders whether an abandoned baby senses its abandonment, whether a trigger is activated within its small body. Does a newborn feel fear? And how does that manifest itself? It must have been hungry. She's sure it must have been wailing. Of course. Yes, of course. How else could it have been found in the first place? The cry – that plaintive plea for survival. How else to let the world know, *Here I am, here I am.*

"But surely, you're not thinking that an abandoned baby, found at Grand Central, is a modern-day version of the Moses story."

Her mother nods, concentrating on her lunch now.

Hannah butters a chunk of bread and takes a bite, regretting it as soon as the rush of guilt for her future expanding body runs through her. "Instead of the Nile," Hannah continues, "and the wishful prayer that he'd be discovered by a princess and raised in a palace, someone wrapped this baby in newspaper and left it in a dirty, dank corner of a commuter train station, where he likely would have remained hidden and starved, rather than found and saved."

"Thank God, they discovered him in time," her mother says as the server shows up with her second glass of wine and more ice for Hannah. "But wouldn't it be wonderful if a loving, well-off family came along to adopt him?" she continues as soon as the server leaves their table.

"Hmm. I don't think it quite works like that."

"It'd be nice, though, don't you think?" her mother says, picking up her glass. "If one could somehow make miracles happen, just by dreaming them into life?" And she takes a long sip, as if any answer

Hannah might have to her question doesn't matter – that in fact, it really has no bearing.

"Yes, I suppose one can always hope for miracles." Hannah inhales a long breath of air, letting it out slowly in a noisy sigh. "As long as everyone is on the same right and honorable page," she adds.

Squinting her eyes against the sun's brightness reflecting off the tables, the silverware, and the glasses surrounding her, she tilts forward to be as far under the awning as possible. How can she get away from all this talk of the abandoned baby? She's sorry she brought it up. Why did she think she needed this prologue to unleash her own story?

"To change the subject slightly," she braves now. "I have something important, a surprise to tell you, too."

Her mother puts her knife and fork down and leans back in her chair. Always in expectation of disastrous news, she folds her arms across her chest, purses her lips, a look of agitation and worry in her purple-shadowed, green eyes. "Everything okay?" she asks.

"It depends on how you look at it." Hannah smiles, feeling the corner of her eyes crinkle. She picks up her water glass, takes a long drink.

"Well . . .? How should I . . .? Are you keeping me in suspense on purpose?"

Hannah puts her glass back down on the table and, avoiding her mother's curious gaze, announces loudly, "I'm pregnant." The words roll out of her with surprising ease, she notes with relief, chuckling to herself for being so cowardly. And as if she's a puppeteer pulling at the strings of her mother's reactions, she watches her mother's mouth open, ready to say something, but close tightly seconds later, followed, instead, by the mixed expressions of disbelief and confusion that cloud her face in the few moments before she's able to turn them into smiles and laughter.

"You are?" she says, her voice unusually loud and shrill as she claps her hands together, attracting the attention of the young couple at the next table who, sidetracked momentarily from their own conversation, look up and over at them.

"Yes. Yes, I am." Hannah nods her head, as if she is as much in need to confirm this news to herself as she is to her mother.

With her eyes fixed on Hannah's chest for a couple of seconds, her mother says, "How far along are you? I must say, I thought you looked a little bustier than usual today."

"Well, now you know you didn't imagine it. I'm about eight weeks." And Hannah's hands automatically fly down again to their protective posture.

"But why have you waited with this fantastic news until now to tell me?" her mother says, hurt and incomprehension showing in her face.

"I guess I was worried you'd think me stupid and crazy."

"Stupid and crazy? What kind of nonsense talk is that? How could I even think . . . I mean . . . maybe I thought you were stupid and crazy to get the two dogs. But a baby?" She leans toward Hannah, uncrosses her arms, and rests them on the table.

"Perhaps I'm exaggerating. I thought with all that is going on in my life between the kids, Jake, the craziness in the business . . ."

"Yes, I do worry you have a lot on your plate – probably way too much."

"When I first found out, I wasn't exactly thrilled, and neither was Jake. In fact, the prospect of having a third child . . . I mean . . . all I could think about was how this," and she points down at her belly and smiles, "would disrupt our lives – mine, Jake's, the kids.' I couldn't imagine how I was going to make it all work."

"Oh, you poor thing," her mother says, reaching for her hand across the table. "Is this why you didn't tell me before now?"

"Well, to be honest, we weren't sure what we were going to do."

"I assume you're keeping it. Right?"

"Oh, yes. It was as if I had woken up one morning and my brainwaves had done a flip-flop overnight. Somehow this baby growing inside me had transformed my thoughts, and suddenly I wanted it, wanted it desperately . . . and . . . well, I came to think of it as a gift, somehow."

"A gift?" The words surprise her mother.

"I don't know how else to describe it. It sounds weird, doesn't it? I mean, isn't a baby always a gift?" As soon as her words are out, she knows they were wrong, even unjust.

Her mother shakes her head. "Obviously, not for the woman who abandoned hers at Grand Central."

The same strange, queasy feeling Hannah had had earlier, as she was getting off the train, comes back to her now. She puts down her knife and fork, takes another long swallow of water. Then with both hands, she once again lifts her thick mop of hair off her neck and wishes there was some way she could get out of the sun. "For me, though," she says, letting down her hair as she inhales a deep breath, "I thought having this baby would give me an opportunity to realign my life in some way – allow me to stop time for myself, to think about what it is I want to be doing for myself from now on."

She can tell right away by the confused expression on her mother's face that she has said more than she should have – that her thoughts are not being followed. Is she following them herself? What exactly is she thinking? Is it all just romantic nonsense? No, it's not, she decides. But then, is her life filled with banality? A question that's haunted her and rummaged around in the back of her mind all day.

"I thought you were happy working in the business with Jake."

"Oh, I am, but . . ." But what? Why does she always feel this slight edge of dissatisfaction with her life? Why can't she be happy? It's most probably true that that stubborn little girl, who sat all by herself at the head of the table with the birthday crown resting on top of her mop of curls, the plates of leftover cakecrumbs all around her, is still the one buried inside her and not as deeply as she might have imagined. Why can't she see how she has grown and changed?

"But?" her mother presses.

"Well, perhaps, like you, I feel my time slipping away from me."

"You're way too young for that," her mother says, a tone of dismissal in her voice, as she leans back in her chair.

"Why? Don't we all have time slipping away from us?"

"Yes, of course. But look, you have two beautiful, healthy children."

"And I'm tempting fate? Is that it? Is that what you're trying to tell me?"

"No, not *tempting* fate. That has such a negative connotation. In fact, no. I was about to say how delighted I am for you. How lovely it will be to have a baby in the family again. Tell me, do you have an actual due date yet?"

"End of January, beginning of February, if you can call it actual."

"It'll be here before you know it," she says, as though her thoughts were roaming away.

"What are you thinking?" Hannah leans back, closing her eyes to the sunlight.

"Just wondering when to go to Basel. What about if I postpone my trip until after the baby's birth? What d'you think?"

"Totally up to you, mom," she says, and then wonders why she said that. Why couldn't she have just said: *Yes, please stay, at least until the baby is born?* Instead, she goes on, "I have Jake. And Miri and Ella are old enough now to be a little more self-sufficient. Honestly, I think I'm covered."

She smiles, mostly to appease herself, and glances over to the next table at the young woman looking perfectly turned out in a beige, silky shirt, and stiletto heels. Suddenly, Hannah feels herself old and frumpy. Beneath the table, flip-flops allow for her swollen feet. Dark curls, frizzy now with the humidity, frame her face and fall over her warm back and shoulders. Her favorite skirt, a simple white cotton with a lacy hem at mid-calf, is wrinkled and damp with the heat. As is her black, faded tank top, machine-washed, and tumble-dried a few too many times. Hannah looks back at her mother, expecting to feel . . . to feel what, though? Beautiful and loved? No matter what? She stares hard, anticipating her mother to feel her gaze and look back up at her, but her mother is busy eating her salad. So, nothing has changed for Hannah. She feels the same. And in all fairness, she reasons with herself, how could her mother even begin to know her, if she doesn't articulate her words, her thoughts, her worries, in a voice loud enough for them all to be heard?

"But then again, on second thought," she says, and waits for her mother to look up at her before continuing. "Maybe you should stay in New York, at least until the baby's born."

There, she's said it.

"Yes, you might be right. But if not, I'll be back in time, I promise you."

At least she's *said* it out loud.

"Well, anyway . . ." she says, trying to sit up more on the wood-slatted folding chair that's tilting slightly backward with the uneven sidewalk, making good posture in the shade almost impossible. "Weren't you going to tell me all about your favorite birthday?"

"Ha! Now it's your turn to change the subject," her mother says, and she laughs.

"I know, but I really can't talk about my pregnancy anymore." Hannah hears the sudden shrill in her own voice and is surprised by it. Leaning forward, her elbows on the table, she whispers, "To be honest, I'm desperately afraid."

"Afraid? Of what?"

"Tempting the gods of ill-fates?" And she laughs. Not at her mother, but at herself. Because deep down, she knows this to be true about herself. After all, isn't she the one who can never resist picking up a lost, dropped penny, because, like a smile beaming up at her from the sidewalk, she's so sure it will magically bring her all the good luck she needs?

Silently cursing at herself for her lack of willpower, she reaches for the breadbasket again, and the butter.

"You're something else." Her mother shakes her head. "Since when are you this superstitious?"

"Since forever." Hannah butters a slice, takes a bite. "But, hey, let's get back to your birthdays . . ."

"Ach! I can't understand what's so interesting about my birthdays."

"Oh, I don't know . . . I'm curious is all."

"Curious? What's there to be so curious about? They are what they are. They come; they go. And all a little too quickly, I might add."

"Actually, to tell you the truth, I want to know how you celebrated when you lived in Berlin."

"Ah! So, you want us to go back there again, do you?"

"Yes. Yes, I do. You okay with that?"

"I suppose. But you must realize I don't remember that much. I was a young kid, don't forget. Besides, I'm sure I must have blocked much of it from my memory. Anyway, as I've told you, I never had birthday parties – not because of Hitler – but because all my friends were away on vacation. And we were too. We either went to the beach on the Baltic or to the mountains in Austria. I've got old photographs from that time. But then, you know, our freedom of movement became sharply curtailed, certainly by the time I was four or five. Every day, more places . . . would put up those horrid signs . . . *no dogs or Jews allowed.*"

Hannah's phone rings. She puts up her finger as if to say wait a minute and digs into her Kenya bag to pull out the insistent ringer, anxious to flip it open before it disturbs the other people around them. "Hello," she says to the caller. "Oh, hi, Jake, we're just finishing lunch. What's up?"

"Pass me to your mother," he says, sounding almost breathless.

She hands over the phone and can hear Jake sing happy birthday to her.

"You're so sweet," her mother says, laughing, and as she passes the phone back to Hannah, mouths "ladies' room," and gets up.

"How's it all going?" Hannah asks, trying to sound calm and non-expectant.

"I was going to wait until you got home to tell you," Jake says, all signs of joking gone from his voice. "But I can't."

"Why? What's happened?" Convinced she is about to hear devastating news, she bends her head down, hiding her face.

"When Artie came into the office super early that last morning, Sally was already here. He had cleared all his shit off his desk, packed everything up in a number fourteen carton and, without so much as a word or a glance in her direction, walked out. What I don't get is why she just didn't call me right away." His voice is unusually loud.

"So odd. Did she think she was protecting him, you know, like a fellow employee?"

"I asked her. She had no answer."

"Hmm." She looks up and sees her mother walking toward their table. "I should go," she says. "My mother's back and I'm not sure how much of all this I feel like repeating to her."

"I don't blame you. We'll talk when you get home. Do you know which train you're catching?"

"For sure, not late. I'll call you when I get to the station."

"Everything alright?" her mother says, as she sits back down at the table.

"Only regular work stuff," Hannah says, shrugging her shoulders and trying to sound as dismissive as possible. And before she needs to make up anything more to tell her mother, the server is at their table asking them if they'd like anything else as she gathers up their empty dishes.

Her mother looks over at Hannah. "Coffee?" she asks.

Hannah nods. "Let's be daring and share a dessert. A slice of whatever you'd like. After all, it is your birthday."

"Two cappuccinos please, a slice of carrot cake with two forks, and I'll take the check whenever you're ready. No rush."

"The check is mine, remember? Your birthday, my treat."

"Okay. Thank you, my darling," she says, though her attention is fixed on an older man and woman passing by their table as they leave the restaurant. He walks slowly and with a cane. She holds onto his arm.

"What're you thinking?" Hannah says.

"Guess." Her mother smiles.

Hannah shrugs.

"Just how wonderful it'll be to have a baby in the family again." She looks back at Hannah and laughs.

"Really? You mean it?" Hannah sounds to herself like a little kid, who's looking for affirmation of a job well done.

The server is back with their cappuccinos and the slice of carrot cake. She's stuck a lit candle in the middle of it. "Happy birthday," she announces loud enough for everyone around them to hear. The couple at the next table look over and wish her mother a happy birthday, too. Smiles are all around. Who doesn't love birthdays? Even Hannah, nowadays.

"I take it you haven't told Miri and Ella about the baby yet," her mother says once the server has left.

"When they get back."

"What a great welcome home surprise for them," she says, picking up her coffee cup.

"Yes. I think they'll be thrilled. A live doll to fuss over."

Something draws Hannah's attention back to the young man and woman at the next table. It's their words. Suddenly louder, they sound curt, spat out. No longer holding hands, they appear angry with each other. Their lunches sit in front of them, barely touched. What words, subject matter, brought to the table now, are harsh enough to clear away those earlier gestures of love and caring? On the one hand, Hannah feels sorry for them. On the other, redeemed. Perfection, she muses, isn't necessarily the path to happiness.

"So, my love, can we talk about you now?" her mother says, still holding her cup in both hands. "You know, you never answered me before, when I asked if you were giving yourself enough time to discover what it is you want out of life. You know, solely for you, for your own self."

"Well, the truth is, whatever time I've allotted myself, for myself, is about to end. The kids will be home soon, and then there's this growing element . . ." Hannah looks down at her belly and laughs.

"But at least you'll be staying at home after the baby's born, won't you?"

"Yes, of course I will." And she's reminded again how silly and optimistic she'd been to have expected Artie to take over her job after she'd had the baby. He never even tried to learn what she did for the company. In fact, he never worked at learning anything at all. He would sit at his desk, and . . . do what? Nothing? What had he expected from her and Jake? Everything for nothing? And he kept repeating the same points he wanted included in his employment contract and Jake had to remind him, again and again, that they'd been off the table since day one.

"Well, do yourself a favor and try not to let the world impose," her mother says.

"Ha! Ha! Easy for you to say," she says, scraping her fork over the leftover icing on her plate.

As Hannah brings the fork up to her mouth, she's caught by her own reflection in the restaurant's large front window. It's disjointed, this mirror image. Like a live Cubist painting, she thinks, with the passing fluffy clouds in the sky above her, and her own image superimposed over white napkins, perched like unfolded fans on top of water goblets, all set and waiting on the white-clothed tables inside the restaurant. *Try not to let the world impose.* But doesn't she need all those disparate fragments of the world to become the whole woman she yearns to be? *Easy for you to say.* Her own mocking words echo back at herself.

They finish drinking their coffees amid talk of her mother's upcoming visit to Leo's married daughters in Basel. Hannah asks if they have jobs. Her mother's not sure. Their children – two boys, two girls – are a little older than Miri and Ella. That's all her mother knows about them for now.

"Updates to follow immediately upon my return," she says, grinning.

After their table is cleared, the check is put down. Her mother grabs it and reaches into her bag for her wallet. Without even looking at the bill, she hands the server her credit card, ignoring all of Hannah's protestations and attempts to pay.

"The day I can't treat my daughter to lunch is the day I don't live for," she says.

When the slip comes back, Hannah watches her mother retrieve her reading glasses from her bag, look up for a moment as she calculates the tip, signs her name, takes her copy and her credit card, puts them and her glasses back into her bag, and brings out a mirror and lipstick. She wipes the mirror with her palm, examines her face, and re-reddens her lips.

"Ready?" she says and, obviously satisfied with her made-up face, she stands. Picking up the bouquet with one hand while smoothing down her skirt with the other, she moves away from the table.

They walk out onto Lexington Avenue and head downtown.

"So, it doesn't make sense to go clothes-shopping?"

"No, not really," Hannah says and can't help but smile as she thinks of the tiny being growing inside her.

"In which case, I'll come with you as far as 59th. Then I'll go home and rest. Leo's taking me out for dinner tonight. A special place, he promised."

They stop in front of Bloomingdale's to say goodbye. As her mother leans forward to kiss her, first on one cheek, then the other, Hannah looks up to see a barefooted young man inside the window. He's struggling with a naked mannequin. Its dislocated arms and legs, sprawled out on the otherwise empty floor, appear to Hannah to be the limbs of a giant-child's doll which, in a fit of temper, have been ripped from its body.

Chapter Three

As Hannah waits at the curb for the light to change, she turns around to watch her mother walk away. There's one thing to be said, she thinks, facing forward again. Her mother certainly knows how to get what she needs out of life. Can Hannah honestly say the same about herself? She doesn't know. Taking a deep breath, she holds it in for a moment, then lets it out in a long sigh. As of late, she sometimes feels more like a lost child than a mother of two with a third on the way.

The light changes. In unison with the surrounding crowd, she steps off the curb at 59th and zigzags her way across the street. It feels like she's in some sort of ancient battle, the way she needs to strategize where she should take her next step to avoid bumping into one or another of the strangers coming at her, their eyes unfocused and seemingly in a huge rush to get ahead of the crowd. Only to beat the next red light?

As is usually the case, after she leaves her mother and is on her way back to the station, she finds herself pushing away the nagging, guilt-inducing notion she should stay in the city, take advantage of the fact that she's already here. There's the Museum of Modern Art to visit. But the idea of walking through the museum by herself feels too lonely if there's no one with whom to share her ideas and views. Besides, once she pictures herself relaxing in the cool quiet of her own garden, inhaling the whiff of freshly mowed grass, she can think of nothing better to do than leave behind all the heat, smells, traffic noises, and crowds of people filling the streets. And today she's especially anxious to get home. Find out from Jake what the lawyer has told him they should be prepared for. This entire episode with Artie has been so disappointing. The initial prospect of their taking over his company and having him work for them was full of promise, such a perfect fit for everyone. Most especially for her.

As she sidesteps a group of tourists stopped in her path and too busy poring over their tour books and maps to notice her, her thoughts drift back to the first time she and Jake met Artie and his wife, Lisa. They were all away in Long Beach, California, exhibiting at one of the annual trade shows. How long ago was that, she wonders, as she tries to place the year in a chronology of trade shows, where each one was about the same as the last and where, whomever you met would make some similar comment, always with a sad shake of their head, about how quickly the year had passed; as if time itself had been secretly compressed.

She looks down at the sidewalk, at the cracks in the cement she avoids stepping on, as though by some miracle, they'll provide her with all her answers.

When she comes to 55th Street, she decides on a brief detour and heads west to Fifth Avenue. The heat, worse now than before, seems to radiate off the sidewalk, like steam from a boiling pot. She counts down the blocks – thirteen to go – and turns left to walk downtown, her white skirt sticking to her legs, her upper thighs rubbing together. With one hand she lifts her mass of long hair away from her neck and, with the other, fans herself to cool down. Every so often, something in a store window catches her attention, but then, knowing there's nothing she needs, she keeps her eyes focused in front of her and walks on. At the corner of 53rd, she notices an empty storefront across the street. A huge "For Lease" sign covers its window. Wasn't there once a Doubleday bookstore on that corner? Yes, she's sure of it. And wasn't this her subway stop? Yes. Yes. And now she can remember that palpable feeling of relief, the rush of dusty air billowing up all around her, as she emerged from the bowels of the station. At the top of the stairs, she would pause for a moment, gather her bearings, and adjust to the sudden sunlight prickling her eyes. Then breathe. Ah! To inhale the city's electrified atmosphere; always crackling with energy.

Of course, all this was ages ago. But as more random, unrelated memories roll around in her head, they seem to become diminished and distanced. She sees those short, dizzying clips of the past as if she were peering through the wrong end of a telescope or, as she can't help inwardly laughing at herself, like seeing the warning signs reversed on her car's side view mirror: *Objects are, in actuality, smaller and farther away than they appear.*

She turns and continues her walk to Grand Central. What has made all this come back to her now? It's not as if she hasn't walked along this street and passed by this corner hundreds of times before today without these memories assaulting her like this. Did the girl-talk on the train tickle her brain, find its opening, and, like a sudden gush of water, flood in? Or was it the abandoned baby? But what makes it odd, she thinks, is that on the one hand, she can trace wide swaths of memory backward and know how she got to where her life is today. On the other, though, thin slices of time seem to have slipped by her unnoticed or to have stood still, buried deeper into her subconscious, the cracks and creases of them like markings on an old map that charts and delineates the path forward. The one, she realizes she can't stop hunting for. Has she always been waiting for an extra something else to happen in her life?

Giving in, she traces her way back through those long-ago times and reimagines her sixteen-year-old self, sprinting up the stairs from the 53rd Street subway station, then heading west toward Sixth Avenue. How magical all those Saturday afternoons were. How grownup she'd felt. How liberated. On her right was the Museum of Modern Art and, at the end of the block, down a step or two from the sidewalk, a small deli, where she would end up ordering the same sandwich each week. *Egg salad, lettuce, no tomato, and extra mayonnaise on rye bread without seeds, please.* After lunch, she would cross Sixth Avenue and walk the block to where her most favorite place in the whole wide world awaited her.

The entrance to the older, red-brick apartment building wasn't fancy. It only mattered to her that the small, dark, wood-paneled elevator brought her up to apartment 5J, where the large bare windows looked down onto 54th Street, and the living room – unfurnished, except for a row of wooden folding chairs placed in a semi-circle at one end of the shined parquet floor – had been reinvented into an actors' studio. Framed black-and-white photographs of actors at work adorned the otherwise plain white walls. This was where she and five other teenage girls would come every Saturday afternoon, eager to learn how to make their dreams of lit-up footlights and starry fame come to glittering life.

Their teacher, Kurt, was an older gentleman. His wild, silver hair jutted out all over his head, giving him a Bohemian aura of brilliance which perfectly complemented his large, craggy face and strong German accent. Like a uniform, he always wore a pair of baggy brown corduroys with a white tee under an unbuttoned, oversized blue denim shirt. But what stood out most about him were his ice-blue eyes, always sparkling with energy and enthusiastic encouragement. He fueled her passion for the theatre. He taught her how to feel the words, to imagine what lay beneath them, to dip into her own young life, as if her experiences and emotions could be wrenched from the inside and fanned out, like the many hues on an artist's palette. And so, she'd poured her whole inner self into those classic monologues from *Joan of Arc* or *Hedda Gabler*.

Funny how things never quite turn out the way you imagine or hope they will in your youth.

And now she wonders about her own words. Can she reach down inside them the way she learned to dig into Shaw's and Ibsen's? Has she dipped far enough into herself to look for her own deeply buried feelings?

Ahead of her, in front of St. Patrick's Cathedral, more groups of tourists block the sidewalk. They talk excitedly to one another in a language Hannah doesn't recognize. She wends her way through the crowd, saying, *sorry, excuse me, sorry,* over and over, and hopes they will understand her, or at best hear her above their yelled directions as they snap photos of each other on the steps of the cathedral. Skirting around the commotion, she walks on and wonders if her own language will be recognizable, understood? If she will ever have what it takes to send her words out into the world? She slows to browse the windows at Saks, even though . . . No, she doesn't need a new outfit for the trade shows this year, her usual excuse to buy at least one.

She's about to turn down 42nd Street when she finds herself staring at a tall set of windows. She follows them around the corner. Fascinated, she moves closer. Staged, as if in conversation with each other, faceless female mannequins with long flowing blonde or red hair are dressed in brightly colored matching outfits, some in wide trousers, others in ruffled dresses. Oddly, it's one of the redheaded mannequins that reminds her of Lisa, though her hair is blonde. From Lisa, Hannah's thoughts automatically slide over to Artie and the FedEx standard overnight envelope which, arriving unbidden at their office yesterday, held all those pages of incomprehensible legal verbiage, with the surprise conclusion; Artie's plan was to return to work the following day. Hannah and Jake's attorney, Louis, responded to Artie's lawyer, saying that in no uncertain terms, will Bloom & Company ever welcome Artie back to work.

At least for the time being, she thinks. Now it will be up to the mediator to provide the actual ending. And as she walks along 42nd Street toward Grand Central, she's brought back again to the first time they met each other at the trade show in Long Beach, California.

After a tiring day staffing their respective exhibitor booths, the four of them, newly introduced over happy-hour drinks at their hotel, decided on dinner together. They walked the short distance from their hotel to the pier, agreed on a restaurant, and sat at a table outside on the deck. The sun, a picture of it coming back to her as she walks through the doors of the train station, was hovering right above the horizon, an enormous perfect circle, colored in the most brilliant, deep red. Below it, the boats bobbed up and down, squeaking and yawning as they pulled against the heavy lines securing them to the dock, while the waterfront mirrored the last of the light as it played on the ripples in the water, bursting at the surface like sparklers.

As darkness fell, a sudden waft of air whooshed around their table, ruffling the paper placemats and menus. Chilled, Hannah rubbed her hands up and down her arms, and with nothing more to look at, finally turned her face fully toward Artie, where she couldn't help murmuring platitudes of commiseration at each gap in the conversation they were having about his ex-partner who had cheated him out of money, left him high and dry, and started a competing company.

Lisa wasn't involved in Artie's company – she was in the costume jewelry business – and remained quiet during his storytelling, only nodding every so often to give credence to her husband's victories and misfortunes. Hannah must admit she felt indifferent to Lisa when they first met, although she liked her more than she ever did Artie. She remembers how Jake's silence that first evening had surprised her. There were things about Artie that didn't quite add up or ring true, he'd told her later in their hotel room. He couldn't put his finger on it, but there seemed to be more to all those sad accounts than met the eye. And he knew Artie's ex-partner – not especially well, but well enough to discount certain things Artie had said about him. Though Hannah shared Jake's unease about Artie, she couldn't help feeling sorry for him, anyway.

Inside Grand Central station, she checks the TV monitor at the entrance. The next train is leaving in five minutes. Weaving her way through the main concourse, where throngs of people are coming and going in all different directions, she thinks of home and wonders how many pitiful letters from Miri and Ella are waiting in their mailbox for her and Jake. Only two more weeks of camp. Which means only two more weeks of relative silence before the house will be filled again with laughter and giggles and cries of happiness, frustration, and sorrow, as well as their sister fights and the tears that inevitably follow. Ah! But she does miss them terribly. Nothing is quite the same without them, even at their whiniest worst. And by the time they're home, she'll know whether she's carrying a girl or a boy, its growth feeling steadier within her now. Best of all, though, she's looking forward to hearing her baby's heartbeat for the first time. She remembers it was such a funny sound, that chug-chugging of blood coursing through its tiny heart. The echo, amplified in the monitor, like a runaway train, knocking at the insides of its barely developed chest. She can't wait for those sounds, those truest of miracles, as she feels the warmth of a smile radiating out from within her.

She arrives at the gate. As usual, she double-checks with the conductor standing on the platform outside the train to make sure she's on the right track for Stamford. Feeling slightly out of breath, she gets on at the first car, digs around in her Kenya bag for her phone and earphones, and calls Jake.

"I'm on the 4:07," she says in a loud whisper, as she settles into the only empty seat she finds, squeezed between two men, both in white dress shirts, both with cuffs unbuttoned and sleeves rolled above their wrists.

"What time will you be in?"

"At 4:50," she says. After she hangs up, she searches for WQXR, her classical music station, rests her phone in her lap, and once again, takes Hannah Arendt out of her bag. The photograph of Adolph Eichmann's face on the front cover stares at her.

What compels her to keep going with it? Looking out of the window as the train leaves the darkness of the station and comes back into daylight, she considers her own words, instead, and how they need to be wrenched from some unknown place inside herself. How the words must sweep over her inner landscape, light up the nooks and crannies of her soul, act like search beams in the dark of night. Is it for her true expression? Her real self? Then again, are all her efforts simply pure, nonsensical drivel? A wasted effort? She lowers her head in the hope no one will notice the stupid grin she can't stop from widening across her face for taking the all-too-serious side of herself *way, way* too seriously. No, not a wasted effort. And the honest answer to her question is, yes, she's compelled to keep at it, to keep digging as if she can eventually uncover some truth she can live with. For one thing, her thinking can't absorb how this man, this most ordinary-looking man, whose photograph stares up at her from the paperback sitting in her lap, could have been responsible for persuading all those many others to do his murderous bidding. And for another, she can't let go of that history, *her* history. She can't let it vanish. She needs, feels bound, to understand the causes of so much venomous hate in the world.

She opens the book, clicks her pen into action and gazes down at the last paragraph she has underlined. She tries to read. Tired and hot, she'd rather nap, but worries she'll miss her stop if she does. So, sitting between the two men – who by now have both fallen fast asleep, one with his mouth slightly ajar, the other snoring quietly – she looks out at the passing scenery in a sort of daze, daydreaming about a vastly different scene from the one that's outside her window now. It was late April, she remembers, the time for their annual trade show pilgrimage. She and Jake were on the train in China, traveling from one trade show in Hong Kong to another in the city of Guangzhou.

She remembers her seat on the train had faced backward, and her neck stiffened as she was trying to keep up with the alternating views: from lush countryside, with all kinds of vegetation popping up out of the red-colored earth to towns and villages, where everything from roadways to buildings appeared to be in disrepair or in partial states of new construction; to clusters of tiny cement huts, houses and buildings, all sheltered by roofs of rusty corrugated tin. Above the narrow streets, ropes of clotheslines zigzagged from balcony to balcony, all crammed with what seemed like weeks of laundry hanging out to dry. The village streets looked muddy and crowded with men, women, and children riding bikes or making their way on foot. There were rows of parked bicycles leaning up against each other on the bridge over a river that led to Shenzhen. Moored on the side of the river, beneath the bridge, was one lone houseboat. And grey clouds covered the sky, as was usual.

It has always amazed her how thousands of people from all over the world come together to attend these trade shows. In those newly built exhibit halls, English is almost always the language of commerce. And commerce, she's come to realize, is the true language of the world.

Pulled away from her dreaming by the conductor announcing that the next stop is Stamford, Hannah gets up out of her seat and climbs carefully over the sleeping man who sits next to her and whose legs sprawl out in front of him. At the door, waiting for the train to come to a stop, she has a growing sense that all this periphery surrounding her life now is about to close in and take over; and all so much sooner than she'd ever thought it would.

Chapter Four

Outside the station, Hannah paces the sidewalk. Where is Jake? Why can't he ever be on time, waiting for her, or at the very least, pulling up as she gets off the train? Not worth the argument, she tells herself and watching his car come to a stop beside her, tries her best to mask her annoyance. Let it go, she whispers those all-too-familiar, well-used words to herself, as she gets into the car.

"How was the city?" he asks once she's shut the door and clicked her seatbelt into place.

"Same as always, except hotter than hell," she says, and feeling the AC's icy cold air blasting from the car's vents, reaches into her Kenya bag for her sweater and wraps it around her shoulders. "Anything new with you? Or should I say, with Artie?"

"Yes. I spoke to Louis, our new lawyer." He turns around to look at the road behind him as he drives the car away from the curb to merge into the trafficked lane.

"And?" She hears her voice rise an octave as she feels herself becoming more nervous now.

"He's going to set up an appointment with the mediator."

"That's a good sign, isn't it?"

"I think so. He's counting on it not going any further."

"What do you mean, any further?"

"He said he doubts the case will be taken to court. He's pretty sure Artie won't find a prosecuting lawyer because, beyond anything else, he'll never be able to pay his bill if he loses."

"I guess Artie didn't think this through before he began all this crap."

"Guess not. But we have homework to do."

"Homework?" She sighs, suddenly feeling heavy with drowsiness as her mind fuzzes out at the prospect of more work.

"He wants us to put our side of the story down on paper. The whole thing. From beginning to end."

"Are you serious? I think we'll end up with a book," she says, laughing.

"Not we. *You.*"

"I don't understand."

"Aren't you the writer in our family?"

"Well, yes, I guess, but . . ."

"Sorry, there are *positively* no *buts* allowed. This job is yours. End of story."

Jake's dead serious. Hannah doesn't know how to take his demand that she alone must perform for him and for their lawyer.

"When does it need to be done by?"

"Not sure. But if I were you, I'd get going on it as soon as possible."

"But once the kids are home . . ."

"Exactly. You'll have less time."

They're stopped at a red light. Hannah watches the pedestrians cross the street in front of them. Downtown is busy. People are just getting off work. It's still hot. Men have their ties loosened, their jackets slung over their shoulders, and women, bare shouldered now, have their sweaters or wraps tightened around their waists. Restaurants and bars are filling up, especially the ones with outdoor tables set up on the sidewalks.

"And your mother? Life treating her okay?" Jake says, shifting the car into first as the light turns green.

"More or less." Hannah feels a sudden shiver of irritation – something like a small gray cloud which darkens the sky for a moment, but she doesn't know why.

"What's that mean?" he says.

"Well, she has this dilemma . . ."

"Dilemma?"

"Yes. She's trying to decide whether she should move to Basel to live with what's-his-name or stay in New York and live by herself."

"Leo?"

"Yes, Leo. And she's planning to go to Basel to meet his daughters sometime in September."

"What do his daughters have to do with her moving in with their father? You'd think they'd be thrilled."

"I suppose to vet her. You know, to make sure she won't steal them blind. . ."

"Christ! Is he that rich?

"No idea."

"Personally, I think she'll chicken out in the end anyway," he says.

"Why? What makes you say that?"

"Because there's no way she's leaving her beloved Manhattan behind to live somewhere else."

"Love for a man conquers all, don't you know?" She looks over at him; he's concentrating on the road.

Turning to her side window, her thoughts go to her new assignment. How will she tackle it?

"You're suddenly quiet. What're you thinking?" he says.

"Nothing much."

"I know you better than that," he says, glancing over at her.

"Well, I'm trying to figure out how to get this whole thing with Artie and Lisa down on paper. Should I go back to the very first time we met them? Start there? Then relive all his shit while he worked with us?"

"I would guess so. But you know best. You're the writer."

"Ha! Ha! You're too funny."

"Remember how desperately you wanted to know what got him into such deep trouble?"

"Yes."

"And I said I doubted we'd ever know the real reasons."

"But I really just wanted to know his pitfalls."

"So, you could steer clear of them?" he says.

"And to make sure all the things we were doing wouldn't . . ."

"Put us in a vulnerable situation?"

"Exactly," she says, clapping her hands together.

"To tell you the truth, I think we have always had excellent controls in all areas of our business. Surely, you must see that."

"I do, except for my constant, nagging worry," she says. "I mean, I know we're on the right path, but there's always a big old *but* or *what would happen if* rearing their ugly faces."

"There's no way to get around all the *buts* or the *what ifs*. The variables and circumstances can change, for better or for worse, in what may seem like . . ."

"I know. A moment's notice. Oh, well," she says, stretching out her arm toward him. "So how was your day otherwise? Good crazy or bad crazy? Did all the orders ship out on time? Anyone miss me? Miss Artie?" She smiles, looks over at his profile, and strokes his thigh, hoping she'll unlock the sudden seriousness in his face she feels she's caused.

"Mostly good crazy, I'd say." And as Hannah inwardly sighs a breath of relief, he adds, "But to tell you the truth, I miss you. I can't wait for you to come back to work on your regular schedule."

"Oh?" Too bad. She was hoping he'd say the opposite – that he didn't need her there as much anymore – though she really knew he'd never say it. "Why? What's been going on?"

"Other than Artie, there's nothing more than the usual. It's just . . ."

His profile still shows furrows of worry lines.

"Hey, what's the matter?" she says. "Are you OK? You sound odd. Have you caught a case of my worrywarts?"

Now he chuckles. "No, I'm fine. I've been thinking about Artie and all the shit he's put us through. I do think we'll be okay in the end, but . . ."

"We don't really know until we're there, do we?" she says.

Jake makes a right onto their street. As she turns to look out of her side window, the angle of the sun, low in the sky, momentarily blinds her.

At the bottom of their driveway, he stops the car. Hannah gets out and walks to the mailbox, leaving her car door open. And there, in the dark little box, on top of the everyday bills and junk mail, lie the two envelopes beckoning her into the unhappy world of her girls at sleep-away camp.

"Kids?" he asks, as she gets back in.

"Yup. One from each."

"Oy!" Jake clicks his tongue.

In the garage, they make no effort to get out of the car. Tired, the cool, semi-dark of the garage feels like a relief from the glare of the sun and these seats in the car are even more comfortable, as they often joke with each other, than the ones they sit in to watch TV.

A groan escapes through her pursed lips as she sorts through the rest of the mail in her lap. Figuring that Miri's letter will be the easier one to read, she picks it up first. There are large capital letters S.W.A.K. printed in blue, red, yellow, and pink on the back of the envelope. Three hearts surround the different colored letters. Hannah slides her thumb under the flap to open it, keeping her daughter's *sealed-with-a-kiss* love message intact, and pulls out the single sheet of lined paper. The handwriting is messy, the spelling atrocious – unusual for Miri. She most probably wrote her letter in the dark after lights out. The first thing she reports is that her sister, Ella, has finally stopped crying. Then complains to them – to her dear mom and to her dear dad – of a sore throat. Please call, the letter pleads. *Please call so I can talk to you.* Hannah can hear her child's voice as clearly as if she were sitting right behind her in the back seat of the car. She reminds herself, as if for consolation, that this is the first letter since visiting day. It must be normal, she thinks. Except, as Miri has sadly pointed out, they won't be seeing each other for another two weeks. Hannah stares down at the unopened envelope in her lap. She can't bring herself to tear open Ella's missive quite yet. She hands Jake Miri's letter, which she has refolded and put back into its envelope. In case he's missed them, she points out the initials Miri has printed in large capitals alongside the seal and the three hearts she's drawn around them. At least Hannah and Jake still feel loved by one of their children. For now, anyway. He reads Miri's letter and smiles.

As soon as they're in the house, their dogs, Zig and Zag, come running. Clutching Ella's sealed envelope, Hannah goes to open the back door for them. They almost knock her over in their excitement to be outside. The air feels a little cooler. It's pleasant out here. She sits at the table facing the yard, watches the dogs scamper about, and then glances down at the unopened envelope in her lap. There is no *sealed with a kiss* on this one, she notes. No hearts either. Their names – Mom and Dad Bloom – and their address on the line below, appear in wavy lines at the very top of the envelope. Jake comes out to the porch with two glasses of Pellegrino and sits down next to her. For a moment, they sit in silence and stare out at the slow waning light, watching dusk drain the backyard of its summer colors.

"Well?" he finally says, turning to her, an expectant expression on his face.

She tears open the envelope, takes out the short, lined, sheet of pink paper, unfolds it and reads the large, scrawled words out loud:

"Dear Mom and Dad,
I'm not having fun. I want you! I'm bored here,
I don't want to stay; I want love, and your warmth. Please call me!
Love Ella
p.s. I also lost my stamps."

Hannah looks over at Jake. "Well, what do you make of this?" she says, holding up the letter for a moment. Then she folds it back up, returns it to its envelope, as if this will force its contents out of her mind, and hands it to Jake.

"She'll get over it," he says, patting her hand as he takes the envelope from her. "The next one will be better; you'll see. She'll be fine, she really will. Besides, Miri's there with her. It's not like she's all by herself."

He unfolds Ella's letter, reads it and sighs.

"Well?" Hannah says.

"She'll be fine," he repeats. "I promise you."

And suddenly she's besieged with all those reasons why – as her mother's voice pipes up inside her head – it's important to stick things out. But those weren't her mother's words, were they? No. They were all her own. Consequently, whatever words she might have thought of – for herself, for her mother – are evaporating slowly, along with the breathy sigh that escapes between her lips.

"Other than thinking of moving in with Leo, there's nothing else new with your mom?"

"No, not really. I still can't believe she's seriously considering it."

"She wants to be taken care of. Surely, you can't blame her for that, can you? But as I said before, I can't imagine she'll go in the end. She'll chicken out at the last moment, you'll see."

"God, I hope you're right." As soon as those words are out, she wonders at her own reaction. Why should it matter where her mother lives? It's never made any difference in the past.

"But aren't I always, right?" he says, leaning over and kissing her on the cheek.

"Sometimes," she says and laughs.

"*Sometimes*? How about *all* the time?"

"Now you're getting ahead of yourself," Hannah says, getting up. "We should call the kids. I should start dinner. You hungry?"

"Starved."

"Now, *that's* all the time."

Chapter Five

The next morning, as Hannah is making her way down the hall toward her and Jake's shared office, she hears the front door open behind her and an unfamiliar-sounding woman's voice asking to speak to the manager. Hannah turns around, retraces her steps. The woman, looking to be in her early forties, stands at the opened door with a large, loose-leaf binder hugged to her ample bosom. Her graying hair is cut short like a man's, and her oversized glasses are propped on top of her head, flattening her bangs. Her black-and-white-striped, button-down shirt, unbuttoned and left open, covers a black tee-shirt that's barely long enough to hide her thick middle or her thighs, squeezed into too-tight chinos. She wears a camera around her neck and a small black pocketbook across her body. Before Hannah has the chance to ask who she is, a business card is thrust in front of her face. There's a certain smug officiousness about the way she holds up her name card. This woman has obviously watched too many cop-shows on TV. Hannah doesn't even have to glance at the card to know who this stranger is, what she's doing here. The sudden quickened pulse in her neck tells her. Those four letters – the dreaded acronym for always finding violations in the workplace and then charging what they consider to be the appropriate, punitive fines, no matter what – are there in large type at the top of the business card the woman still flaunts in front of Hannah's face. Hannah takes the card. The woman's name in the smaller print below the four letters is Sandra

Brown. She looks up at the woman, at her pale blue eyes, her steely face.

O-S-H-A. The Occupational Safety and Health Administration. This isn't the first time. They've had surprise visits before. And it's always a surprise. Of course.

And always an unpleasant one, to say the least. Not that she would expect it to be any different. After all, this is a stranger who, uninvited, comes into their company, walks through the place, inspects every aspect, each detail, then, without question, finds infractions, like plugging electric cords into the ceiling outlets which bring power to the machines on the factory floor. To Hannah, the intrusion into the place in which they spend almost all their waking hours feels personal in a strange, inexplicable way. It's as if they've been invaded by the enemy, where all the things she's always thought of as belonging to her and to Jake are somehow overturned and in question.

"I'm Hannah Bloom. My husband and I own the company," she says, handing the card back to Sandra Brown, the woman from OSHA.

"Yes, yes," she says, a slight hint of distraction on her face as she waves the offered card away. "I have your names in my notes."

Hannah eyes the loose-leaf binder still locked against Sandra Brown's chest and wonders what other information she has about them in those thick set of pages.

Does she know, for instance, that they publish a new catalog yearly and mail it out to current and prospective customers? Or that, in their factory, they imprint the ordered items with the customer's logos and goodwill messages. She will also explain to Sandra Brown, how the pad printers, silk screen machines, and engravers are used and that the printing inks they use come from Germany, Switzerland, and Italy. Finally, she will tell her that their total operation fits into 7500 square feet of rented space in a pre-World War II factory building. For Hannah – and she would smile now – the best part of their space is its bright airiness. Loads of old, leaky windows don't only let in waves of drafty air but fill the place with the brightest sunlight as well.

And so here she is, Ms. Sandra Brown, the woman from OSHA, standing at the ready in front of Hannah, all set to do her job. Hannah would like to tell her that the factory portion of their business only takes up approximately one-third of the entire space. It's a fun business. Extraordinarily hectic. Never boring. Each day brings with it a fresh set of challenges, mostly to do with production, although sometimes difficulties arise with their employees. Like figuring out how to hold on to those who work hard at their jobs, as well as knowing when it's time to let go of those who don't.

The factory employs fifteen people for printing and packing. Another two work in the warehouse, pulling inventory for the orders, then shipping them out once they're completed by the end of the day. Three more employees work in customer service.

In June, they hired a new person. By the end of July, they had to fire him. He was constantly late for work and, besides persuading another employee to punch his timecard for him, he would disappear at various times during the day. Hannah told him he wasn't working out for them. He was furious. He called the health department. Made a complaint about the smell of ink in the factory. Though the inks are non-toxic, anyone walking in the door finds the smell overpowering. The woman who came from the health department was upset and called OSHA.

This was the first of their surprise visits, but not the last time they'd had to let someone go. There was Will, who had come to them through a state-run program which helped young adolescents newly released from detention centers to get back on their feet. Will was bright and said all the right things to Hannah and Jake at his interview. They liked him and hired him on the spot for the warehouse, thinking, in naïve arrogance, that they could help make a real difference in his life. Unfortunately, it was only a matter of weeks before they discovered he'd stolen a fellow employee's paycheck along with items from their warehouse. They had to let him go. Hannah thought he hadn't cared, by the way he'd walked out of the place, barely a shrug to his shoulders.

But the following morning he was back, all riled up and looking for Jake. Almost immediately, the bruise on Jake's cheek bone caused by Will's punch had swelled up, black, blue, and yellow. Poor Jake. She'd stood by helplessly. No. Not helpless. She must have screamed because she remembers the guys from the warehouse were right there, holding Will down.

That evening, she and Jake discussed how they could have prevented the incident. Unable to come up with a satisfactory answer, they decided it would be best to let it be forgotten. Even the bright coloring of Jake's bruise had faded away after a couple of weeks. Only for Hannah, it was a different sort of bruise that had begun to blossom. It lodged itself inside her, a tight knot of disillusionment and helplessness. Unsure she'd ever feel safe again, she became fanatical about bolting doors shut.

And here she is, Sandra Brown, the invasive woman from OSHA, standing at the ready in front of Hannah, all set to do her job.

"Where would you like to start?" Hannah says, planting her hands on her hips.

"Just point me in the direction of the printing floor and I'll make my way 'round."

"Hi," Jake says, coming up behind Hannah. "What's going on?"

"This is Sandra Brown, Jake. She is with OSHA. Sandra, this is my husband and partner, Jake."

Sandra acknowledges Jake with a nod.

"Okay," Hannah says, turning around, "come with me."

And she leads Sandra Brown through the windowed door and into the factory. As usual, the place is hopping. Directions, commands, and questions bark above the sounds of the working silkscreen and pad print machines.

"If you want to go back to your desk, I'll be fine here on my own," Sandra says, putting her binder down at the edge of a table, where products for the orders are unpacked and readied for printing, and once printed, brought back to the table to get packed up in cartons and afterward, transferred over to the shipping area.

"I'll leave you to it then," Hannah says. "If you need me, I'm over there," she adds, pointing to the windowed door they had just come through.

Sandra turns from Hannah and makes her way towards the metal cabinets that hold the inks.

Natalia, who has been trailing behind them all along, now follows Hannah into her office. She's curious to know who this strange woman is, why she's meddling in their business. When Hannah explains, the best way she knows how, what OSHA is all about and what they're usually after and why they're here, Natalia says, "But that's ridiculous."

Hannah agrees but tells Natalia to please be as helpful as possible to the woman, anyway.

By the middle of the afternoon, Sandra Brown, the lady from OSHA is at Hannah's desk to say she has everything she needs, and after she's gone through all her findings with her superiors, Hannah and Jake will hear from OSHA, most probably in the next week or two.

Findings. Plural. Hannah knows the best thing she could do for herself is to put all of it in the back of her mind. Whatever it is, it's done. Hopefully, their fines – plural – won't be too bad.

"Well, that's settled," Jake says, hanging up the phone. "We have our first meeting with Louis, the lawyer, on Thursday morning."

"What time?"

"Why? Do you have something going on then?" he asks.

"Just wondering is all. And wondering when we'll hear from Ms. Sandra Brown again."

"I wouldn't worry. I mean . . ." he says.

"You don't sound concerned."

"Is there a reason to be?"

"Actually, I don't think so," she says, trying to survey their whole place in her mind. "We keep strict control over what happens back there, how the inks are managed, and the need to keep the place clean and tidy, etcetera, etcetera. But who knows what they'll be after this time?"

"C'mon, Hannah. Let's not get ahead of ourselves here. There's no point worrying until we have something definitive to worry about. Okay?" He smiles at her.

"Okay, okay," Hannah says, smiling back at him, though she knows, he knows she'll worry, anyway. She always does, especially about money. Sometimes more than Jake would like. But for her, there's no better sense of security than knowing there's enough in the bank. A leftover from her childhood, she's sure. Or, more specifically, a learned and passed down lesson from her father, ingrained from his days as a Jewish refugee running away from the Nazis in Belgium during World War II.

"Besides, we won't hear anything from them for at least a couple of weeks."

"Yes, you're . . ." and she stops talking and squints her eyes half shut.

"Go on," he says, laughing. "Say it."

"Yes, I am positive you are one hundred percent *right*. As usual. Satisfied?"

Jake comes over to Hannah. She watches him plonk down on the chair by the side of her desk and groan, as if the effort were too much. "Hey," he says, reaching for her hand. "I get it. Suddenly, we have all this going on. But we'll manage it."

"Deep down, I know we will. It's just . . . well . . . it must be the pregnancy making me a little more crazy than usual." She looks over at him and laughs. "What a pair we make."

"And a very proficient one at that," he says and gets up, leans over to give her a peck on the cheek, then goes back to his desk.

"By the way," she says. "Has anything new come in from Artie or his lawyer? Like more of those unwelcome overnight envelopes arriving unannounced at our doorstep?"

"Nope. I think we're at a *status quo* for the moment."

"That's good, I guess," she says. "Although I do wish they'd hurry it up. I can't wait to have this whole mess behind us."

"Me too, but in the meantime, I'm ready to get back to work. You?"

"Actually, I'm going home," she says. "My attention level has reached its peak for today. I'm tired."

"I understand," he says. "I don't think I'll be here too much longer."

"That's fine, just call me when you're leaving so I can start the pot boiling for the pasta."

"Will do," he says, already engrossed in whatever's on his computer screen.

Chapter Six

Her own little room at home, which is next to the kitchen, feels cluttered suddenly. And claustrophobic. Books and magazines jam the bookshelves in untidy piles. Scattered around her keyboard are the odd bits of paper with notes to remind herself of authors she wants to read, partial lines of a poem she means to complete, phone numbers she has scribbled down but no longer knows to whom they belong, and dates and times of orthodontist and doctor appointments for Miri and Ella, once they're home from camp. Like flags or signposts from the real world, these scraps of paper shoved to the perimeter, though still within view, seem to exist to prevent, to interfere, and to lure her away from what gives her sustenance. It's as if she's isolated in the middle of a tiny island where all the marginal stuff in her life has already begun to close in, to wash over her, like stormy ocean waves on the beach at high tide; a scene in her imagination, she keeps coming back to.

As Hannah sits down at her desk, Zig and Zag lift their heads for a moment. A breeze flutters the loose papers under her monitor. The face of Adolph Eichmann – surprisingly ordinary-looking to her, in his black-framed eyeglasses – stares up at her from Arendt's book cover. She picks it up, fans through its pages. So many important, underlined passages she wants to remember, or go back over, because she can't quite grasp Arendt's thoughts and connections as she first reads them.

Evil, Arendt wrote, *comes from a failure to think.*

Is this true?

To be a leader, doesn't someone have to be a thinker, a planner, and then a plotter? But perhaps it all boils down to empathy. To empathize, one must be a thinker. Or must one be a thinker to be empathetic? And would empathy prevent evil? Would the perpetrators be perpetrators, Hannah wonders, if they could feel another's pain, as if it were their own? She'll have to continue reading to find out what Arendt had meant. But not now.

Sighing, she places the book back on her desk, face-down. Thinking, dreaming. This is what she will need to do now. Allow herself to be seduced by the beckoning cursor blinking at her unfinished thoughts on her computer screen and, at the same time, be blind to the ordinary stuff of her life. While she still can. While these few days stretch before her. But do they? She looks out of the window. The sky has turned completely gray. She turns back to her computer screen; the cursor bobbing where she left off. Sort of like her life, she can't help but think again, bobbing in constant anticipation of what might come next.

Go back to the beginning, she tells herself. Be like an archeologist. Dig and sweep in the dirt to uncover the fragments from an ancient past, haphazardly buried in the deepest layers of the earth. Then create a patchwork of connections, as delicate and sustaining as a spider's web. And finally, fill in the unknown, the sketched, with an imagination as thick and malleable as raw clay. From all this, mold your own story.

Hannah shrugs her shoulders, as if she were giving in to herself, and goes back to re-reading her words, static on the screen, but alive inside her head.

Can you imagine?

                Imagine what? I ask.

Who I might've become,

> you say and pause as if fumbling for the
> words to tell me. But then a sudden smile
> animates your face, and I see how all those
> long-ago fancies are brightening your eyes,
> just like the many distant clusters of stars
> on dark moonless nights.
> But who would you have become?

Ah! Anybody else,

> you say,

Just not me,

> and you laugh.

> But why? I ask.

Because my life
should have been . . .

> Been what? I interrupt.

Oh, you know . . .

> and you close
> your eyes, as if to shutter
> your thoughts from the place,
> where—unlike most urgent dreams
> bleached clean by sunlight—the
> ugliness you've known remains
> rooted deep inside.

A different life,

> you say, in a voice flat and quiet now,
> which belies your fidgety fingers,
> flaking off the skin of an old callous.

But,

you go on, eyes
both fixed and searching,

in spite of . . . yes . . .
in spite of it all, what
must never fade, never
dim, are those long-ago
unforgotten figments
of fancy.

Now Hannah hears Jake come through the front door. He's home at last. She saves her file, turns off her computer, and meets him as he saunters into the kitchen, their two mutts, Zig and Zag, tails wagging in anticipation, behind him. "Hey, do you think I have enough time for a quick shower before dinner?" he says, as he pulls out the large bag of Purina from the cupboard and scoops up enough food to pack their bowls. Then he comes over to the sink, where Hannah is about to rinse off the lettuce leaves for salad, and gently nudges her out of the way. They watch in silence as the dogs' bowls fill with water.

"All yours," he says, putting the bowls back down on the floor.

But before he leaves the kitchen, Hannah watches him cut a chunk of the Manchego cheese she has put out on the table and pop it into his mouth.

"But hurry it up," she says, feeling a sudden irritation rise, the day's stresses clinging to her like the blue mold on rancid leftovers. "We have stuff to talk about, don't we?"

He makes a silly face at her and, grabbing a Ritz cracker off the plate, slinks out of the kitchen, as if he's a naughty little boy with something to hide. Hannah laughs at him. "Are you preparing me for when the kids come home?"

His only answer, footsteps on the stairs.

She turns up the volume to her little radio as she hears Schubert's Spring Symphony being played. It's one of her favorites. Humming along with the music, she flits around the kitchen from one chore to the next, oddly calm now. Cut-up lettuce leaves drain in a colander at the sink, store-bought Bolognese simmers on the stove. She adds salt to the pot of bubbling water, ready for the linguini, then chops up onion, radishes, and tomatoes for the salad.

Zig and Zag, with tails wagging, whine at the door to be let out. Unexpectedly drawn by the fast-changing shades of light outside, she stands and watches her dogs charge out into the yard to chase the squirrels and rabbits, until – as if a thick veil has suddenly dropped and spread out over her backyard – it's become too dim to see too far. August is almost halfway over, she reminds herself and, with a little shiver running down her spine, has a momentary flash of dread for the fall's late afternoon darkness to come.

Flickering in and out of her consciousness, the events of the day reveal themselves like hosts of lightning bugs flashing in and out of the night sky. After her thoughts begin to settle down, what sticks in her mind is the impossible news that after all they've done to help Artie with his bankruptcy, he's now turned around and filed a suit against them, on those exact grounds that both she and Jake had made clear from the absolute start; they were in no position to offer him any guarantees. Whirring about inside her, like a machine without a stop button, all this refuses to leave her head. And she still can't imagine how he could have let his business fail, how he never caught the warning signs she's positive must have been lurking in the background. It freaks her out just to think about it; to even consider the possibility that she might also miss something that would bring their business to its knees. She has always been hyper-vigilant about all aspects of their company, from the cost of importing inventory to buying inks and materials for the factory to buying office supplies. Less straightforward is dealing with employees. She's a tough boss but considers herself fair. She expects them to work hard, like she does, to ensure perfect printing, packing, and on-time delivery of all orders.

She can't help thinking that her brain is divided into two distinct parts. One for this business, the other for her poetry. As much as she would love to step away from the company, consider herself the full-time poet she dreams of becoming, she thrives on the excitement of the business: the daily incoming and outgoing order count; depositing checks into the bank; and solving problems. Of course, she could do without all the daily worries that sap her of energy. But Jake has promised her – and she'll know herself when it will be the right time – to look for the perfect person to take over a portion of what she does for the company. Originally, she'd thought Artie might be her lucky break.

She and Jake work like maniacs in their business. Not so differently – she laughs at her own crazy analogy – from her dogs when they sink their teeth into one thing or another and refuse to let it go. For her, more than for Jake, it's always simply been the fear of what might happen if she did let go, that keeps her at it.

When they first set up Bloom & Company – six years ago – they bought one used silkscreen machine, one used pad printer, and hired two employees. Hannah managed the factory, the unpacking, the packing, and the shipping. She also verified all the orders, ensuring the items were perfectly printed and deadlines were met. There were days when simply taking a long breath seemed like pure luxury. Both she and Jake have certainly put in their time, she decides, nodding in agreement with herself. And now that they can afford to hire more employees and their two girls have grown enough to be a little more self-sufficient, Hannah manages to covet tiny parcels of time for herself and for her poetry. But in the coming months, all this will shift again. There will be a new baby to consider. And to worry about, of course. She closes her eyes, envisions how their lives are about to dip, no, not dip, but plunge, once again, into a rushing river of transformation; too much of it, still unknown.

Night has fallen. It's too dark to see outside her window, but still feeling too wound-up to sit, she paces the length of the small kitchen, stopping every so often to examine each of the little dings and cracks in the cream-colored porcelain floor tiles. A plate or a knife dropped here, a mug or a spoon there. She stops pacing as she tries to recall each of those scenarios. All this, she laughs at herself, to interrupt the flow of uncertainties charging through her head as if her brain were holding a stampede of wild animals.

But those aren't the scenarios she needs to unfold now. Jake's out of the shower. She can hear him opening the closet to look for his comfy, at-home sweats to wear. Time to drop these thoughts of vague uncertainties and come back to what's here on the kitchen counter. Leaning into it, she props one bare foot on top of the other, scoops the salad fixings off the chopping block into a large wooden bowl, adds her dressing, mixes it up, brings it to the table, and sits back down.

As to her earlier thoughts on her poetry, would it help to sift through all those months and years to untangle her own history? Understand how she came to be who she is right now?

No, she answers herself. What she remembers today is different than what she remembered yesterday and then, surely by tomorrow, certain memories will be forgotten, while still older ones will pop into her head, remembered.

But how will she begin *this* story? she asks herself now. How has their life changed since they first met Artie and Lisa at the trade show in Long Beach, California? She remembers the hotel they stayed in was beautiful and, true to Southern California weather, the sun always shone like a welcoming beam in a cloudless blue sky. From the time they first began exhibiting at the trade shows there, Hannah had a routine. Each morning she'd get up at dawn and head out for a run along the beach. Those early morning ocean breezes helped sustain her for the rest of her day spent inside the over-air-conditioned, windowless convention center making small talk, answering questions about the products they exhibited there and later pacing the small area in front of their booth as the day drew down and foot traffic slowed. Working at trade shows has never been her strength. Underneath it all, she's shy and works hard to appear outgoing and garrulous.

But what she did enjoy were the happy-hour get-togethers every evening after the show. A small group would gather in the hotel lounge or at the poolside bar to hash over the day. Foot traffic was always the first topic of conversation. Had there been enough to make the show worthwhile? To this most important question, the answers differed, depending on where each company's booth was located on the show floor. As daylight rolled into nighttime and drinks flowed more freely, tongues began to wag more loosely. For Hannah, this was the part she found the most interesting. She loved to hear how the others managed their businesses. Discussions most often included, for instance, the difficulty of keeping a positive cash flow, levels of inventory to have on hand, pros and cons of accepting credit cards for payment, and the high cost of advertising. There was always something new to learn. Then, as the evening wore on, serious talk would turn into chatter and laughter at all those self-impressed, impossible-to-deal-with customers and problematic employees. Everyone had at least one story to tell.

The story of Will was the one she'd told the group, now gathered in a circle by the pool. It had already turned dark. The sole source of light – shimmering in reds, blues, and yellows from the underwater pool lamps – cast deep shadows across each one's face, making them almost unrecognizable.

Before she spoke, Jake announced it as the ultimate no-good-deed-goes-unpunished tale and let out a laugh. To Hannah, though, it was more a story of how harmful letting down a kid, like Will, could be. It was a story of society's failure and, at the bottom of it, sad defeat.

She closes her eyes for a moment. Fortunately, nothing like that had ever happened before. Or since. As the backyard shifts into focus again, she has a strange feeling. It's as if she's been in the pool, swimming underwater, and is just now able to raise her head, and open her eyes. With her attention drawn back to the darkness outside the window, she catches glimpses of her two dogs – sister puppy mutts, they'd rescued from the pound one Chanukah – as they chase each other back and forth across the lawn. She gets up to turn on the outside lights hoping to see them more clearly than her relived memory of Will. Shaking her head, she discovers another ding on the floor's tile and asks herself if the story, about Will, keeps coming back to her because of its failure. It's as if her mind keeps working on it, looking for answers; even though she knows there are none.

Now there's Artie she needs to think about again. She can't help wondering if she and Jake were set up from the start. How had Artie got himself into such trouble in the first place? They never found out. He most probably hadn't sunk his teeth into his business quite deeply enough. And she smiles at her own silly analogy.

Conscious now of her dogs barking, their paws scratching at the door, she gets up to let them in. They follow her back to the kitchen, sprawl out on the floor under the table, their damp noses to the cold tile, the snorting and puffing to cool themselves down, their only sounds.

And suddenly, she wonders – was it Artie who called OSHA?

Chapter Seven

When she hears Jake on the stairs, she grabs a handful of pasta from the package, drops it into the boiling water, and sets the timer.

"Feeling refreshed?" she says as he comes to stand next to her at the stove. She wraps her arms around his middle and leans her face against his still damp, bare chest. "Mm . . . you smell so nice and clean."

"And how's our little peanut coming along?" he says, placing his hands over her slightly rounded belly.

"I would say, well. Very well indeed." She turns away from him.

"What's the matter?" he says, stuffing his hands into his pockets.

"Honestly, I'm not sure . . . Perhaps weirded out, having to think about Artie and his company and now this lawsuit."

He looks over at her. "The lawsuit I understand, but what's different about him now? What has you so weirded out?"

"Honestly, it's everything. And on top of it all, the stupid woman from OSHA. Treating us as if we've purposefully done things against the law to harm our employees. And then keeping all her findings top secret, including, of course, who tipped OSHA off." She looks at him.

"Are you thinking . . .?" he says.

"Let's just say, I wouldn't be a bit surprised."

The timer dings. The pasta's cooked. Jake drains the pot and pours the Bolognese sauce over the linguini. Hannah brings the Pellegrino and their glasses to the table. As if to acknowledge them, the dogs lift their heads for a moment, wait for Hannah and Jake to take their seats, then rest back on the floor again.

"When are we meeting Louis?" Hannah asks him.

"Day after tomorrow, around ten, I think. And I can't believe it, but I forgot again which day next week the girls are coming home."

"Tuesday."

"Right. Do you think you'll have something written for the mediator by then?" he says.

"I hope to." She grates the Parmigiana over Jake's pasta, then over hers. "Artie's become embedded in my mind. I can't stop thinking about him now. Ugh!"

"I'm sorry," Jake says, twirling his fork around the linguini.

"Not much to be done about it," she says. "Hopefully, my story will be convincing enough for the mediator."

"You'll do your best, which will be the best we can do." He lifts his fork, a mass of linguini wrapped in a roll around it, but as strands of pasta slip off, he shoves it all into his mouth in a noisy slurp.

Hannah looks over at him and laughs. "Good thing the kids aren't here to see you eat."

"Ha! Good thing," he says and laughs, too.

"Do you remember what made you realize it was never going to work out with Artie?"

"Not exactly. I remember that it was early on, though. But there was never just one incident I could point to and say . . . this was it. No. There were too many things about him that drove me crazy." He soaks up the sauce on his plate with a chunk of bread and takes a bite. "What about you?" he adds, his mouth full.

"The same," she says. "Never especially cooperative. He always seemed to have his own stuff going on. Stuff, which was only important to him and had nothing at all to do with our business."

"Yes, I never got the sense he felt fully invested in our merged companies."

"So, how could he be demanding all those guarantees?"

Jake shrugs. "Why not?" he says. "He can always demand."

Every time she thinks of Artie, there are always those same few stubborn snapshots rolling around in her head: Artie making one or another of their employees burst into tears for no good reason; Artie trying to solve a printing problem he should have never tackled to begin with because, as we found out, he'd had no experience with the printing aspect of his own company; Artie and his inability to get his own inventory under control, which meant they never knew, with certainty, what they actually had on their shelves to sell; and then Artie with his litany of facial expressions, as good to her as warning flags flying in the wind.

But all this was later, when she was becoming more and more convinced that it would never work out. For now, though, she needs to go back to the beginning. Report to the mediator on the ways they had tried to reconcile their two companies. The most curious "how comes" of what happened to his company with what she would always see as the scary, multiple, unknown "what ifs" of theirs.

"Doesn't it suddenly feel like it was only yesterday when we were sitting here at the kitchen table eating dinner and trying to figure out how he got to be in such deep shit?" she says, remembering the thrill of satisfaction she'd felt when she'd first learned about Artie's problems. It was his arrogance that'd got to her, his boasting about his brilliant business acumen. And how wrong, she now knows, how terribly wrong she was to have been the slightest bit envious of him.

"Yes, in one way it does," he says. "But then in another, like an age ago. Besides. . ." And standing up, he continues, "you were much more curious about all of it than I was." He picks up their dishes, brings them to the sink, and turns on the faucet.

"You're actually doing the dishes?" she says, getting up too.

"Yup." He opens the dishwasher and begins to load it.

"If only he'd presented us with an actual proposal, before we went up to see his place in Rhode Island, perhaps things might've worked out differently." She comes to stand next to him at the sink.

"Maybe," he says. "Although, looking back, I seriously doubt it."

"We never found out what had gone wrong with his company, did we? But I remember being in shock over it."

"Really?" Jake says surprise in his voice. "Wasn't it you, who wondered how he could've effectively run the factory up in Rhode Island from his office on Long Island?"

"Yes. But regardless . . . it seemed to be working. I mean, the company grew, at least according to what he made us believe, and to be honest . . ." She stops talking and bends down to pet one of the dogs. "I was envious . . . I thought he had all the answers to faster growth – answers we had somehow missed."

Jake smiles. "He had investors. Remember?"

"Yes, but so what?"

"So what? They provide the cash for you to buy the inventory you need to grow quickly. But what's scary is that when things don't quite go to their liking; they pull the plug."

"And that's what you think happened to him?"

"It's possible, especially if he talked a good game and they believed him. But then, when he couldn't live up to their expectations. . ."

"They dumped him, like he's trying to do with us," she says. The picture of Artie coming to her now is the one of him sitting across the table from her in the Italian restaurant, with his white dinner napkin draped like a bib across his chest. He'd said he needed to protect his starched, pale blue shirt from any accidental drippings of the red sauce smothering his veal Parmigiana.

She remembers the October evening – the frosty chill in the air, a portent of those bleak winter nights to come – and how Artie seemed to have changed in the year and a half since they'd first met in Long Beach. What she noticed most of all was how his own sense of importance and pride had puffed up his chest, the words of self-aggrandizement urgently spilling out of his mouth as if he were afraid they'd be stolen before they were fully formed, and then how those expressions of disgust or happiness on his large face seemed to be interchangeable at a moment's notice, depending on his mood or where the conversation was going. But no matter what else was happening in his life, it didn't matter, because his business was thriving. That evening, he'd also told them he'd moved his factory from a small space in Long Island City to a 30,000-square-foot building in Cranston, Rhode Island, bankrolled by one of his suppliers. His smile spread wide across his face, as if it were the exclamation point to his news.

Hannah and Jake fared well enough in their 7500-square-foot space. But while listening to his tales of success, she'd felt envy seeping in through the cracks of her own insecurity. Though, admittedly, the longer he talked, the more distrustful of his success she became. Understanding what it takes to run the day-to-day operations of a small business, she wondered how he could control his company from afar. When she asked him about it, he said he traveled up to Cranston at least once or twice a week from Long Island, where he and Lisa lived, and usually stayed overnight. Hannah remembers looking over at Lisa to see her reaction. She never minded his being gone during the week. Fewer dinners to worry about, she'd said, laughing. And her own TV shows to watch at night.

"But you were right," Jake says, starting up the dishwasher. He comes back to sit at the table, and picking up his glass of Pellegrino, adds, "He and Lisa should've moved up to Rhode Island."

"We're all different, I guess," Hannah says, watching him empty his glass. "But I know I could never completely depend on my employees to do what I would in certain situations, no matter how good or trustworthy they are. Or expect them to always act in my best interests or make the same logical financial decisions I would. How could they? Their necks aren't on the line. It's not their business."

And just as her words are out of her mouth, it comes to her; for all the times she'd love to walk away, give her job to an employee, she knows she couldn't. In the end, she'd spend more time worrying about whether they were doing things the way she'd want them done. Hannah looks down to see both dogs standing on either side of her thighs. They nuzzle their noses into her lap in the hopes she'll pet them.

"And yet you envied him . . . for what?" Jake says.

"Obviously not for what he lost. Oh, I don't know. He seemed so far ahead of us, making money, getting beyond the struggle. Do you know what I mean? Didn't you feel the same way?"

"I don't think so. Growing quickly is never the answer. Things can become too easily unmanageable and risky, which, for sure, is not a good place to be. We know what that's like."

"Yes, we do," she says, thinking of how often they've had to work hours of overtime to meet deadline ship dates, pack up the car with the filled cartons and bring them down to FedEx to ship overnight at their own expense. All this to avoid letting a customer down. Luckily, Sophia, their elderly neighbor, has always been available to meet Miri and Ella when they come off the school bus, even at the last minute, if Hannah should be delayed.

"Anyway," Jake says. "I can imagine him pissing off his employees big time."

"Yes, but who doesn't from time to time? I'm quite sure I do."

"You have a point," he says, and chuckles. "You certainly do have a point."

"Ugh! Getting people to do things the way you want them done isn't always easy."

"I'm only glad you're the one with that job and not me, is all I can say."

"Tell me," Hannah says, "do you remember what made us get together with Lisa and Artie in the first place? It's driving me crazy . . ."

"Short trip . . ."

"But seriously, can you remember?"

"Not a hundred percent," Jake says, as he slices more of the Manchego. "A couple to go out with after a long day at a show? We didn't know what he was like back when we first met him, did we?"

"In Long Beach, no. But afterward?"

He arranged the slices of cheese on the crackers and lined them up on the wooden board.

"Don't tell me you're still hungry."

"A little. This is my Continental-style dessert. Don't the French always end their dinners with cheese?" A sudden smile spreads across his face. "Bangkok," he shouts. "Remember? It was Bangkok."

"Oh my God, I'd totally forgotten . . ."

"Perhaps it all goes back to that one chance encounter. I mean, who'd have thought you'd run into a couple you barely knew from business in front of a pots-and-pans display in the middle of some home goods store, you had wandered into, while meandering around the second floor of the largest shopping mall in Bangkok, just to get out of a torrential downpour outdoors?"

"Serendipity?"

Jake nods as he pops another cracker with cheese into his mouth.

"I remember how you and he were chatting away, not about business," she says, "but about how you both liked to cook and what ingredients and spices you used for various dishes. Meanwhile, Lisa and I stood by, silent and smiling."

"It must've been after the Hong Kong show. How surprised we all were to run into each other. I mean, how odd to see familiar faces in a foreign country, and so far from home."

"And you think that's what bonded us in some sort of weird way?"

"Maybe."

"How random life is sometimes," Hannah says.

"I remember we were hoping to get information from him on his overseas sources, but most of all, we were interested in which domestic companies were supplying him. Finding new products and not having to buy inventory in quantity from overseas would have been great for us. Obviously, he never shared that information."

"You can't blame him for that, though, can you?"

"Probably not. Though, here we are, irony of ironies, and how few years later? With the whole shooting match in our laps anyway."

"Serendipity."

"You and your serendipity," he says.

"But did we ever know for sure what he actually wanted from us?"

"Yes, absolutely. He needed us to take over his business, give him a job. But mostly, he needed security."

"And the kind of security he was looking for, we obviously couldn't give him."

"Right," Jake says.

Rings of moonlight glow in the cloudless summer sky, silvering portions of their backyard. Trees sway slightly in the breeze, and every so often, the motion of a squirrel, a chipmunk, or a rabbit surprises her; the flash of its tail caught in the light as it darts across the lawn.

"Do you remember?" she says, patting his arm to get his attention. "The night we met them for dinner at the Italian restaurant in Queens?"

"Yes, vaguely. Why?" He cuts a couple more slices of the cheese, lays them on crackers, then turns to face her, signs of impatience – or was it fatigue? – barely hidden in his movements.

"I can't tell you, exactly," she says. "But there are certain fragments of that evening which keep coming back to me. I mean, it's as if I'm a detective scouring for clues to solve a mystery. I know it must sound crazy, but I feel like all the jagged pieces need to fit together perfectly."

He doesn't say anything at first; only picks up one of the crackers topped with cheese.

"How else can I best explain what I mean?" she goes on. "I guess what I'm looking for, what I need, is a complete picture of them. Do I make any sense to you?"

"In a way. Yes. Although . . . and please don't take this the wrong way . . . But I do think you're taking this whole thing way too . . ." He shrugs and pops the slice of cheese and cracker into his mouth.

"Too seriously? Too much to heart? Too much . . ."

"Look," he says, still chewing. "All we need to do is produce our story of what happened. Nothing more. There's no point in all this searching for deeper meanings, ulterior motives. You'll only exhaust yourself."

She gets up to clear what's left on the table. He gives her a peck on the cheek and leaves the kitchen. She continues to stand in place for another minute or two, feeling as though something has knocked her off-kilter and she needs time to regain her balance.

Hearing the voices coming from the TV in the den, she pictures Jake sitting in his chair, his legs stretched out, his feet on the hassock, the newspaper in his lap. She wipes down the counters and rinses out the sink and despite Jake's warning, she can't help being caught up in her Artie-and-Lisa riddle again. But isn't this how it should be? Especially since she'll be writing about them for the mediator. As the memories of them continue to roll through her mind, she realizes that the puzzle, for her, lies most especially with Lisa. What was it about Lisa when they first met that made Hannah feel like an insecure little girl? The blonde highlights in her perfectly straight, blow-dried hair? Or her perfectly manicured fingernails painted bright red? Or was it her expertly applied black eyeliner surrounding her large brown eyes? Or her creativity in designing and fabricating her own jewelry and making a business out of it? And why did Hannah always feel this way? Not good enough. Not bright enough. Not pretty enough. But her feelings had all changed, she remembers, the day they'd stopped for lunch on their way to Rhode Island to see Artie's factory. Hannah had begun to feel equal to Lisa – had even enjoyed being with her. She wonders how these circumstances are affecting her. Will she be at the mediator's meeting with Artie? But mostly, Hannah wonders how she, herself, will feel toward Lisa. Lost friend or new foe?

She turns off the light and leaves the kitchen, her thoughts still spiraling away uncontrollably, but this time they flit back and forth between her unhappy children away from home, to the desk in her little study, to the view from her study's window, to the way the rays of sunlight slant across her desk and below it, to where her two dogs are always sprawled at her feet.

"One thing's for sure," Jake says, as Hannah comes into the den. "No matter what the verdict will be, you and I will be okay. In fact, I'm sure we'll be better than okay. So, please, you must stop worrying. It does neither of us any good."

"You're right," she says, the word escaping out of her mouth without thinking until, seeing the expression on Jake's face, she's unable to stop the smile dimpling her cheeks and crinkling her eyes. "Yes, yes, I know you are. But for one stupid reason or another, I just can't help worrying." She takes a long drink of her Pellegrino and, leaning back in her chair, realizes how tired she is. And how her thoughts have become preoccupied, all over again, with her unhappy children.

"What are you watching?" she says, suddenly aware of the flickering light coming from the TV.

"Nothing. There's absolutely nothing worth watching."

Hannah looks down at her watch. "We should call the kids before it gets too late."

"Sure. Okay." But, as though frozen in his chair, he stays sitting, his head bent, the unread newspaper in his lap. "You think he might've expected to be put in charge of our business?" he says, looking up at Hannah.

"No, of course not. It would've been an impossible situation," she says. "We barely knew him then. And he didn't know us, either."

"Right. And if he'd fucked up his own company, who's to say he wouldn't have done the same with ours?"

"Jake, what's going on with you now?"

"On the other hand," he says, hardly listening to her. "He might've proved quite useful. Another perspective in the mix. Ugh! My head is in a spin. I can't think about this anymore."

"Good. Then let's phone the kids and call it a night."

Chapter Eight

As if she's been shaken awake, Hannah's eyes suddenly snap open. The light in their bedroom is still dim. But the sun outside her window, barely above the horizon, is a flaming, orange-colored semi-circle. She doesn't have to check the time on her clock to know that the alarm won't be going off for a while and that if she gets up now, she won't have to listen to the dreaded radio announcers sharing their gloomy news of the day. Leaving Jake fast asleep in bed, she tiptoes to the bathroom and afterwards makes her way down to the kitchen. She turns on the espresso machine, puts a slice of bread in the toaster, and sits at the table, alternately daydreaming and skimming the front page of yesterday's paper, while waiting for her toast to pop up.

After a time, and she doesn't know exactly how much has passed, she hears footsteps on the stairs. "How long have you been up?" Jake says, coming into the kitchen.

"A while," she says, stifling a yawn as she folds up the paper.

"You'll be exhausted later on," he says, as he puts a cup under the nozzle of the espresso machine.

"My life is exhausting." The muttered words, barely audible over the whooshing sound of coffee spurting into his cup, land on deaf ears. Thankfully, she thinks. Then, in a voice loud enough for him to hear her this time, she says, "Well, anyway, I can always nap in the car on the way to work."

"What kept you up?" He sits down across from her.

"I slept the night. I woke with the sun is all."

"Hmm."

She gets up, puts her plate and cup in the sink. "Do you want me to put your muffin in the toaster for you?"

"Sure, thanks."

Right after she's left the kitchen, she hears Jake say, "You should stay home today."

She comes back. He's leaning on the counter, staring at the toaster, as if he'll make his muffin finish toasting sooner.

"Stay home?" she repeats, but doesn't understand, or rather misunderstands, what he's telling her.

"Yes," he says, turning around to face her. "I mean, so that you can get as much written for the mediator as possible."

"Oh," she says, a little relieved.

"Well, what d'you think?"

"Umm . . ." The toaster dings.

Jake reaches for a plate, a knife. And takes out the muffin. "The way I see it," he says, now buttering it, "the sooner we can get this done, the better. Don't you agree? Whatever you were going to do at work today can wait."

She looks away from him. As far as she can remember, there's nothing urgent waiting for her. No payroll to administer, no rush orders to oversee. Anything else that comes up during the day, Jake can take care of, or yes, it can wait until tomorrow. And, yes, she might even steal a little time for the poem she's been struggling with. Yes.

"Great idea," she says, turning back to him and smiling. "I'll do exactly that."

Armed with a fresh mug of steaming black coffee, she goes to her little room off the kitchen, turns on her computer, and stares dreamily out the window as she waits for the familiar scenic picture to appear on her screen. But where to begin? She feels stuck before she's even begun.

She goes upstairs. In the bedroom, she stands in front of her open closet. What is she doing? She doesn't have to get dressed today. A tee shirt and sweats will do. But she supposes, as she idly pulls and pushes the hangers back and forth across the closet bar, her brain might need this extra time. And sure enough, the wintry outfit she wore to dinner the evening they'd met Artie and Lisa at the Italian restaurant in Queens is staring her in the face. She shakes her head. A force is guiding her. She'll hop in the shower and let those memories flood her thoughts.

She can feel the touch of Lisa's hand, ever so lightly on her arm. She had a new venture, she'd said to Hannah, raking her fingers through her highlighted, shoulder-length hair. Although Hannah was more interested in hearing what Artie had to say about his business, she didn't want to appear rude. So, she turned in her chair to face Lisa, who was busy rummaging around in her oversized Louis Vuitton. Ah, she said, pulling out a clear, plastic baggy filled with glitter and setting it on the table between them. I have my own jewelry store now; maybe, one day, you'll come and visit me there. Her red-painted nails were fluttering over the baggy. Hannah was about to turn it over to get a better view of its shimmery contents when Lisa made space on the table between them and tipped everything out. Here, she said, you can see all the pieces much better now. And, please, feel free to pick up whatever you'd like and hold it up to the light.

As the shower rinses off her soap-covered body, Hannah's thoughts stay fixed on that evening. She remembers the odd sense of coercion she'd felt, like a vise clamped tight inside her chest, as the colorful, shiny items tumbled out of the baggy and scattered across the red-and-white checkered tablecloth. Was becoming Lisa's customer a requirement for their friendship? A test perhaps, she'd thought, as her fingers gingerly pawed through the glitter. She looked for earrings. What color should the glass jewel be? The wire? Gold, not silver. She thought of the clothes hanging in her closet, tried to visualize their colors. Most were jeans. Blue was her color. Now to find the earrings she liked that didn't appear too expensive. She looked for the least fussy. Found a pair. Thank goodness. How much are they, she'd wanted to ask. But asking would make her seem cheap. Instead, Hannah held up the earrings and, taking a deep breath, said she'd like to buy them. Would that be okay with her? Of course, Lisa responded. And as Hannah remembers it now, Lisa smiled as her hand went up to a strand of blond hair that had fallen over her face and, curling it around her finger, wound it behind her ear. Hannah then turned to Jake, interrupting his and Artie's conversation, to ask if he had cash on him. He reached into his pocket, pulled out a ten-dollar bill and a couple of singles. He never carried too much cash with him. What do you need? he asked. Hannah looked over at Lisa for the answer. Don't worry, you can always send me a check, she'd said in such an offhand manner, it was almost as if she never expected to get paid in the first place.

She remembers she'd held up the earrings she'd chosen – gold hoops with small, turquoise-colored glass beads – to show Jake and Artie.

When the waiter arrived with their oversized portions – veal parmigiana with spaghetti for the men and white clam sauce over linguini for the women – Lisa shoveled all her glitter back into the baggy and dropped it into her Louis Vuitton. Then she brought out a tiny black velour drawstring pouch, slipped Hannah's new earrings into it, pulled the drawstring tight and with a flourish, tapped her hand on the table as she deposited the little black pouch by the side of Hannah's plate.

Stepping out of the shower now, she remembers that while she was eating her dinner, she couldn't keep her eyes from drifting every few minutes to the space next to her plate, where Lisa had placed the little black pouch. How expensive were these earrings going to be? she couldn't help wondering. Surely not enough to have made her that anxious. Then, while they were saying their goodbyes to each other in the parking lot and Hannah had asked again how much to send the check for, Lisa had waved her hand and told her not to worry. Consider them a gift, she'd said, and blew her a kiss.

Throwing on a pair of sweats and a tee shirt, Hannah goes back downstairs to her little room next to the kitchen.

Ready – or as ready as she thinks she'll ever be – to embark on her and Jake's year-long saga with Artie and Lisa, Hannah brings her keyboard nearer to the edge of her desk, pulls her chair in closer, sits up straighter, reopens her new file in Word she's named ARTIE, and starts typing:

We first noticed Artie and his wife, Lisa, at a trade show in Long Beach, California, where we exhibit each year in August. In early May the following year, we ran into each other in Bangkok, Thailand. We talked for a while as we looked around the store together. We learned Artie liked to cook, as Jake does, and that Lisa had her own jewelry business. The next August, we met again in Long Beach. We went out for dinner. Then, once we were back home, we met in Queens – the halfway point between where they live on Long Island and us, in Connecticut. I remember him talking about the factory building he'd recently bought in Rhode Island and how proud he was. But this last time we met for dinner; he seemed a little off. I wasn't sure if he was mad at us – although I couldn't understand why he would be.

Chapter Nine

After rereading what she's just written, Hannah plants her fingers back on the keyboard, and is just about ready to start typing again, when her phone rings. As she picks it up, Zig and Zag stand, nudging at her thighs, then satisfied she isn't going anywhere, lie back down under her desk as before.

"Hi, my darling." It's her mother. Before Hannah has the chance to respond, she hears the usual question, though this time in a higher-pitched tone. "Everything all right?"

"Yes, of course it is. Why?" Hannah answers, a sense of impatience brewing inside, as her hard-earned concentration is broken.

"I called you at the office and whomever I spoke to said you weren't coming in today."

"Well, I've been allotted the arduous and painful task of writing up our history with Artie for the mediator. So, Jake has given me the day off to get working on it." She chuckles. The day off. Ha! Ha!

"Oh, I see," her mother says. "I should let you get back to it, then. I only phoned to chat."

"I'll call you later this afternoon. Will you be home?"

"Sure. I'll be here."

The dogs stir beneath her, assuming she's been talking to them. She gets up, stretches her arms above her head and goes into the kitchen, pours herself a glass of water and comes back to her desk, to her ARTIE file.

The following June, Artie phoned Jake. He said his company was in trouble and would Jake be interested in working something out with him? Yes, of course, Jake said. His product line fits perfectly with ours. So, Artie and Lisa came up to Connecticut to see us. They arrived at our house at around three in the afternoon and didn't leave until ten that evening. They told us how Artie had brought in Lisa's cousin to work in his business and that the cousin had embezzled over $400,000 from Artie's company, leaving him high and dry. Although we couldn't understand how a small company, with approximately $2.7 million in sales, could lose any amount of money, let alone such a large sum, we continued with the proposition, anyway. Lisa said the match between our two companies would be perfect – a win-win situation. We understood from this conversation that Artie was mainly interested in having a job.

Hannah is stuck again. She gets up and walks from room to room. The dogs follow her. In the family room, she puffs up the cushions on the couch and the chairs, and as she folds the blanket that covers her up while watching TV in the evenings, she notices her plants look droopy. In the kitchen, she fills a jug at the sink and goes around to water them. Afterward, she refills her own glass and takes it to her little room, where she sits back down at her desk and stares out of the window. The day is gray. The dogs saunter in behind her, once again taking their place at her feet.

Two weeks later, Artie and Lisa came to our office and from there we drove up in his SUV to see his factory in Rhode Island.

How will she best describe that trip? "What a day it was," Hannah whispers to herself and, shaking her head, stares back out of the window again.

Then smiles at the sudden memory that comes to her. She and Lisa were settling into the back seat of Artie's SUV when these unexpected few words tumbled out of Lisa's mouth.

—Haven't you wondered, she'd asked, clicking her seatbelt into place, —what kind of ride we're in for? And before Hannah had the chance to let those first words sink in, she added, —both literally and figuratively, I mean.

Hannah felt Lisa's hand on her arm, felt her gently squeeze it, and heard her laugh, as if she had told the most hilarious joke; or was it, perhaps, a mask for her own anxiety?

She can't imagine she'll ever forget it.

•   •   •

Hannah and Jake were at their office, waiting for Artie and Lisa to show up. How odd it'd felt, she remembers, waiting for them, as if she were a foreign visitor inside her own world. She'd felt nervous, too, though she didn't know why. Miri and Ella were all set. Their neighbor, Sofia, was going to meet them at the bus stop this afternoon, take them out for Big Mac dinners this evening, then stay with them until she and Jake got back home, whenever that would be.

It was already past ten-thirty. Artie and Lisa were late. She took one last look at the stacks of paperwork on her desk. Annoyed, she began rearranging and neatening them – all the piles in desperate need of a thorough-going through. What would be the point of beginning, though? The law of probability told her that as soon as she did, they'd show up. And sure enough, as she brought one of the piles closer to her, they came bustling through the door like a great gust of wind.

—Traffic was horrendous, Artie said. —The bridge . . . you should've seen it. Bumper to bumper.

—No worries, Jake said and, getting up to greet them, repeated, —No worries at all.

—Before we get started, could you point us toward the ladies and gents? It's been a long ride, Artie said, a sheepish grin crossing his face.

Jake showed them to the bathrooms. A few minutes later, Artie reappeared.

—It's so good to see you guys again, he said, still drying his hands with a paper towel from the men's room. —You both look terrific, as usual.

After a couple more banal exchanges, Jake walked Artie around their office, introducing him to their employees. Then they disappeared into the factory. Hannah watched them through the glass panel in the door. Jake was laughing as he presented each of the women in the factory as his next wife. It's a stupid little joke he tells and the women, eager to please, always laugh every time he goes through his routine.

—Wow! The earrings look great, Lisa said, coming out of the ladies' room. —And Artie's right, they match your eyes perfectly.

—It just depends on the weather, Hannah said, pleased she'd thought of putting them on that morning.

As the two men came back into the office, they joked with each other, like long-lost bosom buddies.

—The place is great, Artie said, a little too loudly. Hannah didn't believe him.

Since Artie had the bigger car, a Suburban SUV, the men decided he should drive.

—We'll let the guys sit up in front. You okay in the back with me? Lisa said, raking her manicured fingers through her hair, just as blonde, blow-dried, and highlighted as the last time they'd seen each other.

Hannah agreed, though she had hoped to spend the trip up to Rhode Island gazing dreamily out of her window. What would she find to talk to Lisa about besides her glimmery jewelry?

—Are we all ready? Artie said, rubbing his hands together and oddly sounding quite jovial – as if they were off for a day's vacation trip rather than the viewing of his bankrupt company.

In the black SUV, Hannah sat behind Artie; his cell phone's microphone still attached to his right ear. As he drove, she watched him glance over at Jake now and then as they talked. She only listened peripherally. They'd returned to their shared love of cooking, discussing recipes for clams with pasta, their secrets for grilling steaks and burgers, and the ingredients they used to make their marinades for chicken and pork. Were cooking recipes all they could find to talk about? The road trip was feeling more than a little surreal.

Meanwhile, she and Lisa chatted about their kids. Safe ground, Hannah remembers thinking. Lisa's son, Ethan, was about to start college and she already knew how badly she was going to miss him. Hannah told Lisa that Miri and Ella were in day camp. She said nothing more about her own life and luckily, Lisa never asked. Luckily, Hannah thought, because she wouldn't have known what to tell her. For whatever reason, she couldn't figure out why it always embarrassed her to explain how much the threading of words into poems and stories meant to her. And how inept the slow process made her feel.

—Anyone else hungry but me? Artie called out, breaking the momentary lull in their conversations.

—Always, Jake said. —And I know the best place to stop for lunch.

—Great. How long before we're there? Lisa asked.

—Fifteen minutes.

—Perfect, Hannah and Lisa shouted out together, and they both laughed.

•   •   •

Out of the corner of her eye, Hannah notices a large racoon sauntering across her lawn. She continues to watch it waddle along, convinced the animal can feel her gaze when it suddenly speeds up as if in a huge hurry to cross the grass to arrive unharmed at its shelter in the woods.

She pushes her chair back, stands, and goes into the kitchen to make herself an espresso. The mail truck has stopped at the end of their driveway. An arm stretches out of the truck's window and deposits a bunch of envelopes and circulars into her mailbox. She waits for the truck to drive off, slips her feet into her flip-flops and rushes down the driveway. She knows there will be letters from her girls, even though sleep away camp is almost over. They must be enjoying it by now. She opens the mailbox. Sure enough, sitting right on top of all those unwanted bills and circulars is one letter from Ella. Hannah feels a sudden dryness in her throat. She rushes back up the driveway. And as soon as she's in the house, she flicks through the mail to make sure that this is the only one from her girls, and goes back to her desk, Ella's words tight in her hand. She sits down, takes a deep breath, and tears open the envelope.

Dear Mommy and Daddy,
*Today was Deborah's birthday. I'd **die** if I had to spend my b-day without you guys. I'm very homesick.*
*I **hate** being in camp and want to come home as **soon** as possible.*
Do you remember where I hung up all my pictures and postcards on the wall above my bed? Every night before I go to bed,
I look at the pictures of you and start to cry.
2 nights ago, the bears were very wild.
Jerry tried to set traps.
It didn't work, only for the baby cubs.
*Now the mama bear's **very** mad and growls **a lot**!*
I miss you & love you!
Love, Ella

Hannah lets out another longer and deeper breath. She remembers the space around Ella's bed from visiting day; how she'd filled it with her photos and postcards and pasted them with stickers in the shape of hearts in bright red. Hannah misses her girls. More than missing – it's like a hole punched into her chest. She wishes they were here to hug and to kiss. Her tears brew. "But they'll both be home in no time," she says to console herself, imagining each of them, arms tight around her middle, heads leaning against her body. Then she wonders how Miri is doing. Not as homesick as her sister, she's sure of it.

Her focus drifts back to her screen. She looks over at the words she's put there. It's past three o'clock. She's tired and too distracted now to continue working. But she must. She gets up, goes into the kitchen, and makes herself another espresso. As the machine sputters the coffee into her little cup, she's brought back to Lisa.

·   ·   ·

They'd sat across from one another at one of the wooden picnic tables set up in the garden outside the restaurant.

Artie and Jake were inside, ordering the lobster rolls the four of them had decided on. Hannah remembers she was curious to know if Jake would feel compelled to pay for all four lunches. She had tried to push that possibility from her mind along with the thought of the American Express bill she'd have to pay. She was sounding mean and stingy, even to herself.

—What a beautiful day, Lisa said, closing her eyes and pointing her face into the sun.

Hannah looked over at the people sitting at the tables surrounding theirs, and at the kids running and playing. She turned to face Lisa again. A deep breath helped bring her into the moment and, as her thoughts drifted into the background, she asked, —How is your store going?

—Well, I've moved it inside a hair and nail salon. And although the space is much smaller than what I had before, I now have a ready-made clientele, which is good, plus it's not costing me nearly as much. I'm also designing my own stuff now.

—That's fantastic, Hannah said.

Lisa, cocking her head to one side and moving her fingers in a circle around the wood knots in the table, continued, —I have pictures of my latest creations on my phone, if you'd like to see them.

Hannah told her she'd love to, and immediately pictured the oversized costume jewelry, the colored glass sparkling in the dim light of the restaurant, and the red-and-white checkered tablecloth strewn with the pieces pulled from her oversized Louis Vuitton. Then she asked Lisa where she got her ideas from.

—I search through vintage shops for old pieces, she said. —And if I'm lucky, I come across those big brooches and pendants the women used to wear all those years ago. Remember them?

Hannah nodded.

Lisa explained how she would take apart the pieces of jewelry for their stones and create new pieces with them.

—Oh my God, that reminds me of two stories about my pendant. The first, the oldest, is about the piece itself, Hannah said, twisting it on its chain and leaning closer to Lisa. —At first, I believed this piece of jewelry commemorated a son's birth for his mother; however, I later learned it memorialized a husband's death for his widow. *William Isaac Allgood,* died on *April 20th, 1868.*

—How sad. And the second story?

—That one began, or most likely ended, with the death of my grandfather. The pendant had been sitting in its own special silky satin-lined leather box, on a bookshelf, in my grandparents' living room. The inscription is printed in gold on the satin lining and, beneath a picture of the crown, reads,

H & E Tessier, the Jeweler on New Bond Street
TO THE QUEEN
and their RH The Prince and Princess of Wales
and the Royal Family.

The piece had always fascinated me, even as a young girl, and after my grandfather died, my grandmother gave it to me. I bought a chain for it and didn't think more about it until months later when I was in a jewelry store with a friend. The jeweler spotted my pendant and explained that the heart-shaped golden cage on the front of the piece was originally the setting for diamonds. As soon as his words were out, I knew the rest of the story and, although no one had ever confirmed it, I believed it to be true. My grandfather, a poor refugee recently arrived in London from Antwerp in May 1940 to escape the Nazis, had bought the piece of jewelry in London – with the same idea you had with the brooches and pendants you search for at yard sales. Only, my grandfather wasn't interested in creating something new. He bought it solely to remove the diamonds from their setting and then resell them. I guess he must've kept the pendant as a memento – perhaps to celebrate his first transaction as a diamond dealer in London.

—Wow, what an interesting story, Lisa said. —Amazing.

—Odd how it came flooding back to me. It must've been when you mentioned how you take apart jewelry for the stones. I bet whoever bought those diamonds from my grandfather created pieces of new jewelry as well.

—Have you ever thought about putting diamonds back in the cage?

—Yes, but only for a moment, Hannah said. —I get a ton of compliments on this, the way it is.

—I don't blame you. It's beautiful, just the way it is. And what an amazing history it holds. My greatest joy is in the creating of new designs. And . . . well . . . to be perfectly honest, besides all the fun, the pleasure, and the money this work gives me, it also helps me to keep my mind off other things, if you know what I mean.

Hannah understood perfectly, and planting both elbows on the table, she crossed her arms and leaned in toward Lisa – a new and different Lisa.

—What about you? She was asking Hannah now. —Do you have, or do anything, you would consider yours alone?

Hannah didn't answer right away. Partly, because she was too busy following her index finger as it traced over the gray, patchy weathered wood of the table, but mostly because she was unsure of how to vocalize what she hadn't even been able to set straight in her own mind yet. —I'm writing, she finally said. —Yes, I'm writing.

She remembers Lisa saying, that's great. But there was a slight hint of disinterest in her voice, or perhaps it was only a distraction as she dug around in her large bag for her phone and, holding it up, began to scroll through her photographs in search of, Hannah had assumed, her jewelry designs.

. . .

Although disappointed again that Lisa never asked her what she was writing about, Hannah knew she'd never be able to explain what exactly it was, she did. Her successes and failures remained, as they still do, as immeasurable to the outside world as . . . as to what, though? Her writing is not like looking at a painting, a sculpture, or a piece of jewelry. If she can't get the words for her thoughts set down in their proper order, they're meaningless. But a piece of art can be appreciated, even if it's unfinished – for the colors, the brushstrokes, the design. And the beholder's eye, able to fill in the rest, has the freedom to imagine, even without direction from the artist. Not so with writing. It needs to be all there, in full, from the very first. And only then can it be open to interpretation.

. . .

—It's nice that we both have . . . Lisa said, but stopped short, as she looked up, past Hannah, and immediately put her phone back in her bag and sat up a little straighter. Hannah turned around. The guys were coming back toward them. The serious expressions on their faces didn't quite match the bright, colorful trays, loaded with French fries, lobster rolls, coleslaw, packets of mayonnaise, tartar sauce, and ketchup, as well as large paper cups of drinks, that each of them were carrying.

—Yes, all the cash, Artie said, putting his tray down on the table. —Can you believe it?

—Artie, please, Lisa said, touching his arm and shaking her head.

—I'm talking to Jake, he said, and turning his back on her, moved a little away from the table.

—That's quite something, Jake said, setting down his tray in front of Hannah and, after grabbing a fry, moved back toward Artie.

Hannah watched them. She knew Jake was expecting to hear more of Artie's story. It was also obvious Artie didn't want Lisa to hear what he was telling Jake. So, he came to the table, sat down next to Lisa, and began doling out their lunch. Jake took his place beside Hannah. She handed him his lobster roll.

—Delicious, he said, after the first bite, coleslaw dripping from his bun, the mayonnaise rimming his top lip.

Hannah was suddenly quite hungry, as were the others, judging by the sudden silence at the table.

After lunch and once again seated in the back of the SUV, Hannah sensed a restless energy zigzagging back and forth inside the car, as though lunch had pepped them all up.

The men were telling each other business war stories. Which one of them, they teased each other in friendly competition, would win for having had the worst employee, the biggest pain in the ass customer, the largest screwed-up order. They were laughing and cursing. Business locker-room talk, Hannah told herself, mentally rolling her eyes. Though this was completely out of character for Jake. He neither cried nor bragged about their business. She looked out at the passing scenery and began to wonder and worry about the money that Artie had mentioned, and Lisa hadn't wanted him to talk about. Had it been her imagination, or had Jake been avoiding eye contact with her since then? She remembers harboring an uneasy feeling that there was more to Artie's problems than he was letting on. Or was she merely being her usual paranoid self?

—Almost there, Artie said, as if he were talking to a group of young kids, impatient to get to where they were going. They'd crossed the state line and arrived in Rhode Island. Hannah felt a gentle pat on her arm and turned from looking out of the window to face Lisa, who was about to ask her a question when Artie's cell phone beeped.

—Yes? he shouted into the mouthpiece protruding from his ear. —No, no, he continued loudly. —I can't deal with this today.

Though it was barely audible from where she was sitting, Hannah could still hear indecipherable chatter coming through his earpiece.

—Look, I'm telling you, my hands are tied right now. You know that.

More indecipherable chatter.

Hannah remembers how she'd felt her body tighten as Artie banged the steering wheel with his fist.

—Again, he said, sounding as if he were speaking between clenched teeth. —My hands are tied. If the effing bastard hadn't ripped . . .

More indecipherable chatter from the other side.

Hannah felt bad for Lisa now. —So, when does your son start college? Hannah asked, wanting to draw her away from the drama in the front seat.

—Too soon, she said, but Hannah knew Lisa wasn't really listening to her at all, she wasn't listening to Artie either. She appeared to be in another world.

The phone call ended. The caller had calmed Artie down before hanging up.

—I'm sorry, he said, first looking over at Jake, then at Hannah and Lisa in the rear-view mirror. —That was my lawyer.

—No worries, Jake said in a mumble and turned sideways to look out of his window, surely not only to take in the passing scenery.

If only Hannah could decipher Jake's thoughts. She crossed her arms, her fingers pinching them to help calm her anxious butterflies and peeked over at Lisa, who was back on her phone, her perfect vermilion fingernails busy click-clacking letters in a message. And Hannah found herself counting out various exit strategies. For just in case, she allowed herself. They could always catch a train from Rhode Island back to Connecticut, she confirmed, then a taxi from the station to their house. Worse comes to worst, of course. Exit strategies; a tactic to foresee or is it to forestall the future? A way out. A plan *B*. She wished she could have told Jake how incredibly nervous she was feeling.

The car's navigation system announced the arrival at their destination. Artie parked the SUV in front of a small, one-story, red-brick building. It looked nice, Hannah thought, getting out of the car, and stretching her arms over her head. Really nice. She walked over to

Jake. He put his arm around her shoulder and asked how she was doing. --Fine, she lied.

Artie unlocked the front door and once they were inside, went to turn on all the lights from a junction box.

—Well, here we are, he said, coming back to them. —Let me give you a quick tour and afterwards we can sit down and talk. All right with you?

—Sure, Jake said, looking around, obviously as surprised and impressed with the building as Hannah was.

Chapter Ten

The inside was just as remarkable. To the right of the entrance hall was a small conference room, where six black Herman Miller chairs sat around a long, cherry wood table. The table was bare except for a generous coating of gray dust and the fingered words, *CLEAN ME,* scrawled at the far end by the back wall. Across from the conference room, a small, glassed-in office held three desks, each with its own computer. The large screens, all turned off, were shiny, like black looking glasses. As Hannah walked by, she caught a dark and strangely warped reflection of herself, the rendering of it, a little unsettling.

Go ahead, Lisa signaled to them, as she rummaged around in her Louis Vuitton. —I'll catch up with you.

—Are you okay? Jake asked. —It is rather hot and stuffy here.

Lisa only waved in response as she turned from them, retrieved a small packet of tissues from her bag, took one out, and blew her nose. The guys looked at each other, shrugged, and turned away from Lisa. Artie chatted noisily as they went through a set of double doors leading to the factory. And just like that, Hannah found herself alone in this unfamiliar, dimly lit entryway. It felt odd. She felt odd. Out of place. Why had she even bothered to come? Jake didn't need her. And what had happened to Lisa? They seemed to have connected with each other over lunch. She'd even begun to like her, Hannah thought, standing at the open doorway to the conference room.

Lisa was sitting at the table, cradling her head with one hand, while holding up her phone to her ear with the other. Her feet were resting on another chair, her Louis Vuitton on its side in the middle of the dusty table with the little black cotton sweater she had been wearing earlier, now flung carelessly on top of it. Hannah watched her until her own anxiety started to churn in her belly once more. Perhaps, she mused, anxiety can be propagated by the germ of a thought, which then spreads, just like the flu or the common cold.

She turned away.

The all-too-familiar whiff of inks and thinners hit her before she'd even pushed open the double doors that led to the factory area. The space was huge. But the lack of windows surprised her. Instead, fluorescent lights flickered and buzzed from the wide skinny bulbs hanging low on chains from the high ceiling.

Unlike her and Jake's varied assortment of used printers, all of Artie's appeared quite new and uniform. Otherwise, this factory's layout was similar enough to theirs to feel familiar, including the colorful ink streaks and splatters on the cement floor – a Jackson Pollock in the making, as someone would always joke. The machines were set up in neat rows according to whether they were one-color or multi-color printers. Conveyers lay dormant between them. Tables lined the perimeter of the room for assembly work with open boxes of merchandise stacked next to them, ready to be unpacked.

Hannah wandered around the factory floor, checking out each of the different pad printers and silk screen machines. Some of the machines still had ink sitting in the trays with silicone pads in place, ready to print. It looked to Hannah as if the operators had set them up to begin their workday but were then told to leave at once. While she walked up and down the aisles, taking in everything around her – the brick walls, the high ceilings, the machines – she tried, and still tries, to imagine how awful this loss must've felt. But what had caused this place to become such a veritable ghost town? With her hands tightly squeezed over her folded arms, she pinched and poked at them, as if she needed to feel the little stabs of her fingers to remind her, she wasn't dreaming; perhaps there was no more to all of this than pure bad luck in his choice of business partners to finance him.

She shook her head and thought of her and Jake's much smaller factory floor, always in a whirlwind of chaos, always in perpetual panic mode. At least that's the way it must look to an outsider, with their employees running in all different directions: picking inventory off the warehouse shelves; unpacking the items; printing them; repacking; labelling the cartons; and bringing the completed orders to the front of the building for the UPS driver to pick up.

But here, at Artie's, it was eerily quiet. She stood in front of the ink mixing station. Next to it were bright-yellow metal cabinets, stocked with quart and gallon cans of ink in all imaginable colors. And now in front of her was a cart piled high with sealed cartons, their outgoing printed UPS labels and packing lists already attached. How long, she wondered, had they been sitting here, waiting for a pickup?

Too depressing, Hannah couldn't help repeating over and over to herself. Neither could she stop her thoughts from going back to the night at the Italian restaurant, to those shiny pieces of jewelry Lisa had spilled out onto the red-and-white checkered tablecloth. And, ringing through her mind, Artie's voice going on about his new factory. When was that? Surely, no more than three years ago. She shook her head again in disbelief. What had gone so terribly wrong with his business? And in such a brief time. She couldn't help shivering, even though the room was overly warm and stuffy. She wondered when the air conditioner had last been turned on. Probably quite a while ago, but then again, she reminded herself, someone had set up the pad print machines, as if ready to run his orders.

She was catching up with Jake and Artie, who were only steps ahead of her. She hung back. The next area the men were inspecting was the warehouse where the inventory was kept. Mostly bare, heavy-duty metal shelves lined the concrete brick walls from floor to ceiling. The few cardboard cartons, stored haphazardly on the shelves, were each stenciled with his company name, the item's product number, and the quantity. Half empty, this was still way more than she and Jake ever had. How could he have blown it? She was sounding like a scratched record to herself. The men had stopped walking and were leaning against the shelves. She watched them, half listening. They were talking numbers: items in inventory, which then translated into dollars sitting on shelves in the warehouse; orders per day, per week, per month, per year; employees; cost of payroll; and on it went. Not that she lacked interest, it was just too much for her to process at that moment. Overwhelmed, Hannah turned back, walked through the factory and out to the front to look for Lisa.

She found her pacing up and down the conference room, crying and talking on her cell phone. Hannah stopped at the door for a couple of moments, then walked across the hall to sit in the office with the turned-off computers. She checked her phone. No new emails. No new messages. Thank God Miri and Ella didn't own cell phones. How full her inbox would always be if they did. She wondered about Ethan, Lisa and Artie's son. How was he doing with all this disruption? Luckily for him, he was starting college this fall. But was Lisa only crying for the loss of Artie's business? Hannah began to imagine there was more to her story than that.

—Hey, Hannah. Lisa was standing at the open door, her large bag slung over her shoulder. —I'm sorry . . .

—No need. You guys are going through such a difficult time right now.

Lisa nodded in agreement and came into the room, dabbing her face with a balled-up tissue. Smudges of mascara streaked her flushed cheeks and darkened the circles beneath her eyes. She looked almost feverish.

—I never realized there was all this. And she opened her bare arms, as if to embrace the entire space around them.

—You mean you've never been here before today?

Lisa took a deep breath, let it out slowly. —No, I'm ashamed to say. This is my first time, and I guess, by the sound of things, it'll be my last, too.

Hannah, feeling confused, was unsure of what to say. How was it possible that Lisa hadn't been here at least once before?

—It's complicated, Lisa had gone on when Hannah didn't respond.

Complicated? Hannah wondered. What could have been so complicated about taking a three-hour drive to see the pride of her husband's life?

Once again, Lisa pulled out her phone, checked for new messages, then slipped it back into her bag.

—And hard to explain, she added. —Anyway, what do you say we go find the boys?

—Sure. The last time I saw them, they were in the warehouse, talking numbers.

As they walked through the door to the factory, they found them checking the handcart filled with outgoing cartons.

On the way here, Artie had told us that he was broke and that his bank accounts had been frozen. When we arrived at his factory, we saw a cart filled with orders waiting for a pickup by UPS. But UPS was not coming to pick up; Artie owed them money. He and Jake piled all the cartons into his SUV and went off to the UPS depot to use our UPS shipper number to pay for the shipments.

Hannah and Lisa followed the men out to the driveway. They watched in silence as Artie and Jake struggled with the boxes, initially loading them into the car in no set order, then taking them out again when they didn't all fit. Finally, with the cartons rearranged perfectly inside the SUV, the men drove off, leaving Hannah and Lisa staring after them.

Later, we had a problem with UPS. They held up our orders at the depot in Rhode Island. There was a mix-up with the accounts. Our UPS rep in Stamford helped to get the money issue squared away for us. But because the orders were held up, Jake and I needed to ship them out overnight—an added expense. But from then on, our UPS rep made sure Artie could ship out his orders from his Rhode Island facility using our shipper number.

Back inside the conference room, Hannah and Lisa sat across from one another at the dust-laden table.

—Well, as I'm sure you're quite aware by now, Lisa said, digging around in her bag again, this time for her tissues. —The long and the short of it is . . . we're flat broke. She looked up at Hannah, an air of defiance on her face, blew her nose, then went on, —But what you're most probably *really* wondering is how we got here. Am I right?

The sharp-edged coolness in her voice took Hannah by surprise. Not that she blamed Lisa for her anger. It was as if all this had just hit her. What she'd lost. Certainly, her way of life – the one she'd always known.

—Well, to tell you the truth, she continued, before Hannah had a chance to respond. —I'm not so sure I can answer my own question for myself. Artie's company never particularly interested me. Occasionally, I'd go to the trade shows with him to help him out. Like the time we met you at the Long Beach show. But that's been the extent of it. Personally, I don't know how you do it. How you can be there with your husband all day, every day . . . No offense meant, of course . . . I mean, I'm sure he's a great guy and all, and a loving husband, but. . .

—None taken, Hannah said, the words rolling out of her mouth in one quick and easy breath without thought, though inside herself, she remembers feeling as if someone had pinched the skin covering the entire outside of her body, to bruising. Whose dream was she pursuing, anyway? Hers or Jake's? Was the business as much hers as Jake's? She shifted in her seat and uncrossed and re-crossed her legs in the opposite direction.

Lisa reached out her arm and said, —I'm sorry. I think I've overstepped. Have I offended you? I didn't mean to.

—It's okay, Hannah said, wanting to believe it.

—Though Artie and I live together, we have quite separate lives. And if it weren't for our son . . . Well, anyway, that's a whole other discussion for a different day. But truly, I find it amazing and admirable how you and Jake can work together the way you do.

—We have our disagreements and fights, like anybody else, Hannah said, hearing the defensiveness rise in her voice. —It's not as easy as you make it sound.

—God, no. It's not what I'm suggesting. No, not at all. I'm only thinking about myself. I can't imagine what it'd be like to work every day, all day, with Artie, let alone sit across from him. I'd be afraid one of us would end up like the proverbial corpse in the middle of the room.

—Well, hopefully, Hannah said, as much to dispel that disturbing picture presenting itself inside her head, as to reassure Lisa, —We'll be able to come to an agreeable arrangement between the four of us, and all our lives will calm down without finding anyone unbreathing in the middle of the room.

—Believe me, it's exactly what I'm longing for, Lisa said as she pulled a fresh tissue from her bag and dabbed at the tears welling in her eyes again.

Chapter Eleven

But now Hannah can't let go of the awful picture in her mind – of Artie lying flat on his back motionless, his legs splayed, his phone contraption attached to his right ear, his mouth opened in a lopsided scowl, and his eyes half-closed.

Exhausted, suddenly, she realizes she needs to keep Artie and Lisa out of her thoughts for at least a short while. Another cup of coffee might ease her mind from its running in maddening circles. And, yes, she says aloud to herself; she needs to call her mother back. But Hannah doesn't move. It's as if she's nailed to her chair, the air in her little room suddenly too oppressive to even get up. She scans her desk, glimpses Ella's letter out of the corner of her eye, reaches for it . . . and studies her daughter's handwriting. There's no need to read the words again. She can remember each one. Had they made a mistake in sending Ella away to camp? Would she, Ella, ever forgive her mother? Would the pain of it always be there, ready to prick Ella's consciousness whenever her brain finds a connection, however remote?

Connection. Is this what Hannah's looking for now? Yes, she decides. And for now, the connection is her mother.

But as she reaches for the phone, her attention becomes lulled by the lush view and the summery sounds outside her open window. The sun, a hazy circle now, barely shows through the woolly-looking clouds graying the sky. Moths and butterflies bat their wings in metallic pings against the screens of the open windows, while the cicadas screech from their hiding places up in the trees, their racket rising in unbearable waves, like a crescendo in unison to a high-pitched hysteria. Then there's the sprinkler click-clacking around a circular patch of parched lawn, like a sped-up metronome, rudely marking off her time – a constant reminder that she only has a few more days left before her children will be home again. Beneath her desk, her two gray, shaggy dogs lie on their sides, ears cocked, paws and shiny black noses spread out on the beige-carpeted floor. They're resting.

Wasn't it only the day before yesterday when she saw her own time stretched before her, each day shiny-new and sparkly with expectation, like the warmth of sunlight beckoning her as it rose from far out on the horizon? What was it her mother had said to her about taking advantage of this free time? Huh! Fat chance. She shakes her head and smiles at the image she has summoned up of the questioning look on her mother's face.

She dials.

"You know," her mother says, by way of greeting. "I've been racking my brain, trying to think back, ever since you asked me at lunch. . ."

"Asked you?" Hannah feels like her head is thick with fog.

"And oddly enough, it just came to me out of the blue. I mean, I *have* been thinking about it, but then, as I was watching some stupid show on TV last night and hardly paying any attention, it struck me."

"What did?" Hannah says into the phone, although what she really hears, reverberating noisily inside her head, are her own words, *never leave New York*.

"My favorite birthday."

"Favorite birthday?" Now she's beginning to sound like a parrot.

"You asked me at lunch, which was my favorite birthday."

"Yes, I know, but . . ."

"Well, it wasn't exactly *my* birthday," she says, and the words tumble out of her in a rush, as though, if she were to hesitate for a single moment, she'd lose her courage. "But *yours*."

"*Mine?*" Hannah whispers, all at once stunned. "What do you mean, mine?"

"The day you were born was my favorite birthday."

"I don't understand."

"Remember when I said how important all those silly children's birthday parties were, to our family of refugees?"

"Yes."

"Well, if you can imagine, what all of us had gone through and how lucky we were to have survived. A miracle. And here we were, saved and safe with you, our children, this next new generation, the absolute proof that a normal life is waiting to be led. Just around the corner. Am I making any sense to you?"

"I think so," Hannah says. "But now I feel even worse . . ."

"Worse? About what, my darling?"

"Being such a spoiled-rotten kid."

At first, there's no response. Only the monotonous whirring of the fan on the floor, which does nothing to stir the stifling air hanging over her like the thick haze that shrouds the sun and darkens the sky outside her window. To feel the closeness to her girls, all she need do is look straight up at the shelf above her desk, where the latest photo of them taken only a couple of weeks ago, is propped up against a short stack of books. The camp's name is barely visible on the tee shirts they're wearing as they stand at the edge of the lake, smiling. Their arms are wrapped tightly around each other, their curly hair tied up in ponytails, Miri's dark, Ella's blond. So sisterly looking, she thinks. It makes her so happy to see them like that. Next to the photo are the two clay pieces the girls had made for her – one a tiny replica of a typewriter, the other a small pot, ideal, Ella had insisted, for holding paperclips. She can visualize how their small fingers had worked to press the clay into a recognizable shape. Not so different, she muses, from her own need to whittle her thoughts into a form and for them to be recognizable, if only to herself.

"Spoiled, yes, and sometimes, even rotten," her mother says, blurting out the words quickly. "But honestly, it didn't matter at all to us then. It really didn't." There's also earnestness in her voice Hannah doesn't recognize. "What was important was that I gave birth to you. That you, my child, exist. That, in spite of everything that'd happened, in spite of Hitler wanting to rid the world of all its Jews, we are still here. *We*, the survivors. And we, the survivors, could, and did create the next generation. We *created* you. It was as simple and difficult as that. But what's so ironic about it all," her mother goes on, her words tumbling out of her. "What I find so truly incomprehensible is that I didn't even know I was Jewish before Hitler, no idea I was any different from the rest of my classmates at school. I mean . . . we never celebrated the Jewish holidays."

"I don't remember you ever talking to me about any of this."

"No, probably not. Right or wrong, I always thought it best to lay all those lousy memories to rest, keep them buried deep."

Hannah has a sudden childhood recollection of her grandmother poking her finger in anger – or was it from angst? – at the golden Star of David hanging from a gold chain around her neck. "Why must you wear this?" she remembers her grandmother yelling. "To advertise to the world, you're a Jew?" She had no answer for her grandmother, hadn't understood the fury. But from then on, she wore the golden star out of sight, keeping it hidden under her clothing.

"Anyway," her mother says, sighing into the phone. "I just thought . . . well . . . I do love you, you know. And . . . oh, never mind."

"And what?"

"Forget it. It's not important. But I do have to get off the phone now. Leo is on his way over. Call me again soon, okay?"

"Sure," Hannah says, but her mother hasn't heard her. She's already hung up.

Convinced it's her pregnancy muddling her up, Hannah realizes her fingers haven't touched the keyboard in these last few minutes. She saves the file with her notes on Artie and opens the one with her latest poem. She looks at her words on the screen. On the right side, they create a pattern that loops in and out like a curl. Are the strings of words, their shapes – the curves and lines of their individual letters, as well as the whole words themselves – no more meaningful than a pattern, a design in . . . what? But these are the words she has picked, the form she has created as well as the order in which they appear on the screen. She didn't select them at random. But . . . *but* does she like what they are saying back to her? It's kind of like looking at herself in the mirror. There are days the reflection staring back at her shows her one image, other days, quite something else. But is there a true day? A true self? Or is the eye of the beholder always fickle? Changing its mind from one moment to the next, depending on what it has seen, touched, or heard only moments beforehand? She looks at her words on the screen.

But then . . .

Closes the screen with her poem and reopens the file with her notes on Artie and Lisa, reminding herself that she needs to keep them at the forefront of her mind; unfurl the year, day by day, the mysteries, one by one. But it's her mother's insistent voice that comes back to her. Her mother's memories. She turns up the volume to her little radio and rests back in her chair. She stretches her legs under the desk which had once been their dining table, and folds her arms carefully over her growing, overly sensitive breasts. The overture to *The Magic Flute* fills her ears. She continues to stare lazily at the blink-blink of the cursor on her screen. It seems to both beckon and dismiss. She closes her eyes. August is always depressing. She can't help it. She hates the idea of summer ending; the sun setting earlier, the leaves on the trees turning a darker green, their edges curling inward with the heat and shortage of rain.

Along with the doctor and dentist appointments for Miri and Ella, there will be excursions to the mall for new fall clothes and trips to Target and the five-and-dime for notebooks, glossy-covered three-ring binders, paper, pens, pencils, and magic markers. And after they're back at school, instead of afternoons spent alone in the quiet of their house, sitting in front of her computer in this small room of her own, she'll be at the bus stop, waiting for them in her little red car to drive them to their after-school activities. Miri for piano lessons.

And Ella for tap and ballet, but only after Hannah has bribed her daughter with a toy or an ice cream first. It's the same tiresome game each week. While Hannah waits for their classes to end, she'll sit in her car reading more of Hannah Arendt, or else stare out through the windshield in a dream, allowing her thoughts to brew over one or another of the quotes from the book; exactly the way a cup of tea, steeped in boiling water becomes darker and more flavorful, the longer it sits.

Now a Mozart symphony, one she recognizes from the movie *Amadeus* but can't name, bellows into her room. To her, the music is brilliant, wild, frenzied. But frenzy was also in her mother's voice, the words cascading out of her with the memory of the day she'd given birth to Hannah. She pushes her chair back and stands in front of her desk. Zig and Zag stir, lifting their heads. But she and Jake do mark the holidays, she insists, as though she were still talking to her mother. And as if the dogs have concurred with her, they settle back down, stretch their paws out, and rest their chins on the carpet once again.

The importance of celebrating the Jewish holidays came unexpectedly to her one afternoon. She was sitting on a bench at the playground, watching her two girls as they scooted down the slide, pushed each other on the swings, and rode in circles on the roundabout. Perhaps it was the roundabout that did it. For the first time, she saw those celebrations as rites of passage – from not knowing to knowing, from not belonging to belonging – that she'd felt compelled to pass down. Call it a remembrance of the people and the lives who'd come before her. This was how she'd explained it to Jake. And to bring it to life for herself, for him, and for their girls, she began by decorating their house for Chanukah. She hung blue and white streamers from the ceiling and filled every shelf and side table with cardboard cutouts of dreidels, menorahs, and silver Stars of David. Shaky little hands, held in hers and Jake's, lit the candles on each of the eight nights. Springtime brought the Seder. And first Miri, then Ella, learned how to ask the four questions. Why is this night different from all other nights? Although talk at the table began with the question of the Jews' deliverance from slavery in Egypt, it would always digress, with equal regularity, to the stories their grandmothers told. Those floods of memories escaping their lips, yearning to be spoken out loud, and demanding to be heard, would inevitably lead to Hitler and those questions which stubbornly still have no answers. Will Hannah remember all their sagas when it's her turn to deliver them? Eggs, the symbol of life. Infinity. No beginning, no end. Rosh Hashana, Yom Kippur. Family get-togethers for dinner, lunch, or the breaking of the fast. Surely *her* children know now and will always remember what it means to be Jewish.

She clicks save on her own thoughts and re-opens those of Artie and Lisa.

There were most definitely things that struck me in a very odd way about that trip up to Rhode Island. The first was the factory, which was obviously in close-down mode. Artie assured us that two or three people still worked there, but when we arrived in the middle of the afternoon, the place was empty. Another was Lisa, who although had never been to see the factory before that day, was crying about the loss of the business.

Chapter Twelve

—Honey, I'm home, Jake's voice rang out, as he and Artie, back from their trip to UPS, came through the front door of Artie's building.

Hannah remembers rolling her eyes at Lisa, as if to exclude herself from what she called his silliness.

—He always does that, she explained, still sitting across the table from Lisa. —It's a kind of joke, I guess. One of his dozen or so regulars.

The two men appeared at the entrance of the conference room. They looked hot and beat.

Artie came into the room first, dropped a folder of paperwork on the table, causing the dust to rise then spread as it settled. Jake followed him in.

—We're just going in the back for a bit, we won't be long, Artie said, and they left the room.

Hannah and Lisa both cried out, okay, in perfect unison and, as if a wall of formality had suddenly shattered, they giggled like two nervous, nine-year-old schoolchildren.

—Jinxed, Lisa shouted, wiping away her giggle-tears. —Isn't that what we used to say as kids?

—I think so, Hannah said, feeling as though their laughter had pushed open the imaginary locked door between them a little further. They both shrugged their shoulders and continued to laugh.

—I'm getting a cup of water from the cooler. Do you want one, too? Lisa asked, standing.

—Sure, Hannah said, and stood as well. She stretched her arms over her head and walked around the table to have a look at the folder of paperwork Artie had dropped there. God Almighty, she thought, rifling through the papers. All these shipments, charged to Bloom & Company's UPS account.

—Didn't you ever want to do anything else? Lisa said, startling Hannah for a moment as she came back into the room with a paper cup of water, which she put down on the table in front of where Hannah had been sitting.

—Like what? she asked, going back to her chair.

—You know, a profession, a career. Something to call your own, Lisa said, punctuating the words *your own* in a way that made Hannah feel small, inconsequential.

But, as Hannah remembers now, she'd had to remind herself that she already did have something all her own. And hadn't they talked about this exact topic at lunch? Hannah wasn't sure what to think now.

Suddenly Lisa sat up straighter, leaned forward, and stretching her arms out toward Hannah, rested them on the table. —You know, she said, —We all go through this. You aren't alone. It's hard to give equal time to all the things in our lives. At times, it's impossible for us to figure out, or even to understand, when or which part of our life must take precedence. Especially when we're young.

•   •   •

It's not only *especially when we're young*, Hannah thinks now, watching a young deer outside her window munch away at the Hosta, flowering along the border of a small island of trees, bushes, and other nameless shrubberies, mostly devoured by the host of animals passing through her yard all day long. No, it doesn't matter the age. Her mother has the same dilemma. She doesn't know what part of her life is the most important to her – moving to a man in Basel, Switzerland, or staying put, here in New York, with her family close by.

•   •   •

But she hadn't known this when she was sitting across from Lisa in Artie's conference room. Instead, she had looked over at Lisa, who was smiling, waiting for her answer.

—Well, to be honest, Hannah began. —My younger self wasn't particularly good at staying in school – or holding down a job, for that matter. I did eventually get my degree. But I never found anything I liked to do or was any good at.

—And this kind of work? Lisa asked, pointing her chin up and moving her head about, as though with one sweep of it, she could encompass the whole thing within and without the space around her.

—I just sort of fell into it, Hannah said.

— *Fell* into it?

Yes, she'd thought, *fell* was exactly the right word, and she held her breath for a second before taking the plunge, as if all those memories hid in deep water.

Slowly, letting out a breath of air, she said, —I'd just dropped Miri and Ella off at nursery school. It was Ella's first day. She was clingy, I remember, hesitant – not sure she wanted to stay – and it took me a while to calm her before I could leave. She was only two-and-a-half. And then I felt so awful, so guilty because . . . well . . . you know . . . I couldn't keep my eyes off the large, round clock hanging on the wall in front of me. You see, these were the first few hours I was going to have all to myself since God knows when and my precious time was evaporating like smoke into thin air, the longer I needed to stay . . .

—Where were you going? Lisa asked.

•   •   •

Indeed, Hannah thinks now, where was she going? Where *is* she going?

Every night before I go to bed, I look at the pictures of you and start to cry.

Hannah can't stop looking at those awkwardly written words in Ella's letter. She wishes she could simply close her tear-filled eyes and magically send her arms out to wrap around her daughter for all the hugs and love she needs.

•　　•　　•

—Well, that's the thing, Hannah answered Lisa. —Nowhere. I really had no special place to go. Then to top it all off, after I got back into my car, put the key into the ignition, looked up at the rearview mirror – force of habit, you know – glimpsed the two vacant car seats behind me and the ugly stuffed monkey I'd succeeded in wresting from Ella, as I hugged her goodbye at the nursery school door. With those big black button eyes staring hard at me, as if in accusation, I found myself . . . well . . . like . . . paralyzed in a way. For the first time in four years, there were no little voices chattering, laughing, whining, or crying for my attention. The silence was deafening. And at that moment, it was more terrifying than freeing.

The minute she finished telling her story, she asked herself why she'd bothered. And felt like a fool for opening herself up. She glanced down. The paper cup filled with water sat on the dusty conference table in front of her. She picked it up and drank, closing her eyes so as not to see Lisa's reaction. But when she heard the sudden excitement in Lisa's voice saying she had a similar memory, Hannah opened her eyes, surprised and relieved.

As if to emphasize or validate what she was about to say, Lisa put her elbows on the table, her head in her hands, and leaning in toward Hannah, she said, —What I remember the most is having this strange feeling of loss, as much for the child growing up and away from me as for who I'd become in those last few years. And then, of course, the realization that I'd have to figure it all out again – the person I'd need to be for the foreseeable future and where my priorities would lie.

—Sort of like suddenly finding yourself at another of life's crossroads, Hannah said, leaning back in her chair.

—Exactly, Lisa said, drawing out the word and folding her arms at her chest, as if for emphasis.

And Hannah couldn't help it; she began to laugh. —Sorry, she said. —It's only my old hilarious self I'm laughing at.

—I don't understand, Lisa said, a puzzled look on her face.

—This conversation's reminding me of the *me* I was striving to become in those early days of motherhood. And what I used to do with those treasured downtimes when the kids were napping or watching *Sesame Street* on TV.

—You mean the best part of the day? Lisa said, a bright smile lighting up her face.

—Yes. It was during those times I'd be at the kitchen table with one of those black and white notebooks, busily making up lists for myself.

—Lists?

—Oh, my God, yes! Lists and more lists. Or I'd write . . .

—I'd forgotten. About your writing, I mean. Please forgive me.

—Don't worry, I forgive you, Hannah said, a wave of delight sweeping through her; Lisa had remembered, after all.

—But what were your lists for? Lisa asked.

—Oh, stuff like novels or poems I thought I should be reading. You know, Shakespeare's sonnets, the English classics, the Russians. Very erudite. I would also make up lists of graduate schools to apply to. Not that we ever had the money for it, mind you.

•   •   •

Hannah laughs out loud now at her younger self. Hearing her, both dogs, still at her feet, raise their heads and finding nothing amiss, go back to their prone position under her desk, their damp noses once again to the floor. She remembers how she'd gone on talking, as if Lisa were her best friend, until her enthusiasm came to a sudden halt and she realized there was nothing more to say. The lists had turned out to be fantasies. She did apply to one graduate school. They rejected her. And that was the end of that. Even her erudite list of books became longer and more complicated than she could've ever managed. But, looking back, she recognizes she was growing up, pushing herself outward, to become . . . she didn't think she even knew who or what.

•   •   •

—I was just desperately afraid of my life passing me by in a flash, as easily and quickly as watching the scenery roll by outside a train window. Do I make any sense to you? she asked, searching Lisa's face for her answer.

—Absolutely, Lisa said.

—So, nap time and *Sesame Street* became not only my sanity saviors back then but they also, Hannah barged in, afraid to lose her momentum and bravery,—afforded me the space for those invaluable spurts of self-awareness to help me grow. Have I said too much?

Of course, Hannah absolutely knew she had. After all, Lisa wasn't her best friend, wasn't even a regular, ordinary acquaintance of hers.

—Not at all, Lisa said, sitting forward in her chair. —I know exactly what you're saying. I must admit, though, I squandered my free time away. I couldn't help but nap when Ethan napped, and after we woke, the two of us would lie on my bed, like two zombies, and watch *Sesame Street* together and afterwards *Mister Rogers*. I had memorized all the songs from both programs by heart. Honestly, I was too tired to do much else.

—And I was too afraid my brain would become as mushy as the baby food I'd fed to my babies.

They both laughed.

—But to be honest, Hannah said, shrugging her shoulders as she went on. —I haven't totally come to grips with my whole situation yet. And as you can see, despite all my efforts, life keeps shifting me in all different directions.

—I hate to make this sound cliché or unfeeling, but truly, isn't that what happens to all of us?

—I guess. Hannah looked down at the table. And glancing back up at Lisa, she added, —I'm sounding like a spoiled brat, aren't I?

—No, no. You misunderstand me. All I'm saying is life is like a heavy wind . . .

—It's okay . . .

—Hey, Lisa said, her voice upbeat. —You were going to tell me what you did after you left Ella at nursery school.

Hannah chuckled. —I went to see Jake at his office.

—Aha! Lisa said, and a smile of comprehension spread across her face.

—And, of course, the going joke is that I never left.

—That's a funny story . . .

—Considering I never wanted to work at a regular job in the first place, it is pretty funny, Hannah said.

—And did you ever figure out what it was you wanted out of your life back then?

—I'm not too sure the word *want* has had anything to do with it, Hannah said, as she looked out of the window at the empty parking lot, all in shade now.

•　•　•

But if she were to be completely honest with herself, thinking about this now, she would have to admit that there's nothing she can imagine doing in her life other than working with Jake. She's had her writing for as long as she can remember, but any passion she harbors for it is overshadowed by her feelings of insecurity, of being afraid she's just not good enough. But does it matter? She always ends up asking herself. If she continues to work at it, even sporadically, as time allows, her answer will have to be no. No, it really doesn't matter at all.

•   •   •

—That's enough of me. Now tell me about you, Hannah said, turning her attention back to Lisa. —Are you doing what you always wanted to?

—Hardly. Jewelry-making wasn't exactly in my scope of thinking in those days. Nope. I wanted to be a lawyer. You see, I had a big mouth when I was a kid. I'd always defend my older brother and sister whenever they got into trouble. Frustrated and annoyed with me for always butting in, my parents would yell at me: What are you? Their lawyer? Those words became my signal to shut up. But they were also the words which propelled me into thinking that a lawyer was who I was meant to be.

—So, what happened?

—I got into law school after college but never could attend. My father died of a heart attack suddenly the summer before I was to start, so I had to get a job instead.

—I'm sorry, Hannah heard herself say.

—Yeah, well, shit happens.

She remembers Lisa looking around the conference room as if, perhaps, to hold back the images of that long-ago summer day, when her whole life was turned upside down. And probably not all that different from today.

—Anyway, Lisa went on. —Over the summer I found work at an art gallery to help support me and my mom. The couple who owned the gallery were great bosses. And I grew to really love that job. I learned all I know about art and design from them.

—Then why did you leave?

—I didn't. Business became sluggish, and they were getting on in age so . . . they decided to pack it in. They offered me the gallery. But at the time, I wasn't ready for that kind of commitment. I was twenty-two. Way too young. How could I have known what I'd want for my future? Though I must confess, I've often regretted my decision.

It sounded to Hannah as if she were still debating this issue with herself all these years later.

Lisa sighed. —You could almost believe there are certain predestined coincidences in life. As if fate, with a great big capital F, were the dealer in an extremely global-sized game of cards.

•   •   •

Here again is that word, fate. Is that what life is all about? Fate – as if no more than an all-powerful card dealer running our lives or the accidental arbitrariness of a magician's sleight of hand? Is this what her mother believes in, too? Fate? No, can't be. But then wasn't she, Hannah, the one who ordered up the queen and knave of hearts to play in her imagination as she stared out at the moving landscape from her window seat on the 10:55 to Manhattan . . . in a dream . . . while Hannah Arendt sat perched on her lap, opened to a page, the text already messy with ragged underlines, her scribbled notes and question marks taking up most of the white space in the surrounding margins. But what had fate to do with her walk uptown from the station to meet her mother? The flowers she'd bought for her birthday, cradled in her arm. The heat. The abandoned baby. Her pregnancy. Their talk of Leo. And now she wonders if her mother has already booked her flight to Basel to meet Leo's daughters. Or listened to Hannah and thought twice about moving there? No, surely, it's too soon for her to have made up her mind definitively. Funny how that hot and muggy afternoon, only two days ago, feels as far away to her, as if the whole day itself were merely a figment of her imagination.

She shakes her head and can't help the slow smile that erupts on her face, broadening her cheeks, as she answers her own question. Yes, it's all in the cards.

•　　•　　•

—What's so funny? Lisa said. —You don't believe in fate?

—Truthfully, Hannah said. —I find it a bit of a scary notion. I prefer to think of it as . . . serendipity.

—Serendipity? Fate? It's all the same to me. Aren't we all shuffling, like the dealer, to make some sense of what we've been dealt with in our world?

—I'd prefer not to think of myself as either the dealer or the dealt. I mean, thinking that way implies giving up, or giving in. Don't you agree? Hannah asked, and moving in closer, put both hands flat on the table.

—I suppose you might have a point, Lisa said. —But living my life has always felt like I'm constantly having to push against the tide. And right now, I have neither strength nor will.

—You sound very pessimistic.

—It's probably because my boy is going off to college, and to tell you the truth, I've no clue what's going on with Artie and his business, or even, to be totally honest, with Artie and me. All I know for sure is that I feel helpless and scared shitless.

—But, Hannah said, and for a moment, she was tempted to stretch her arm out across the table and take hold of Lisa's hands to stroke them, but instead she clasped her own. —You know, she added. —You really do have to keep pushing.

•   •   •

Pushing, she thinks now. Who is she to have given her that advice? Especially since she always feels she's being pushed and pulled by everyone in her life, but herself.

•   •   •

She kept her eyes on Lisa, who was biting at a loose bit of skin around the cuticle of her thumbnail.

—Yeah, well, Lisa said, looking down to examine the rest of her painted fingertips. —I'll work on that once my life's sorted out and I know exactly what it is I'm pushing for.

She looked up and smiled at Hannah. And Hannah smiled back, finding herself liking Lisa more and more. Although she was wondering how they'd be able to maintain a friendship, if this was what she dared to call it, considering they're on opposite sides of the playing field.

Chapter Thirteen

Jake and Artie were sitting at each end of the long, dusty conference table. Slumped in their chairs, they looked as if they'd been to the wars and back. Jake had his arms in a tight cross over his chest. And Artie's hands, clasped behind his head, had caused his black golf shirt to ride up his middle and reveal a strip of white belly. Hannah remembers she'd looked from one to the other, expecting their discussion to begin.

Instead, Artie yawned noisily, only covering his mouth at the last moment as he pulled down on his shirt. Then he reached for the folder he'd dropped to the table earlier, and shuffled through the papers inside it; more, it seemed, to give himself something to do than of any genuine interest. Mindlessly, that was the word that came to her. And why not? Those papers weren't his responsibility. Those UPS bills now belonged to her and Jake. She would have liked to put her head down on the table, close her eyes, dream all this away. Instead, she looked across the table. Oddly, Lisa appeared oblivious. She was picking at her cuticles again, while checking her phone. Now Hannah was feeling as though she was the only one who was aware of their situation and anxious to move on it.

But then Jake came to life. He straightened up and leaned forward in his chair, took a long drink from his bottle of water, dropped the plastic empty onto the table and began to peel off the paper label, scratching it away with his fingernail. His eyes remained fixed on the task.

He cleared his throat.

The words coming out of his mouth were said in a slow, measured kind of way, as if each one needed to be tested in the atmosphere before the next could be released. —Artie, he said, without looking up, —has been working on a proposal for us. But, for us to discuss it, he needs to hear from his attorney first.

—What the fuck? I don't understand. Hannah practically jumped out of her seat. She couldn't believe what she was hearing. —I thought that the entire purpose of our coming up here today was to begin . . . at the very *least* . . . begin sorting all this out.

—Hey, Hannah. Jake was glaring at her, trying to calm her down with his eyes.

She stared straight at Artie. Ignoring Jake's pleading looks, her mounting anger rose through her voice, octave by octave. —So, when do you expect your lawyer to get back to you? But then, if I'm not mistaken, he'd called you while we were in the car on our way up here. Why didn't he give you the go-ahead to talk to us?

Hearing herself, she wasn't sure where this sudden hysteria had come from. Maybe she was only tired. Or impatient to know the outcome or, more precisely, what all this was going to mean for her. Across the table, Lisa continued to stare down at her lap, her face mostly hidden by a curtain of hair as she continued to press the buttons on her phone. Hannah kept her eyes fixed on Lisa, silently imploring her to look up. Had she known about this all along?

—Believe me, I'm just as annoyed and frustrated as you are, Artie said. —I told him he needed to get back to me A-SAP. I told him I needed his input by today.

Hannah looked over at Jake. He shrugged his shoulders. She wanted to shake them. What was the use, though? She leaned back in her chair, straightened her legs out in front of her, and clasped her hands together over her chest.

Suddenly, Lisa slammed her phone down on the table. —Artie, I have a suggestion, she said, turning to look at Jake as she spoke.

—Why don't you call your attorney and ask him if there's anything at all we can talk about without him?

—Great idea, Artie said, and clapped his hands, obviously thankful for the reprieve.

He got up without another word, walked out of the conference room, and went outside, letting the front door shut noisily behind him. Jake and Hannah watched him through the window. He was pacing the parking lot, kicking away pebbles in his way, while gesticulating wildly with his hands as he talked. It was like watching a silent movie, Hannah thought. And now, Lisa appeared annoyed and fed-up, too. She scraped her chair back from the table, stood, grabbed her oversized bag, and announced, —I'm going to the ladies'.

That left Hannah and Jake alone at the table.

—When did you know? Hannah turned to Jake.

—Know?

—Yes, when did you know we wouldn't be talking about any of his company stuff today?

—He mentioned something about it on our way to UPS.

—Aren't you pissed off about it?

—Not really.

—How can you . . .?

—Look, he said, interrupting her. —We have two choices. Walk away from him now, in which case we'll have gained absolutely nothing. Or be patient . . .

—I think we've been taken for a ride . . . more than literally. She sat up straight in her chair, folded her arms over her chest, and turned to face him.

—You have such a pessimistic attitude, he said. —Why do you always believe people are out to screw you?

—Not always. She shook her head back and forth, pawing her memory for the truth, like a dog for a buried bone.

—It certainly seems that way to me, he said, pushing his chair away from the table and crossing one leg over the other.

She wanted to yell at him: What the fuck do you know? She didn't, though. Instead, she said she was going to pee. And stood. Anything to get out of here, she remembers thinking.

As she left the conference room, Lisa returned, her hair freshly combed, her makeup reapplied.

—Down the hall on the left, she said, even though Hannah hadn't asked her for directions.

—Thanks, Hannah said, and walked on.

It took her a couple of panicked seconds, after she let the door slam shut behind her, to find the light switch on the wall inside the pitch-black, airless, two-stall ladies' room.

Hannah took her time in the bathroom. Looking at herself in the mirror, she brushed her hair, then leaning in closer, searched, as she always did, for any new wrinkles showing up on her face. Satisfied enough with herself, she finally wandered back toward the conference room only to find Jake, Artie, and Lisa waiting for her in the lobby, each in their own world as if they were strangers waiting at a bus stop. They had decided it was time for dinner.

Before heading home, we stopped for dinner and devised a plan for us to take over all the existing orders that had been sent to Artie's factory and prepare them for production. Any future orders coming to him would be sent directly to our place to process.

The choices, Artie told them, were either Italian or Chinese. Both restaurants were down the block from his factory. Chinese got the vote. After Artie turned off the lights and locked up the building, they piled back into his SUV, the men up front again, the women behind. Minutes later, he pulled into the parking lot of a small strip mall. At first Hannah didn't see the restaurant, only a shoe store, a laundromat with fogged-up windows, a pizza joint, and a dark-looking pub. Turned out, the restaurant was around the corner.

—I must say, I could eat a horse, Lisa said, as they were led to a booth by a window overlooking the parking lot.

—Are you into sharing dishes? Jake asked, putting down his menu.

—Sure, Artie said. —What do you like?

—Dumplings and spareribs, for starters? Jake asked.

—Perfect, Artie said, nodding his head. —And for the main?

Jake checked the menu and reeled off his and Hannah's usual selections. —Moo-shoo pork, orange-flavored beef, General Tso's chicken or any shrimp dish as long as it's not sweet.

—Works for me, Artie said and closed his menu.

—Me too, Lisa said.

Hannah's eyes stayed fixed on her menu, not to read it because she didn't care one way or the other about what they ordered for dinner, but to keep herself focused and her confused thoughts from jumping all over the place.

—What about you, Hannah? Lisa said, patting her hand.

—Yup, no problem, she said, and closing the menu, looked up at Lisa.

But what she wanted to know, would have loved to ask, was where these sudden muddled feelings about Lisa had come from. If this strange thickness, which had sprung up wider even than the table between them, was totally in her imagination.

—Now that that's settled, Jake said, gathering the menus and stacking them at the table's end for the server. —What did your lawyer say we can discuss today?

The room was noisy with the two- and four-tops filled around them. And this booth, smaller than normal, felt claustrophobic to her. And so narrow, Hannah could have easily stretched out her arm, if she'd wanted to, and touched Lisa's, the way Lisa had reached for hers. But now Lisa was busy rearranging the tableware in front of her. She was in her own world and oblivious to Hannah's staring and silent appeals for her to look up. Hannah took a sip of water. What had caused this change?

Artie leaned forward. He cleared his throat. And was about to speak. But the server arrived at their table, pen and pad in hand, to take their order. A necessary, momentary reprieve. After the server left, the four of them fell into silence once again. Hannah, almost afraid of looking directly at Lisa and Artie, was worried about what might come out of Artie's mouth. She had the feeling there'd only be more of those 'poor me' stories. Had the day turned out to have been a huge waste of time? No, not huge, she told herself. She did get to satisfy her curiosity about his factory. She glanced at Lisa, who smiled back at her. Meant to reassure, she thought, though she couldn't help looking at the expression in Lisa's eyes and thinking she was doing the exact opposite. Why did Hannah have the distinct feeling Lisa knew full well what Artie was about to tell them? That, in fact, she'd known all along. And now an awful thought hijacked Hannah's mind; it wasn't only Artie who'd taken them for a ride. The butterflies inside her were beating their wings like crazy again.

The server brought them their orders of spareribs and dumplings.

Artie picked up his chopsticks, peeled off the paper covering, pulled the sticks apart, and plucked a dumpling from the serving dish. After stuffing the whole thing into his mouth, he took a swig of water, cleared his throat, and said, —The long and the short of it is this; all my bank accounts and credit cards have been frozen. His nose was running and his eyes filled with tears. —I'm totally out of money. Christ, I don't even have enough to pay for the gas we need to get us back home.

Lisa took out a packet of Kleenex from her bag and passed it to him. He pulled out a tissue, wiped his eyes, and blew his nose. No one said a word. Instead, there were only the sounds of chopsticks clicking, mouths chewing, and occasional, satisfied *mmm* sounds; everyone was hungry for dinner, as well as the welcome diversion it created. But Hannah's butterflies persisted.

As if to justify his ugly situation, Artie explained that his lack of money was due to his cheating partner, who happened to be Lisa's cousin, Mark. Artie gulped down all the water in his glass, slammed the glass back down on the table and, as his voice rose and his eyes filled with tears again, he blurted out, —Lisa's cousin, Mark, *her cousin*, embezzled $400,000 from my company.

What? How the hell . . .? Impossible, Hannah thought. And as she sat there in total disbelief, she worried her mouth was hanging open like an imbecile's. Or was that what he thought of her and Jake? Imbeciles. Ready to believe any story he'd dish out.

—He left me high and dry, Artie continued, more quietly now.

Hannah had to look away. She turned to the window, watched a couple get into their car, and drive off. Hadn't she heard this exact same story from him before? She didn't dare turn around in the small booth to face Jake but settled her hand on his thigh instead and scratched at it, as if the itch were his as well. This can't be true, Hannah wanted to say. As if Lisa had read her mind, she glanced back at Hannah and shrugged. Shrugged?

—So, going forward, how do you envision your company becoming part of ours and, more importantly, how we will work together? Have you given some thought to any of this?

Artie shook his head in slow motion. —I haven't completely worked out the details yet. And to be honest, I had to promise my lawyer I wouldn't go into too much of it without his say-so.

Hannah felt Jake turn toward her. Afraid of what his face would tell her, she kept her eyes focused straight ahead of her, directly on Lisa, who still seemed strangely oblivious.

—But I thought you were going to ask him what we could talk about now, Jake said, planting his curled fists on the table.

—Yes, I know, and I did, but he wants me to wait.

—I'm confused. I mean, then why are we here now?

—Because, well, I thought we could . . . Artie began to say, but then, looking down at his plate, shrugged. —Unfortunately, I just don't have enough of my shit together yet. I didn't realize. I need a little more time. I'm sorry.

Between large forkfuls of the chicken, rice, and string beans, Artie continued to make more excuses. Sometimes he talked as he chewed, spitting a little as he grew more upset. At other moments, his eyes glazed over, becoming shiny with tears.

To Hannah's surprise, there was a part of her beginning to feel a little sad for him. It was as if a tiny fissure had opened and let in a glint of light. She found herself nodding or shaking her head in commiseration, as she repeated the same few words over and over, whenever there was a break in his monologue. *I can understand perfectly.* Or, *how awful it is for you to have to go through this.* What else was there for her to say? Although she couldn't help thinking now and then as he went on, to that other time they'd sat across from each other at a restaurant on the dock in Long Beach and she'd watched the sun play with the ripples on the water while he talked and complained about his ex-partner. But this time, the more he told them, the worse she felt for him and the more she fantasized. If he came to work for them, perhaps she could go home and become the person she had always dreamed of becoming. She would raise her two children and concentrate on her writing. Yes, she decided she was going to make him her liberator.

Chapter Fourteen

For a short while, she remembers, they were lulled into the privacy of their own thoughts by the darkness and the monotony of the drive home. Until Artie's phone rang, unsettling the calm. As he pushed the button on his ear-piece contraption, he announced it was most probably one of his Chinese suppliers.

After listening to his caller for a bit, Artie cried again. —All my money has been stolen, he said, banging one fist after the other on his steering wheel. —I'm so sorry, but I can't pay you.

Artie repeated this over and over, as though it were a mantra, his voice becoming hoarse through his tears and stuffed-up nose. Finally, he could hang up. A heavy silence blanketed the SUV once again. And Hannah still couldn't think what it was that bothered her about Lisa. Why she felt she'd been put on the defensive? She stared out at the highway, numbed by the cars in the fast lane zipping by, their headlights blinding. She closed her eyes against the flickering brightness for a moment. It had been a long day, she told herself, as if to absolve all those mixed-up thoughts she couldn't untangle or push out of her head. Was it Lisa's smile, when they first settled down across from each other in the narrow, red-vinyl-covered booth that'd unnerved Hannah the most? Her smile? But why? Was she being unfair? Or imagining . . .? There was something about it, though, that radiated insincerity. She couldn't shake the feeling that she'd been taken for a fool. The way she'd opened herself up. But, then again, so did Lisa. Then why this feeling? Was it how she'd said the match between their two companies was a perfect fit, and sure to be a win-win? *Win-win.* How would Lisa know? She hadn't even bothered to come up to see Artie's factory in operation. Besides, Hannah had always hated that expression. It reminded her of someone else, someone she didn't like. Although who that person was, she couldn't remember.

Out of nowhere, a set of hi-beaming headlights blazed like a sword across her face, bringing back memories of the dock in Long Beach; how she'd watched the low sunlight pierce the rippling water while at dinner with Artie and Lisa that first time. They'd sat across from each other, Hannah from Lisa, Jake from Artie. Just like they were tonight. And how she and Jake kept nodding in agreement with Artie while offering him words of commiseration. Just like they did tonight. But then, it was his ex-partner who'd left him high and dry to start-up his own new company. Now it was his wife's cousin who had embezzled money from him. Who would he blame on the next go-round? She and Jake?

—You must understand, Artie suddenly blared out into the darkness of the SUV, disturbing the silence. —You'll have to be ready to buy new inventory as needed for ongoing business, as well as pay me for my stock.

—Yes, yes, of course, Jake said, stumbling over his words.

And as if Artie's bravado had suddenly and inexplicably returned to him, he began to outline his concerns and expectations.

They were to purchase his machines and take over the existing leases he still owed on his equipment.

—Plus, he said, hitting the steering wheel. —We need to agree on a timeline for your company to produce all my current orders. As for future orders, I'll make sure they're automatically sent your way.

He rattled off his words in quick succession, as if he'd memorized and rehearsed them. Before Hannah or Jake could respond with anything more than a quick nod of their heads, which he couldn't have seen in the dark anyway, he continued with his list. —And don't forget I have to be out of Rhode Island by the end of the month. You should also check into acquiring additional space in your building as soon as possible. You'll need it for all the extra machines and inventory you'll be getting from my place.

—Absolutely, Hannah heard Jake say. —We're prepared to accommodate you however we can.

Artie didn't respond right away. He drove on, the night fully enveloping them now.

—If you hire me, which I hope you will, he finally said, —I expect to be reimbursed for my daily commute from Long Island.

This time, Jake said nothing.

After a few minutes of silence, Artie spoke up again. —And lastly, but obviously far from the least, if you decide to employ me, you must agree to my salary requirements.

—I'm assuming you'll let me know what those are, Jake said.

—My lawyer is drafting contracts as we speak.

—Ah! Yes, Jake said.

If his lawyer was drawing them up now, as they spoke, Hannah wondered why he couldn't have drawn them up yesterday, before they were to speak? And now, she also wondered, who had suddenly given Artie permission to talk to them about any of this, after all?

—So, to reiterate, to be sure we're all on the same page, Artie went on. —You have agreed to process and produce all my orders, starting immediately. You have also agreed that if I do come to work for you, providing, of course, you accept my terms, I will take charge of running production and keeping track of inventory. And speaking of inventory, you will buy what I have on the shelves and take over the leases owed on all my machinery and equipment.

—Just to be clear, everything you're telling us now will be in the contract your lawyer's sending over to us, Jake said.

—Naturally, Artie responded, as if all this really were the most natural thing in the world.

—In that case, it sounds to me like we have the perfect fit. What do you think, Hannah? Jake asked in a jolly voice while twisting his body fully around to face Hannah in the back seat. —We're looking to hire someone to run production, right?

—Right, she said, trying to discern by the expression on his face, if there was a message underlying his words. She couldn't find one; it was just too damn dark to see.

With all of Artie's list of needs to make this work, Hannah realized that her own private fantasies, of him relieving her of her obligations at the company, hadn't even lasted for half of their ride home. They'd begun to flag and fade in equal measure to the darkness of night, which had taken over the light of day.

•　　　•　　　•

Coming down the driveway at night alongside one of the two buildings, which makes up the small complex where Hannah and Jake rent space for their company, always surprises her; it looks and feels different than it does in daytime. The parking lot had emptied since the morning. Only Jake's old black BMW, resembling a great, hulking, pre-historic beast, stood in the center of all the marked spaces, as if it too was resting from a hard day's work. All the lights were off inside the building; the large windows stared out, shiny black. No sounds. No delivery trucks. No people coming or leaving their jobs. Only an eerie stillness and the stars pin- pricking the spring nighttime sky.

Hannah leaned over in the car to give Lisa a kiss on her cheek. Jake got out of the car and walked around to the driver's side. Artie rolled down his window. They shook hands. As Lisa got out of the back seat to reclaim hers in the front, she and Jake exchanged quick kisses. Hannah poked her head through Artie's open window and kissed his cheek, too.

—Drive safely, Hannah and Jake shouted out and waved as they watched the SUV pull away from them.

—I'm beat, Jake said, unlocking their car doors.

—Me too.

—So . . .?

—You go first, Hannah said, as she got in, and opened her window.

—Four hundred grand . . .?

—Missing? Stolen? It's got to be a load of crap.

—How would it be possible? Jake said, snapping in his seatbelt, and starting up the car.

—You mean on 2.7 million in sales?

—Exactly.

—Makes no sense at all, she said, turning to look at him.

—It's pure bullshit, is what it is.

—But why make up a story like that?

—Good question.

—I'm too tired right now to think straight, Hannah said, starting up her phone to look through her emails. —I only hope he's not a con man.

—An exaggerator, maybe. But, in any case, he can only con those who allow themselves to be conned. We need to be wary, careful, that is all.

—What does it mean? To be wary, careful? Hannah asked.

—It means that so long as we have our lawyer and don't sign or promise anything we're not one hundred percent sure of, we'll be fine.

—Hope you're right, Hannah said, not altogether convinced.

—I know I am, he said, a smile crinkling up the skin around his eyes. —Think of this as an incredible opportunity for us to expand our company . . . and way more quickly than we ever could on our own. But we will have growing pains, no doubt about it.

—Growing pains? Hannah repeated, adapting to the idea that growing pains in a human body could apply equally to a business.

—Yes, and don't assume it's all going to fall into our laps easily, Jake said.

Hannah turned to look at him as he stole a quick glance at her. They smiled at each other.

—So, anyway, Hannah said, determined not to dwell on the negatives. —What did you think of them? I liked Lisa, but then over dinner . . . I don't know. Something seemed to change.

—She seems okay, just not my type. And he? God knows.

—I agree, Hannah said, and as they turned into their street, she looked out at the familiar houses.

—I'll get the mail in the morning, she said. —The bills can wait.

Jake drove the car up into the garage.

As soon as Sophia, their babysitting neighbor, had opened the front door, Zig and Zag came running to Hannah. While she was getting the rundown on her girls' activities for the evening from Sophia, the dogs stood next to her, wagging their tails and licking her hands. They were itching to go out. As was Sophia. It was late.

—Go on up to bed, Jake said, after she let the dogs out. —I'll watch a little TV while I wait for the pooches to come back.

Since he hadn't done the round-trip drive up to Rhode Island, she didn't have to feel too guilty leaving the dogs to him.

—Make sure they have enough water, she called out in a whisper, already on the stairs and afraid to wake the kids.

•　　•　　•

She wonders, as she sits in this little room of her own, and stares at her computer screen, if her words are saying what they need to, if they will provide the mediator with enough proof to counterclaim all of Artie's twenty-four points against her and Jake. She hopes so. How tired she was that day. She remembers she never heard Jake come upstairs to bed; she must've fallen fast asleep before he'd even made it to the stairs.

She saves and closes her ARTIE file.

Chapter Fifteen

Soon after our expedition to Artie's factory, he sent us about fifty orders. More than half of all those orders were extremely overdue, going back to April. From one day to the next, we had a completely new product line that we knew nothing about but were expected to start with its production at once.

Glued to her desk chair at work, Hannah was struggling to stay focused on what she needed to accomplish for the day, but lapsed into daydreams instead, her mind splintering off into a million different directions and feeling as overwhelmed as Hydra must have, with her multiple heads. A week had gone by since their trip to Rhode Island and still they'd had no word from Artie or his lawyer. She and Jake chalked it up to Artie being too busy packing up his small Long Island office and making the arrangements to empty his Rhode Island warehouse and factory. Even with his lawyer in Southern Florida, they couldn't imagine why he should have held things up or taken this long to draw up a preliminary contract. Hannah, impatient as usual, wanted the whole thing over and done with immediately. All this, *may be* and *what if*, was driving her crazy. Her brain felt thick with the possibilities for potential, as well as her worries of a downfall.

She was staring so hard at the list of payables on her computer screen; the lines blurred into a meaningless, murky pattern. Payables. Her grand juggling act of the week. Who would scream the loudest if they weren't paid on time? Who would cut her off? Then there was the added burden of paying Artie, which loomed large and expensive in their future. How would they manage it all?

It'll work out, you'll see, Jake always told her whenever she presented him with an added concern. It was as if his voice – always cheery with optimism in those days – was on a kind of upbeat autopilot the minute she opened her mouth, knowing that one objection or another was about to come out.

Never mind.

She sent the accounts payable report to the printer. While she waited for it to finish, she checked her email, stared out of the window some more, scanned over the dusty knick-knacks accumulated on her even dustier desk, and half-listened for the printer to stop churning out her report.

She was so caught up in her daydream that she hadn't noticed Jake standing next to her desk and was startled by the sound of his voice when he spoke.

He held a mountain of paperwork up against his chest.

—These are all Artie's open sales orders, he said, shuffling them like a deck of cards.

Her hands flew up to cover her wide-open mouth. —When, she finally said, —I mean, how did all those get here?

—UPS.

—On our account, no doubt, she said, and conscious of the sudden quiet of the printer, swiveled her chair around, pulled out the report from the tray, rotated back, and slid herself closer into her desk. With a yellow marker in hand, she pored over the report, ready to put a stripe through those she absolutely had to pay.

—We need to look through these right now, Jake said, his impatience curdling around his words.

—Okay. But give me a little time to go over my payables first.

Jake dropped half the stack of orders on her desk. The stack gave way and spread out in front of her like the moraine of a warming glacier, impossible to ignore.

Returning to his side of the room, he dropped the other half on his untidy, paper-filled desk and sat, his head bent down, his face hidden by his computer monitor.

She brought her attention back to her list of payables, trying hard to concentrate on them. But the morass of paperwork fanned out in front of her, beckoned like a well-guarded, dirty secret. She glanced over at Jake. She could see the top of his head resting in his hands, his fingers busily massaging his furrowed brow and temples. Something must be wrong. She sighed, put down her yellow marker, and, lifting the batch of Artie's paperwork, assembled it in front of her. One by one, she began sifting through his orders.

Most of them were crumpled, dog-eared, or coffee stained, as if they had come in and out of his overstuffed briefcase, unpacked and repacked again and again. Others had notes scrawled in barely legible script: extended ship dates, changes of shipping addresses, altered shipping methods, instructions for no over-runs or under-runs.

Nothing unusual.

—Wow. I didn't realize how far back these orders go, she said, picking up her yellow marker to highlight the ship dates.

Another problem we had was dealing with furious customers. Artie had not been answering his phones for at least two months prior. These customers did not know what was happening with their orders. There were also customers who sent in deposits for orders which were never processed. This entire summer was extremely stressful.

—I guess he hasn't been operating his business since . . . May, Jake said.

—Well, that's no surprise. His place looked quite abandoned, didn't it?

—It did, he said, letting out a long, loud sigh.

—But what I don't understand, she said. —Is why he couldn't have at least gone through the pile himself before sending it to us.

—Obviously, he wants us to do his homework for him.

—Do we know the status of his inventory up there in Rhode Island? Did he ever give us a list?

—No, not yet, Jake said.

—Then how do we know how to fulfill these orders? Where to get the products from?

—I'll email him right now.

—What if you call instead? she said.

—If I don't hear back from him in short order, I will. I'm just not up for listening to his whiny, bullshit voice right now.

—I can't say I totally blame you, she said. —Although I can't imagine he'll bother checking his email this late in the day.

Shaking her head, she put Artie's stack of sales orders aside and was about to go back to her payables report when she saw Clara coming toward her, a black plastic pen in one hand, the order and template for the artwork in the other.

The bank's name, imprinted in white on the barrel of the black pen, looked a little blurry to Hannah. The order was for five thousand pieces. Too many to let it go like this.

—Don't worry, Clara said, as soon as Hannah looked up at her.

—I need to clean the screen.

—Please, go and make it right, Hannah said, and watching Clara leave, she let go of her annoyance, picked up her yellow marker, scanned the report for her place, and resumed her stripe-marking, adding up the rough dollars in her head as she went.

Minutes later, Clara came back with the sample pen and the paperwork.

—It looks great, but please, make sure the whole run looks perfect, okay?

Clara nodded and walked away from her, disappearing through the windowed door to the factory, where the sudden rush of voices and the whooshing sound of the screen and pad print machines billowed out into the office as the door opened, muffling into silence again as it closed.

Hannah left her payables report in the middle of her desk and went into the factory. She walked around, stopping at each machine to check the imprints on the various products – cups, notebooks, colored pencils, and pens. So far, so good. And best of all, these orders weren't scheduled to go out until the next day or even the day after. From there, she went over to the shipping area. The number of outgoing cartons waiting by the door for UPS had increased considerably, she noted happily. All her employees were scrambling now to get the last of the orders packed up. It was the usual end of day routine. She wondered if it would ever change and, if so, would she miss this frenetic last hour of work? She wouldn't miss the overtime; that was for sure. On the other hand, though, there was a certain feeling, a camaraderie that existed between everyone on the floor, as they rushed to finish up, and which she'd most definitely miss the most.

—Holy shit! Hannah heard Jake hiss as she came back to their office.

—What? she said, glancing at her payables report.

—Look at this. Urgency was in his voice now. There were three stacks of Artie's orders lined up on the desk in front of him. —You see this pile? he said, the deep furrows lining his face. —This is the pile of old orders. Chances are, most of these are useless by now, their event and deadline dates long gone. He was pointing to the highest of the three stacks. —But these, he went on, his hand resting on the shortest pile. —These are the current ones.

—That's it? Doesn't look like too many to me.

—No, but the good news is, with a little luck, we should be able to ship these orders out on time.

—Some consolation, she said.

—Better than none.

—God, what a frigging mess.

—We'll sort it out, he said, picking up the shortest pile to count how many there were.

—Just to let you know, we've already had calls, Hannah said.

—Calls? What kind of calls?

—I've been meaning to tell you. Nasty calls. Distributors demanding to know where their orders are and why they haven't been shipped.

—I guess we're in the business of damage control now, he said, as well as organizing and producing Artie's orders. As well as making sure we don't fall behind on our own.

An obvious irritation he couldn't hold back seeped out between his words.

—I hope this won't affect our own reputation. The people I spoke with were really pissed. One woman even threatened to sue.

The summer was becoming more and more stressful. Artie came to our place about once a week for hardly a full day. This once a week was supposed to be enough to teach us about his product line.

—He let no one know he was out of business, Jake said.

—The woman threatening the lawsuit said she was in danger of losing her biggest client.

—When was this? When did she call?

—A little while ago, Hannah said, looking down at her payables report, still needing to be tallied, the bank balance figured out, and the difference reconciled. She stifled a yawn.

—What a shit, he said.

—But I can't say I totally blame her, after all . . .

—I meant him, not her. I don't blame her, he said.

—Have you heard back from him about his inventory?

—No, not yet.

—I think you should call, she said.

—I will . . . first thing tomorrow.

—And what do we do? I mean, how do we get a handle on all this mess going forward? Hannah rifled through the orders on her desk. She hadn't separated her pile yet.

—Honestly, I see no other alternative than to call these people. We do need to know if their orders are still viable, and if they are, how long their clients are willing to wait for them.

—Just be prepared, I'm warning you, she said.

—Do you have a better idea?

She didn't, she told him and glanced back at the report she needed to finish going through. It was almost seven o'clock. Dinnertime. She was hungry and tired. At least Sophia was at home with the girls. Worst of all, she would have to be back here again first thing tomorrow. Was she beginning to sound like that spoiled child she used to be? No, not spoiled, she assured herself. Her feelings of responsibility and frustration curled around each other in equal parts, like dual strands in a tightly woven braid. She felt stuck.

Jake stood up and went into the factory. Now he seemed to be annoyed with her too, as if all this were just as much her doing. She heard him walk around and curse occasionally, as she imagined him finding a mess of garbage near a machine or ink-filled paper cups that should have been returned to the cabinets. Then she heard the slam of the back door closing, saw the factory lights go off one by one, and finally there was quiet as he came back into the office and once again settled down at his desk.

Looking up at her, Jake said, —Artie just emailed me. He's coming up tomorrow.

—Surprise, surprise, she said, unable to stop the cynicism coating her words.

—You have got to stop with this negative attitude; it's getting to me.

—I don't mean to be such a downer. But I'm already feeling overwhelmed, even without Artie's shit. And being interrupted all day long with stuff, I don't want to be bothered with anymore, is getting to me as well.

—Not sure what to tell you.

—I know, I know. I'll try to have a more positive outlook. I promise.

—I'll hold you to it, he said, getting up, and laughing, as he pointed his index finger vaguely in her direction. —Meanwhile, I think we should call it a night. I don't know about you, but I'm dead tired and starving.

—I just need to . . .

—Whatever it is, it can wait until tomorrow. Let's go. With a little luck, Sophia made enough dinner for us, too. If not, I'll go back out and pick up dinner from Boston Market. Okay with you?

—Sure, Hannah said, arranging the paperwork on her desk into neat piles so she could pick up tomorrow exactly where she left off today.

Making neat piles. Was her world really coming to this? Making neat piles? Good God.

In the car, she stared out of her side window at the houses, yards, and shops they passed. She couldn't help wondering now if this was going to be worth all the trouble. She turned to look at Jake.

—Is it . . .? she began.

—He said when he comes up tomorrow, he'll help sort things out.

—Hmm . . .

—Look on the bright side, he said.

—What bright side?

—You promised, he said, turning toward her.

—Oh, yes. Sorry. Bright side. For sure.

—Bright side is the increase in our business.

—But too many of those orders are worthless.

—Maybe, and maybe not. But think. Whichever ones we can salvage are ours. We're taking over his business, don't forget, folding it into ours. Of course, you've got to expect there'll be blips along the way. I told you there would be. But don't forget, it's still a fantastic opportunity. It'll all be worth it in the end, I promise you.

—Are you that sure of it?

—Absolutely. If we're smart about it and have a positive outlook.

—But do you trust him? she said, and as they stopped at a red light, she turned away from him to look back out of the window again.

A couple were walking with their black Poodle. The woman was obviously pregnant. Her tight, bright-orange tank top stretched thinly across her belly, accentuating its egg shape. Six, no, seven months, Hannah guessed. The woman waddled.

—Well, do you? she repeated, looking at him now, searching his face for a hint of a true feeling.

—No, he said, enough emphasis in his voice for her to believe him. —I don't trust him any further than I can throw him. And you?

—Not at all, she said and, drawn back to her window again, watched as the man put his arm around the pregnant woman, pulled her into him, and kissed the top of her head. The Poodle barked and danced around them. They were laughing. Were those kinds of moments over for her and Jake? As the car drove on, leaving behind the scenes outside her window, she added, —I think he's a fucking creep. And what's up with his lawyer, for God's sake?

—No doubt about it. We should've had his lawyer's paperwork in our hands before he sent us all those orders.

—It's as if Artie could give a shit about what happens.

—Too odd, I'll grant you that, he said.

—And what's with *our* lawyer? What does he have to say about all this?

—We'll be talking to Louis tomorrow.

—So, my summer days of writing are over, huh?

—Sorry, he said.

· · ·

That word, *sorry*, and the way he'd said it, had registered in her brain as unconvincing, she remembers thinking, as a repeat offender.

What else could he have said, she reasons now, as she walks down to their mailbox, her fingers crossed in the hopes there won't be another unhappy letter from Ella, hiding under a bill or tucked into the folds of an advertising circular. They'll be home next week, she says, as if to gird herself. And there'll be no more letters.

But they're not here at home yet. And as she opens the mailbox, the envelope greeting her has a picture of three bubble gum machines, each half-filled with an assortment of colored bubble gum. The envelope, addressed to Mom and Dad Bloom, has a round gold sticker to keep it closed. The postage stamp stuck onto the front of the card has the word LOVE printed along the top and beneath it, the face of a forlorn-looking brown puppy dog with exceptionally long ears. Hannah takes a deep breath and walks back up the driveway, Ella's card clutched in her hand.

Back at her desk, she slides her finger under the gold sticker, opens the card and reads:

Dear Mom & Dad,
Tonight, I get to call you,
the only reason I wrote
today is because I want you
to know I was thinking about
you, here's a poem

When you're happy, share it
With me.
When you're angry, I'm depressed,
When you're upset,
I still care!

That poem is a poem I found
 on a card and I'm not sure if
I wrote it.
I miss you so much. I want
 to go home. Last night I fell
out of bed again!
Love, Ella
 p.s. Let me come home!

Could she really have written this poem? Hannah wonders if she gets that angry and upset with Miri and Ella as regularly and often as she thinks this poem suggests. She doesn't believe so. But where did Ella find it? Surely, she didn't write it herself. It doesn't even sound like her.

Hannah closes the card, puts it down on her desk, and turns her thoughts back to her required task at hand – Artie and Lisa.

Chapter Sixteen

She remembers how Artie had burst into their office the next day, with the same whirlwind of energy as the last time he was here. Beach traffic, he'd announced, disgust in his voice. And before uttering another syllable, he'd dropped his briefcase along with a bouquet of alstroemeria – a mixture of pinks and whites – on the nearest desk, bent his head to his chest, and strode off with great determination and speed toward the men's room. Artie was very, very late for his first day of work – if that was what it could be called.

Hannah looked over at Jake. He made a face, shrugged his shoulders.

—Is beach traffic supposed to excuse his life away?

—So sorry, Artie said, rushing back out of the men's room. —It was a long ride.

He smiled at them, scooped up the flowers, held them out to Hannah and apologized once again for being late. She thanked him and, taking the bunch, told him it really wasn't necessary.

—But it's my pleasure, he'd shot back, grinning from ear to ear.

Watching him bend to retrieve his beat-up, over-stuffed, brown leather briefcase, she couldn't help but think how scruffy he looked in his khaki-colored shorts which needed pressing and the short-sleeved shirt, a flashy plaid in reds and yellows, perhaps a size or two too small, stretching tight across his rounded stomach and pulling at the buttonholes. Discolored white leather sneakers clad his sockless feet. His dyed brown hair was combed straight and slicked back off his forehead. And, of course, there was that stupid phone thing sticking out of his ear. What an incongruous picture of a man he was.

—Before I forget to tell you, Lisa sends you both her best regards. She's sorry she couldn't make it here today.

—Thank you, Hannah said. —Please give her mine and Jake's as well.

—Of course, Artie said, almost bowing. —And here's a little something she wanted me to give you, Hannah.

As he pulled a little black, familiar-looking pouch out of his pocket, Hannah's stomach lurched. And again, the dinner at the Italian restaurant in Queens flashed like a series of stills across her mind. The baggy of glitter. The earrings she had chosen and, afterward, the worry throughout dinner over how much they were going to cost her.

She also remembers there were questions she would've liked to ask Artie but never did. Would his answers have helped mitigate the envy she'd had of him?

Taking the little pouch from him, she untied the drawstring. Coiled inside lay a beaded choker, the blue beads identical to the ones in the earrings Lisa had given to her.

—Wow! This is beautiful. What a memory she has, Hannah said. —Please give her a big kiss for me when you get home. I'll call her a little later.

—She'll be delighted to hear how much you like it.

Hannah put on the necklace and turned from Artie to Jake.

—Gorgeous, Artie said. —We'll have to take a picture before I leave. Okay?

—Absolutely, Hannah said, fingering the beads.

—So, Jake said, slight impatience sneaking out through his voice. —Are we ready to go into the showroom now?

—You guys go ahead. I just need to put these gorgeous flowers into water. It won't take me a sec.

She went in search of a vase but had to settle on using an oversized coffee mug instead. After cutting the stems down and arranging the flowers to fit into the mug, she put them next to the monitor on her desk.

Back in the showroom, she took a seat at the table next to Jake. Artie had already settled across from them. The table was tidy and clean. Usually, it overflowed with all kinds of samples they brought in from China to consider for their product line or various artwork and layouts to review for their next catalog and weekly email blasts. Sometimes she would find abandoned half-filled paper cups of coffee and then occasionally, to Hannah's disgust, a takeout box with someone's leftover lunch. Now there were only Artie's orders, categorized into three separate piles, sitting in the middle of the spotless, dust-free tabletop. The setup felt like an interrogation. Well, perhaps it really was, she thought. To keep her eyes off Artie as well as the three piles on the table, she concentrated on surveying the room as though she were the stranger here. Framed catalog covers, one for each year they'd been in business, hung along the back wall. Behind Artie, a bookshelf held their prize samples of challenging, multi-color imprints. Memories of late nights, treks to the FedEx depot to ship out the deadline-dated orders, and her pride in their accomplishments drifted through her mind. They'd put everything they had into this, worked hard to create a stable, well-run company with outstanding employees in place and a solid product line to sell from.

And now, sitting across from Artie, she couldn't help but wonder if they were ready for this next step with him. It'd hardly begun and already it was taking its toll. She and Jake had fought on their way into the office that morning. She was desperate to talk it out, have a clear idea of what they were going to demand of Artie. But Jake had pulled away from her. There was nothing to talk about yet, he'd said. Nothing? He needed the time to think. Yeah, tough guy. He was acting as though the muddle of thoughts whirring around inside his brain would have little or no effect on anyone else but himself. So, by the time they arrived at work, fifteen minutes later, Hannah had reached her boiling point. She got out of the car, slammed her door shut, and walked ahead of him into their office, feeling as though she was no more than an addendum, a conjoined twin, forever stuck to her husband's side. No matter what.

Artie cleared his throat. She looked over at him. He was fumbling around in his battered briefcase.

—Where would you like to begin? he said, buckling up the straps and putting his bag on the floor next to his chair.

—I'm sure you've figured out by now, Jake said, putting his hand on all three piles, one after the other. —That these are all the orders you recently sent us. We've separated them according to their ship dates. The highest pile makes up the oldest. The next highest has ship dates we may be able to work with. And these, in this small pile, are the orders we can get out on time, provided, of course, you let us know *a-sap* where we can order the products from.

Jake sat back in his chair. Hannah looked at the three piles on the table. An image of Goldilocks and the three bears came to her. How silly, she thought, and while she tried to dismiss the image from her head, it stayed there, as stubbornly as the story itself.

Artie cleared his throat, poked around inside his shirt pocket for his glasses, put them on and asked, —Have you been able to reach the distributors from this tallest pile?

—You know, you have quite a few extremely angry customers out there, Jake said, leaning in over the table. —Not only were their orders not processed and shipped out to their clients, the way they would've expected, but some had even sent in deposits for those orders. You haven't been answering your phones.

—I know. I've been out of business since . . .

—Yes, but the least you should've done was to notify them, so they could've sent their orders elsewhere and, more importantly, had their deposits returned. How do you have the nerve to keep their money?

—I've told you a hundred times, Artie said, and rolling his eyes, he folded his arms across his chest and leaned back. —I'm out of money. I have no one to answer the phones, take care of customer service. My hands are tied. I told you about Lisa's cousin . . .

—Please, let's not go down that road again, Jake said. —We all know it's bullshit. Keeping those deposits is, to my way of thinking, stealing. Pure and simple.

Jake sat up straighter in his chair, and with his arms still outstretched, his fingers drummed impatiently on top of the folders in front of him while his eyes remained glued to Artie's face.

Artie took off his glasses, put his elbows back on the table, and dropped his head into his hands again. After some moments, he lifted his head. Tears filled his eyes. Wiping them away with the heels of his palms, he said, —I can assure you; it's not bullshit.

—Do you have receivables? Hannah asked, steering them away from where this conversation was taking them, as well as her own growing discomfort.

—Yes.

—You still have money coming in? she said.

—Yes.

—Well, then, Jake said. —You'll hopefully have enough to at least make good on the deposits.

Exaggerating a groan with the exertion, Artie lifted his overstuffed brown leather briefcase from the floor, laid it down sideways on the table, unsnapped the latches and pulled out a stack of paperwork.

—Here's the latest aging of receivables, he said, sliding his report across the table toward Jake.

Hannah grabbed it, sifted through the few pages. To her surprise, hardly anything remained owed to him.

—This it? she asked.

He nodded.

She looked up at him.

—What about a list of your inventory? Do you have it with you?

He shuffled his papers. —I do, he said, laying the pages down on the table in front of himself. Hannah stood up and reached over to retrieve them.

Hmm, the voice inside her head, nudged. Passive-aggressive? She put the report down in front of Jake.

—Tell me, he said, sifting through the pages. —Is this a list of the items you have stored in your warehouse in Rhode Island? Or does it also include the list of items you don't inventory, but buy directly from your domestic sources?

—Of course it includes the lot, Artie said, as he pushed his chair away from the table and got up. —Hey, I'll be right back. I forgot something in my car.

He left Hannah and Jake sitting side by side, staring at the windowed wall opposite them.

His inventory count was completely inaccurate from the beginning. We still had to learn where the various products came from and how much they cost. He gave me a list of his inventory. It was obvious he had not updated it in quite a long time. Even more frustrating was discovering, on the day an order was supposed to ship, that we had no stock in any of the locations. Artie kept telling me that as soon as he could come to work full-time, all these frustrations would be behind us.

—This is painful, Hannah said. —Do you think he's being purposefully evasive?

—Maybe, Jake said, as he brought the batch of reports closer to their side of the table and began flipping through the pages. —But I bet you, he's on the phone with his lawyer right now, trying to figure out what his next move should be. Looking through this paperwork, there doesn't seem to be much here. No receivables to speak of. And who knows if the inventory count is anywhere near correct? My guess is it's not.

—I'd agree with your assessment, Hannah said, picking up the report. —Look at all these negative numbers.

—From what I can see, there's nothing of value to buy here. He's driven his company into the ground.

—So, once again, I'm asking you, Jake . . . What're we doing with him here?

—Incorporating his product line into ours and giving him a job. And that's exactly what we're going to stick to, okay?

—I guess, she said, still trying to figure out the inventory report. —Though there are way too many things here that aren't making any sense to . . .

Before she'd finished her sentence, Artie had returned, rubbing his hands together, as if he had exciting news to report. She lifted her hair off her shoulders and fanned the back of her neck with Artie's inventory report.

—I apologize, he said, taking his seat back at the table. —I'd left my jotter in the car. It has all my notes and my questions for you. I think I'd leave my head behind if it weren't screwed on tightly.

They all laughed. Hannah felt relieved. A little of the icy seriousness had cracked, at least for the time being.

—Listen, Jake's tone of voice had deepened and become serious again. Artie sat further back in his chair. Looking at him, Hannah thought that if he could have shrunk up his entire existence – or better yet, sprouted wings, spread them wide, and flown away from all this – he would have.

—You sent us these orders, around fifty, I believe. Excuse my confusion, but I'm not exactly sure how we should proceed. I mean, besides finding out how many of them are in fact, workable, we need to figure out how we're going to get them all printed and shipped out . . .

—You know, Artie interrupted, —I still have a couple of people up in Rhode Island. Since we have until the end of the month before I need to be out of there, they could produce a bunch of the orders for us.

Now it was Hannah's turn to be confused. She was sure when they were at his factory, his employees were gone, and nothing was happening up there.

—Okay, Jake said, slowly, as if trying to process this latest piece of information, as well. —I didn't know that. Do you now have a handle on all your inventory?

—Yes, of course . . .

—But if memory serves, Jake interrupted him. —You weren't too sure about what you had on your shelves when we were up there.

—But see for yourself. It's all right here, he said and pointed to the report now sitting in Hannah's hands.

Hannah shook her head. —But this report isn't making much sense to me. Could you explain . . .

—Look, Artie said, cutting her off, tones of impatience driving his voice. —We'll send the orders to my factory in Rhode Island and the two guys I have working up there will figure out what we have in inventory and what we will need to buy. It's not a problem.

He forced a smile.

—Actually, Jake said, sitting back. —It is, though, because first and foremost, we don't have a fucking contract from either you or your lawyer to sign. In the end, we could be doing all this work, paying for it, and getting nothing in return.

—And what's to say, Artie said, —That you won't cheat me out of everything you owe me thus far?

Hannah felt an involuntary shiver run through her whole body.

—Excuse me, I'll be right back, she said, getting up.

She left them sitting across from each other, Jake staring at Artie's face, waiting for a response and Artie staring down at the tabletop, looking for one to give. Hannah didn't want to think about it anymore. First, she went to sit at her desk. She checked her email. Most of the people writing to her these days were from Chinese manufacturers she'd never heard of before, seeking to sell her products she had zero interest in, like power banks or gym bags. Clicking through her inbox, she deleted them all. Then she got up and went to the bathroom. Sunshine blasted heat through the old windows, which never did quite line up properly, letting humidity sneak in through the gaps. Her eyes stung. She closed them for a moment. Blinked. But it didn't help. She washed her hands, splashed her face with water. Still made no difference. She stared at her reflection in the mirror and noticed the purplish-colored skin underlining her eyes; she looked tired. Bringing her hand up to her neck, she rolled around the beads strung on her new choker. In the sunlight, she could see all the different colored blues in them, ranging from teal to sky to blue-jean blue. Lisa must have created this especially for her. The thought, the gift touched her. They hadn't spoken since their excursion up to Rhode Island. Had she sensed Hannah's confusion about her that night? Distracted, she looked out of the window for a moment. A car in the parking lot below kept honking, as though it were the car itself crying out with impatience. She turned back to her reflection in the mirror.

•   •   •

There are days when she wishes she could simply remold the features in her face – make her eyes larger, her mouth sexier, her nose straighter. But more importantly, she scoffs at herself as she leans back in her chair and stretches her arms high over her head, she wishes certain parts of her daily life would fit together as neatly and easily as . . . And then she suddenly remembers how her own reflection had caught her off guard that day at lunch with her mother; it was the way it had looked back at her from outside the restaurant's large plate-glass window, superimposed, like a collage, over the white cloth-covered tables inside and the matching starched napkins folded into triangles, as if standing at attention inside the wine glasses.

Like an artist's collage . . . and not so different, she muses, to her own life. Partner in marriage and in business, mother both outside and in, and finally, poet. But can she align, or realign as needed, all those parts artfully, gracefully, as if she alone owned the code to piece them together? Again, there's that pang going right through her, like an arrow; she really does miss her two little girls. Her life without them feels useless and somehow . . . unfamiliar.

The house, as well, is too silent and still. Everything's put away. Nothing's left out. No half-undressed dolls to move away from the chair she's about to sit in. No cookie crumbs sprinkling the floor in front of the TV. No plastic cups half-filled with milk or juice, abandoned on kitchen counters. She promises herself she'll never rail at her children's untidiness ever again. Well, maybe not *ever* again. She smiles at the promise she knows she'll never keep. Envisioning their homecoming, she can't wait to know how they'll react to the news of a new baby on the way? Excited, she's sure. With a little luck they might be able to feel the baby kicking by the time they're home from camp. God, how fantastic would that be? She closes her eyes and can imagine their small, dimpled hands, splayed and tentative on her stomach, and hear their giggles with the fluttering movement of their baby brother or sister, and then the amazed and astonished expressions on their faces. She can't wait.

•   •   •

She had turned away from the mirror in the overheated bathroom, thought of the showroom, took a deep breath, and wondered how Jake and Artie were surviving with each other, if they were staying civil without her. Despite her worries, she knew that Artie's company would help provide them with that push to the next level – to the place they'd been working toward to where she wouldn't have to worry about every little decision they made, or each cent they spent. Yes. They just needed to get through this sticky part with Artie. They had to get to understand him, to know his requirements, and he, theirs. Yes. Surely, it would be that easy. Smiling, she left the bathroom, the conditioned, fresh-feeling air in the office, soothing and cooling her skin.

As she came to the showroom, she could see the two men through the square of window in the shut door. Neither looked happy. Turning the knob to open the door, she had a sudden feeling of being dragged down into a deeper place, where the ground shifted and fought to absorb her, like quicksand.

Once inside, she took her seat and looked from one to the other.

—What's going on? she said.

—What is going on, Jake repeated in an obvious huff with his eyes fixed on Artie, —Is that *we* will have to provide all the inks and supplies for his guys up in Rhode Island, as well as pay their salaries for them to produce *his* orders . . .

—No, no. These are not *my* orders. Artie practically jumped out of his chair. Leaning forward, he pointed his finger at Jake. —They are now *yours*. One hundred percent yours. You will be shipping them under *your* account, invoicing them under *your* company name, and then collecting the payments. No. They are definitely not my orders.

Hannah looked at Jake. Artie, it seemed, had given away the shop.

—Apparently, they're out of plate material right now and certain inks, so we'll need to order whatever it is they need. And the next issue, or perhaps I should say the first, is that Artie doesn't think he'll be coming to work for us on a full-time basis until late September. Which means . . .

—We'll be sucking wind until then, not knowing what's what, Hannah said and, looking at the three bears in the middle of the table in front of her, realized there would be little or no help in sorting out the mess. That job, she knew, would end up falling to her.

—I'll still come up once a week and you know you can always contact me . . .

Jake let out a laugh. —I'm sorry. I just don't get this.

—There are things I need to take care of.

Jake stood, put up his hand to silence Artie, and began to pace back and forth behind Hannah in the small room. After a few moments, he said, —Okay, we'll give it a couple of weeks. But Artie, I need your lawyer to send us a contract. If we don't get it by the end of this week, I'll have our attorney draw one up. We can't let this go on. It just isn't right.

Artie said nothing. He only pulled off his glasses and lifted his hands up over his head in a conciliatory gesture. Looking at his face, his eyes brimming once again with tears, Hannah's heart sank with the distinct and unfair feeling that they had somehow beaten him up.

At first, we had his factory (there were two or three people still working there) produce most of Artie's orders. We had to replenish the inks and supplies for the factory in Rhode Island because Artie was out of money. Since we sourced a number of his catalog items from other local companies, we were able to have those items shipped directly to our factory for printing.

•   •   •

Knowing what she does now, she can't understand how she could've possibly felt sorry for him. But then again . . . her thoughts waver. No, no, she says to herself, standing up, she mustn't allow those thoughts in. It must be the pregnancy hormones raging away inside her and doing their best to keep her unhinged and off-balance, as if her trembling emotions were like a pair of unsteady legs tottering on five-inch stilettos. What if all this were an act though? If she and Jake were being played, after all?

She steps away from her desk. She paces up and down her little room. How does she proceed from here? She remembers she had left the office, left the two men in the showroom to battle out whatever they needed to.

But then there was Lisa. Enigmatic Lisa.

Chapter Seventeen

When Hannah started up her car, a flute concerto was playing on the radio. She'd just left Jake and Artie at the office. Needing a breather, she sat back in her seat, closed her eyes, and listening to the music, tried to guess the composer. Until she remembered that she'd forgotten to have Jake take a picture of her with the new choker necklace Lisa had made for her. Which reminded her. Better now than to forget later, she said to herself, as she reached for the key to turn off the ignition, silencing the flute concerto as well. Unclicking her seatbelt, she stretched out her small body as best she could and searched on her phone for Lisa's number. Yes, it was best to get this out of the way now.

—Hey, she said as soon as Lisa picked up. —It's Hannah.

—You're calling to tell me how much you love your choker, right?

—How'd you guess?

They both laughed.

—Don't let on, said Lisa. —But I'm actually a brilliant mind reader, as well as a mighty talented jewelry maker. You love it, right?

—Absolutely, yes. The beads are magnificent. Those fabulous blues. Where'd you find them all?

—Ahh! That's my little secret to be shared with no one.

—You're too funny.

—Is Artie still there?

—Oh, yes.

—Any idea how it's going?

Hannah would be lying if she hadn't said the picture of Artie, a broken, tearful man who was about to lose everything, was a pitiful one. She also knew that she shouldn't be talking to Lisa about any of it.

—No, not exactly, she said. —I left the boys to themselves. I figured they're better off working things out without me.

—You'll most likely think this too weird and premature for me to say, but . . . I've missed you. Lisa's last words tumbled out of her in such speedy succession, Hannah wasn't certain she'd heard them correctly.

—Yes, yes, me too, she said.

•   •   •

And now can remember how, even to her own ears, her response had sounded forced, automatic. What Hannah would have preferred to say, in all honesty, was that her days were, as they are right now, too full to think about, let alone miss anyone who isn't in her direct line of vision. She would also have to admit that although she does try to remember friends' birthdays and such, she isn't always successful at it; and when she isn't, she ends up berating herself for living within the imaginary confines of her impenetrable, square box of a life.

•   •   •

—You must think me crazy, Lisa said. —I realize we barely know each other, but after our wonderful chats up in Rhode Island, I feel like we have this special bond between us. Do you know what I mean? Do you feel it too? Or am I totally wrong?

—No, you're not wrong, Hannah said, stretching out her legs, as best she could, in the narrow spaces between the gas and the brake pedals. —But I'm not sure how we'll be able to maintain . . .

—Because of what's going on with the business? Lisa said, her voice flat with disappointment.

—You do realize we're on opposing sides in all this. I mean . . . there's really no way out of it.

—But you don't think, once the whole thing is over with, we'll be able to resume our relationship?

Hannah traced the rim of the steering wheel with her free hand and stared out at the cars lined up in the parking lot all around her. How could they resume something they never had, to start with? They'd met three or four times, had interesting conversations. Yes, they understood each other, but . . .

—And the girls? How are they doing? Lisa asked.

•   •   •

Her girls. How she misses them now. Even though she's had a great summer. No responsibility, no refereeing, no chauffeuring. But she is *so* ready to have them at home again. She misses her girls desperately. Yet . . . she sent them away. But it's not strictly *sending* them away, she thinks, as much as giving them a new perspective on life, a new way to think of themselves in a different context, another way of learning how to maneuver themselves within this new world. She still hopes Ella will find her way and enjoy her last few days of sleep-away camp.

•   •   •

—They're both fine. What about Ethan? He must be starting college soon, no?

—In another two weeks. He can't wait. I can, though. I know I'll miss him terribly and then I've become overly anxious about what direction my life will take, what I'll do without him. You know, to keep me grounded.

The sun's angle had shifted. Sheaths of light were slanting directly through the car's windshield, lighting up Hannah's face. She pulled down the visor and moved around in her seat to dodge the brightness prickling her eyes. She rubbed her thighs, sore now from sitting in the same position all this time. It was meant to be a quick conversation, a speedy thank-you call.

—What worries you, Lisa? Hannah asked, as she found herself pulled into the awkward position of consoling a woman she barely knew. —You'll have your business, your jewelry-making. You'll be incredibly busy. Besides, don't you think Ethan will come home on weekends from time to time? It's not as though he's going away for good, is it?

—No. You're right, Lisa said. —I shouldn't be complaining. No one listens to me, anyway. She let out a brief chuckle . . . or was it a snort? —Besides, she went on. —I imagine once the four of us have come to an agreement and signed a contract, life will settle down. Don't you think?

—For sure. At first, Hannah's voice sounded far away to herself, as though hope itself was adrift in the middle of an open ocean. But then, she could hear the acquiescence in her own passive tone of voice as brutally banal. And feeling a sudden need to make Lisa know this was not who she was, she brought the phone's mouthpiece closer to her mouth and said, —But tell me, surely you must have some clue as to what's going on. Where the contracts are, I mean. What the hell's taking so goddam long?

—I'm only the bystander, she said. —All I do know for sure is that Artie talks to his lawyer at least once a day, sometimes more often. Why? What's wrong?

—What's wrong is everything, including what Jake and I are paying for, and then without a contract . . .

—I get it, really, I do, Lisa said, interrupting Hannah's sudden tirade. —But, please believe me, I have no say in any of this.

—Lucky you, Hannah blurted out in a nastier way than she had intended.

—Hey, what's got into you?

Hannah's free hand drifted to her neck and felt for the beaded choker Lisa had made for her, the blue beads smooth and cool to her fingertips, a momentary comfort to her muddled emotions. About the same way, she imagined, a rosary, twirling between anxious fingers, might soothe the heart.

—Nothing, really. I've just been sitting in my car this whole time we've been on the phone, the sun beating down on me and suddenly, talking to you feels like such a paradox to me. I almost feel like I'm a traitor to my own cause, if that makes any sense.

She heard Lisa clear her throat, as though she were about to respond, but when she didn't, Hannah continued, —I don't know what to think anymore. When I left Jake and Artie at our office, Jake was losing his patience with Artie or the situation, or both. And Artie looked like he was about ready to burst into tears at any second. Do you really have no idea about what's going on, why all this is taking so goddam long?

—The short answer, Lisa said, —Is no, I haven't a clue. And just in case you have any weird ideas about me and my role in all this, you should also know that Artie never shares his business dealings with me.

—Hmm . . . too bad.

—Honestly, I'm more than happy keeping it that way. The only reason I came up to Rhode Island was to keep him company for the car ride and to see you again. I've liked you ever since we first went out for dinner in Long Beach. Remember?

—Yes, of course I do.

The beeping signals of a UPS truck, backing up to the dock, suddenly sidelined Hannah's train of thought. Her mind spinning in unexpected confusion, she watched the driver jump down from his cab, walk to the rear, and throw open the doors. As the freed doors slammed against the sides of the truck, she was brought back, not to Long Beach but to the oddness of the day in Rhode Island, to the almost hour by hour change in the way Lisa appeared to her – friendly for a while, then cool, reserved, as though she were afraid of letting on what she wasn't supposed to. And Hannah could only react exactly as she did now: Confused. She shut her eyes against the sun, a burning torch on her face. Behind her closed lids, more images of the day they'd spent together at Artie's factory crowded her thoughts, making less and less sense, as each one jostled another for their own significance.

First, there was Artie's insistence that he drive them in his SUV, knowing full well he had neither enough gas nor cash for their trip home. Then his secretive, brief mention of the money gone missing from his company bank account he'd conveniently, and much to Lisa's distress, let out during their conversation at lunchtime. And later, at the factory, Lisa barely budged from the conference room. She'd sat, teary-eyed, at the dust-covered table, her scarlet-painted fingernails busily clacking away, text after text, on her phone's keypad. Hannah remembers her saying that she only came along for the ride to keep Artie company, confessing, moments after they'd stepped into the building, that this was her first time at Artie's factory. Even more of a surprise to Hannah than Artie losing everything he'd ever worked for was Lisa, who hadn't shown the tiniest bit of curiosity about the place. She must've known how proud he was of his building. Hannah kept trying to think back, as if she could push and pull her memory, drill its way through the surface of time, and reveal . . . what?

—Hannah? You there?

—Yes, yes. I'm sorry. A loud truck went by. What were you saying?

—To cut Artie a little slack. This is a real shit situation he's created for himself. It's painful. And not only for him.

—Which is why, Hannah responded, hardly believing what she'd just heard. —You'd think he'd want to push to get the deal over and done with, and as quickly as possible.

—I know what you're saying, and I agree with you, Hannah. But as I've said before, he doesn't listen to me. In fact, I'm the last one in the world . . .

—This whole thing is making less and less sense to me. Doesn't he realize he's making it more difficult for himself?

—Why? What do you mean?

—Well, to start with . . . Her concentration wavered again as she watched the UPS truck pull away from the dock. —We have no contract, which, in case you haven't noticed, is tremendously frustrating for us because we can't move forward without solidifying this deal and then . . .

—And then . . . what? What are you trying to say?

—I don't mean to be vague, but to be perfectly honest, I can't help sensing there's something else going on . . . a hidden agenda of sorts.

—Hidden agenda? Good God! Like what?

With each word, Lisa's voice sounded further away, as if she'd put the phone down and moved across the room. Or that she'd simply put her hands up to her face, closed her eyes, and covered her mouth.

—Like the fact that he won't make himself available to come to work on a regular schedule, because he has 'things' he needs to take care of. What could be more important to him right now than squaring away his company?

—I'm not at liberty . . .

—Pfaff! Hannah slammed the steering wheel, then switched hands, putting the phone back up to her other ear. —So, there *is* something else going on, she said.

—Hey, that something is what you're not remembering. If I'm not mistaken, you're the ones who will reap the benefits of this in the long run. Lisa's voice was loud and high-pitched, as if she'd just put the phone up close to her mouth for emphasis.

—And you think it's okay for him to dump all his open sales orders into our laps, no matter what their status, creating havoc in our company, and letting us take the heat from his customers for late or no deliveries, plus unreturned cash deposits.

Heat blazed through the windshield even hotter than before. Hannah felt feverish. She'd been ranting and hadn't realized how angry she'd become. But it wasn't Lisa's fault. She knew that.

—I understand it's the turmoil you've both been put through, Lisa said. —But you didn't have to do this. You both knew from the get-go, from the day we were up in Rhode Island together, that he has no money, that things haven't been going well for quite a while. Although I can empathize with you, I can't exactly feel terrible for you, either.

—I'm sorry, I didn't mean to take it out on you. I know you must be having an even tougher time . . .

—*Even* tougher? My God, Hannah, do you *even* hear yourself? Excuse my French, but you have absolutely no fucking idea how tough 'tough' really *is*.

Hannah leaned forward. Head down. Chest heavy. Arms bent. Elbows pinned to her thighs. Not a word to, nor a peep from the phone held tight and hot against her right ear. Only the thrumming of a pulse, like an echo inside her head. She shut her eyes, stinging from sudden fatigue and the too-bright light of the sun. What to say now? Her mouth opened. Searched for words. Nothing. What was the use? She knew that whatever words she chose would only have been like those of a spoiled child.

—Hey, Hannah, you still there?

—Yes, I'm here.

Hannah sat up and leaned her head against the back of the car's seat.

—I never meant to blast you like that. Unthinking, the words just flew out of my mouth. I'm so sorry.

—Don't worry, Hannah said. —I'm sorry as well.

—I'm angry, Lisa said, continuing her diatribe. —No. Angry isn't quite the right word. Furious is more like it. But not at you. Please understand that.

—I do. I understand. But you must know how stressed out and frustrated I am.

—Yes, I know you have more on your plate than you'd bargained for. And I know this whole thing is not exactly fair or right. But at least you have . . . Oh, never mind . . . If you'd just believe me. I promise it'll work out. Honestly, I wish there was more I could tell you, but I can't. I'm not in any position to say more than I already have. I hate this feeling of being torn. I barely know you and I'm like . . .

—What are you trying to say?

—Forget it, Lisa said. —Forget the whole thing. I can't understand why we can't simply let the guys figure it out and leave us the hell out of it?

—You know that'd be impossible, don't you? I mean, our company is as much mine as it is Jake's.

—Good for you.

—Yes, it is . . . *most* of the time, Hannah said.

—Well, at least it's *most* . . . And they both laughed.

—Hey, I hate to do this right now, but I need to hang up. I'm boiling hot.

—No worries. I understand.

—And, Hannah said, laughing, —I'm desperate to pee. Are you free to continue this conversation later this afternoon or tomorrow?

Lisa laughed.

—Sure thing, she said, her voice suddenly upbeat again. Perhaps she, too, was relieved their conversation was ending for now.

And just as she was about to get out of her car, Hannah saw Artie storm across the parking lot toward his SUV. She had to crouch down in her seat again. She didn't want him to see her. He didn't get into his car right away. Instead, he leaned up against the driver's door, talking into his phone contraption. No, not talking, shouting. Though she was unable to make out what he was saying, he was obviously upset and knowing that Jake wasn't happy with the way things were going, she wondered if they'd gotten into a fight. They were at a deadlock. And most frustrating of all was that there was still no signed contract.

After a little while, Artie got back into his SUV and drove off. Hannah wondered if he was still on his phone.

Chapter Eighteen

—What are you doing back here? Jake said, almost running into her, as she came out of the bathroom, patting her flushed face with a paper towel which made her think of Artie when he'd done the same thing. —I thought you'd left ages ago.

—I did, she said, laughing as she dried her hands.

—What happened?

—Nothing really *happened*. I was on the phone with Lisa . . .

—This whole time?

—Yup, but listen . . .

—You've been sitting in your car? he said, guiding her toward their office.

—Well, I expected the call to be a quick hello, thanks for the necklace, and goodbye.

At the door to their office, he turned to feel her cheek, then her forehead, a backhanded caress, the way he might've checked the temperature of a child.

—No wonder you look about as hot and boiled as a lobster.

—A pretty sight, I'm sure. But listen, I have something to tell you.

She scrunched up the paper towel, patted her forehead once more, and rubbed her eyes, stinging now from the heat.

—Okay, he said, as they walked into their office. —Spill it out, I'm listening. He crossed his arms over his chest and lowered his head toward hers, as if to help him hear her better.

Hannah sat in the spare chair beside Jake's desk. She pushed aside a pile of paperwork, rested an elbow on his desktop and, with her head cradled in her hand, turned to face him.

—How did it end with Artie? Did you get into a fight?

—Of course not. What makes you say that?

—No reason, she said, and deciding not to let on she'd seen an angry Artie in the parking lot, changed the trajectory of her subject. —Except, I know you were already beginning to lose your patience with him before I'd left.

—Perhaps a little, yes. I mean, trying to get any valid information out of him is like pulling teeth, for God's sake. He's become tight-lipped. His reports are all a mess . . .

—And I'm trying to tell you, I think there's weird stuff going on with him, or with her, or both. Maybe he's trying to chicken out of the deal.

—But what good would that do him? He'd have nothing to gain. No, Hannah, it'd make no sense. None. He needs us more than we need him at this point. Jake took a deep breath, bit down on his lower lip and went on. —Besides, he seemed fine leaving here. We shook hands, civil-like. He even said he'd be back next week to help us out with the inventory.

—Don't hold your breath, she said and immediately looked away, realizing she should have kept her mouth shut.

—There you go again.

—Sorry. I don't mean to be so negative, but it's Lisa who's getting to me now. She's too weird. One moment she says she knows nothing about the business and the next, she's not at liberty to say a word. What do you make of that? A note of triumph seeping into her voice as she got up and went to sit at her own desk.

Jake picked up the phone.

—I'm calling the lawyer. Enough of this bullshit. We absolutely need to have the frigging contract drawn up, he said.

—Wait. There's something else.

—What now?

He put the phone down and glanced at her. He looked confused, his face scrunched up, as if she, the storyteller, had become a strange alien he was trying hard to name.

Well, she thought, maybe that's precisely who she had become.

—I also think there's stuff going on between Artie and Lisa.

—Oh, come on . . .

—No, seriously, she said.

—Like what, for God's sake?

—Well, for one thing, I'm quite sure they're having marital problems.

—How would you know?

—The way she talks about him.

—The way she *talks* about him? What the hell's that supposed to mean, exactly?

She looked away from Jake; her gaze settling on the hazy sky outside the window. How could she explain what she meant when she wasn't so sure she understood any of it herself? Hearing Jake sigh, she turned back to face him again. A new frown of worry rumpled his forehead. He stared down at the pile of paperwork in front of him and began shuffling through it. He jiggled his mouse from side to side and glanced up at his computer screen every few seconds. And with another sigh of frustration, this one loud, he looked across the room at Hannah as if, she thought, she'd been the one waiting for him to speak first all along.

—Well? he said. —What do you mean?

—The way she talked about him. Like she couldn't have cared less about what might happen to him or his business. She only worries about their son.

—You're making stuff up, Jake said.

—No, I don't think so. And why do you always say that whatever I come up with is never real, but an invention inside my head?

The shifting sunlight behind Jake veiled his face in shadow, obscuring his features. She leaned back in her chair, pushed herself away from her desk, and stretched her legs straight out, crossing them at the ankles. But it wasn't only him she was feeling impatient and annoyed with. It was with herself, as well. She could feel her irritation nag at the fringes of her consciousness, as she realized she was wasting her own precious time. If she left the office right this second, she'd have a few spare moments to work before meeting the girls at the bus stop. Her latest poem wasn't going as well or as fast as she'd hoped. So then, she asked herself, while she sat at her desk, trying not to take any notice of the increasing workload impatiently staring at her, what the hell was she still doing here? She shook her head.

—Not true, Jake said. —You know it's not true. Concoct? Why would you even think that?

Hannah shrugged and said, —Because it's just the way I feel sometimes.

—Look, let's get back on track here. This is all about Artie being out of money, the beginning and the end of his story. And it's the only story we need to be concerned with.

—And the money supposedly embezzled from his company? What do you make of that? She sat up, slammed her sneakered feet noisily to the floor.

—I don't know enough about it, and besides, it has no bearing on us.

—Hmm . . . She smiled and leaned back again.

—What's that supposed to mean?

—It means, I'm not exactly sure.

—Not sure? About what?

—That the embezzlement will have nothing to do with us.

Jake stood, walked around his desk and came toward Hannah.

—I think we both need to keep our focus straight, okay? Again, all we're doing with this transaction is folding his business into ours, paying him for whatever of his we use, and providing him with a job and a salary for that job.

As his voice rose to a crescendo, he clapped his hands together in dismissal. He was now standing in front of her.

—Geez, Jake . . .

—Sorry, but I feel like I keep telling you the same old goddamn thing over and over.

—You think I'm dense, she said, more to get a rise out of him, than believing he really thought so.

—What is going on with you?

—Perhaps we keep going over the same thing again and again because there are issues that don't add up. Did you ever think about how I might look at this whole situation differently from you? Or perhaps that I've picked up certain vibes from Lisa, for instance?

She watched him walk back to his side of the room. He didn't sit at his desk. Instead, he paced up and down in front of it.

—You're driving me nuts, she said. —Sit down for Christ's sake.

—You're the one making *me* nuts, coming up with all these phantom problems. He continued to pace.

—They're real, I'm sure of it. There are things, she said, and waved a hand, vaguely pointing it up at the ceiling.

—Things, things. For God's sake, what things? He stood still for a moment then turned toward Hannah and continued. —What goes on in their lives makes no difference to me. This is a business proposition. And from what I can tell, a simple one; at least that's the way it should be. He's out of money and needs a job. Why he came to us in the first place is a bit of a mystery, I'll grant you that. But otherwise . . . And he threw his arms up in the air, —I think we should keep going forward. It's such a fantastic opportunity for us. At the least, we'll double the size of our company right off the bat. Are you, or are you not, with me on this?

—Yes, I'm with you, she said and sighed.

—Don't you want to grow the company? Isn't this what we set out to do in the first place? Isn't this what we've been working for, all this time?

—Of course, and I totally agree with everything you're saying. I want it all for us, too. I do. It's just that I have certain things I want to accomplish on my own as well. You do understand that don't you?

—Absolutely, I do, he said, coming toward her. —I really do. And I strongly believe that once we get past a certain point, you'll be able to take off all the time you need.

—You promise?

—I promise.

Hannah got up. She gave him a hug and a kiss on his cheek.

—I'm going now, she said. —The kids will be home soon. We have leftovers for dinner. What time do you think you'll be leaving here?

—Why? Do you have a secret lover you'll need to hide away from me before I get home?

—Yup, she said. —I do. It's my poetry.

Chapter Nineteen

Taking a break from Artie and Lisa, Hannah is at her desk in her little room of her own. She sits back in her chair with her arms clasped together behind her head and smiles as she takes in the words to the poem she's been working on, for what she feels like has been forever.

As the late afternoon light
* flickers through the woods,*
a sudden squall kicks up a
thick carpet of newly fallen
leaves and shoots them into the air
—a whirlwind of sunlit frenzy—
and tugs at a lone leaf still fiercely
attached to its limb. Crumpled and torn,
it reminds her of the tattered remnant of
a dream her memory will never surrender.

From her window, she catches sight of two frolicking baby deer with another she assumes must be their mother by the way she looks after them. As Hannah watches the deer nibble away at the plants in her garden, she wonders if all these animals, strolling past her window most days, are more protective of their young than human mothers? Would one of them, for instance, swaddle up her newborn in a cradle of dirt and leaves and deposit it in the dark corner of a field or a backyard or a forest? Perhaps animals don't panic about their lives in the same way humans do. Could that be her answer?

Zig and Zag nuzzle their noses into her thighs to gain her attention.

Beethoven's Sixth is playing on the radio in the kitchen. Tuned in to WQXR, New York's classical music station, the volume is way up. Laughing, she's told Jake – who dislikes classical music because, he says, it reminds him of his childhood and those rainy, boring, stuck-at-home Saturday afternoons when there was no escaping the opera broadcasts blaring out from the living room – if robbers were ever to break in to their house, hear a symphony, or a piano or a violin concerto playing at full blast, she's sure they'd run off in the opposite direction. But really, the music is to keep Zig and Zag company when no one's at home. It soothes them. And she's read that classical music is also good for her house plants. They thrive on it. As she does, too. She hates coming home to the quiet of an empty house. Once settled down at her computer with her latest in-the-works poem staring out at her from her screen, the music helps her find that special place in which she needs to be.

She hits the *save* key and gets up. The dogs follow her to the kitchen. She opens the back door to let them out into the yard, but before closing it again, she stays to watch them race away. The late afternoon air has cooled. She's tempted to turn off her computer and go outside – sit with a book or simply vegetate with a daydream or two. But there's her poem. She's promised herself to work on it some more before her opportunities, for alone-time, shut up tight, like a door slamming in her face. But there's Artie and Lisa she needs to be writing about. Then, when Miri and Ella are back home from sleep-away camp, they'll need extra attention for the first couple of weeks, at least until they settle down into their old, remembered routines. Once they're in school again, she'll divide her time, though not equally. Working at Bloom & Company always comes first. But there are instances, short though they are, when she can juggle her time, devoting a little more of herself to her poetry.

Jake will be home in a little while. What are they having for dinner? She opens the fridge. Relief washes over her as she remembers she doesn't have to think about it. Little white takeout containers stare back at her, leftovers from last night's Indian dinner. She takes them out of the fridge and puts them on the counter.

Back at her desk, she looks at this next stanza. Reads and rereads her words to herself, then aloud.

Feeling a shivery chill
in the air, she lifts the collar of
her buttoned-up, navy-blue pea coat,
tightens the knitted scarf around her
neck and then laughs at herself when
the fringed ends, swaying across her chest,
mimic the phantom clock that lives inside
her head, ticking off her time with
its unceasing thrum of loss.

Her thoughts drift away from her writing in a kind of dreamy, disconnected way for a little while. She hopes that Jake's assessment of the situation with Artie and his company is correct and that they will win. But Hannah is such a worrier. It's all those ubiquitous *what ifs*. Jake has dubbed her the queen of the worrywarts. He says she frets enough to cover for the four of them in their family. But right now, she can't get the picture of Artie's sorrowful face out of her mind. And she's brought back to that phone conversation with Lisa.

•   •   •

She remembers Lisa was saying something Hannah couldn't quite grasp; her voice was quiet, muffled, her words spilling out, like an afterthought. And just before Hannah had had the chance to ask Lisa to repeat what she said, she'd seen Artie come out of the building and walk toward his SUV. Hannah couldn't keep her eyes off him. She watched the balding spot at the back of his head, the too-tight shirt, the rumpled khaki shorts, and the well-worn sneakers. As though he knew he was being watched, he'd turned around, leaned back on his car again and continued to look around the parking lot.

It was then that she'd heard Lisa say again, —Hannah, you still there? I seem to keep losing you.

—Yes, I'm here. My phone must've blipped out for a second.

Hannah hated to lie but hadn't wanted to tell Lisa she'd seen Artie. She hadn't wanted to confuse the conversation any more than the direction it seemed to have been going in.

—There's much more to my story than I've told you. But I'm not ready to talk about it right now.

Not ready right now? But if not right now, when?

Then it dawned on her what had been nagging at her. For once, it wasn't Artie, but Lisa. Why would she be looking for ways to pull Hannah into her life and, at the same time, push her away? Had she expected Hannah to plead with her, to open herself up, tell her all that was on her mind? Didn't she know their friendship, if Hannah could call it that, needed to still be superficial? At least until. . . and suddenly she was drawn back to Artie, talking into his phone contraption; the lines in his face curling as his fists slammed against his SUV. It was almost as if this scene, Lisa in her ear and Artie within full view of her, was being played out expressly for her. How did she come to feel herself the betrayer? And to whom? And that's when she told Lisa she had to get out of the car; she desperately needed to pee.

•   •   •

But the real question, she decides, as she stands, aware of Zig and Zag scratching at the door to be let back in, is how she'd be able to disentangle herself if she became too involved? She clicks save on her keyboard and goes to let the dogs in. They rush past her, immediately heading for their coveted place under her desk, where they stretch out on their sides, inch their paws and noses along the carpeted floor, and close their eyes. She strokes their bellies with her bare feet and feels the in-and-out motion of their bodies slowing as their breathing does. She's jealous. Relaxation is such a distant, rarely used word in her own mental or emotional vocabulary. Perhaps it's because, for as long as she can remember, she's been plagued by the idea that there's something she's meant for in this world, though what that might be remains vague, hidden, and hangs stubbornly just beyond her reach; bothering her in the same way a forgotten word or name might sit at the tip of her tongue.

Or like the tattered remnant of the dream, she's been writing about in her poem. She stares hard at her screen – at the words and the pattern they make at the close of each line. Changing one word here, she puts another there. Then, shaking her head, puts back the original arrangement. Nothing is working. She gets up. Stands in front of her desk. Touches her palms to her abdomen, that recent automatic reflex of hers. And as though in response, a flutter rises unexpectedly to her touch. She lets out a laugh. "A flutter! Wow! What do you know?" The dogs lift their heads, glance up at her for a moment, an air of indolence about them. But once reassured there's nothing changing in their world, they shift their positions, and lie back down, their quivering noses to the floor.

Reassurance. Was that all Lisa was looking for? Could Hannah have ignored her? Or even Artie? But as if their names are the notes in a song which keeps on playing in her head, the two of them remain trapped inside her brain now. She needs a break from thinking about them. But how? They won't let her. For instance, she asks herself, why was Lisa itching to tell Hannah there was more to her life than she'd let on? Then hold back on it, as though she were telling her a detective story. Was it to keep Hannah curious and riveted?

Unable to concentrate further, she walks into the kitchen, fills a glass with water from the tap. Gulps it down. She's beginning to feel like a receptacle, not only for the fetus growing inside her, but for everyone else's predicaments. Is she just too gullible?

Her phone rings. Jake's on his way home. Another day gone. She opens the Styrofoam containers, doles out the leftovers onto plates. Sets the table.

Now back at her desk again, she stands and looks at her screen, reads the next stanzas of the poem she's desperately trying to make work. She groans, closes her eyes, puts her hands over her belly, expecting to feel her baby's flutter again. But, no, not right now.

The dogs scamper away,
chase each other,
crackling and scattering the red,
the brown, and the gold-colored leaves.

So peaceful, so perfect a picture until . . .
But . . . wait . . . is it really?
Relationships, she calls out
to the sun, the sky, the bare treetops.
How smoothly the word rolls
off her tongue: soft, sturdy, easy.

The dogs race back, nuzzle
their clammy noses to her thighs.
She laughs.
Off with you, she says,
your names aren't relationships.

And throwing out a stick,
she watches them run for it,
tumbling over each other as they go.
Relationships aren't always soft and sturdy,
and they're never easy.

Nope, she whispers to herself. Never easy.

Only now she can't tell what she needs to do with her poem. She moves around words, whole phrases. But she discovers her original meanings keep shifting with the changes. Back and forth the words go until she can't figure out, in the end, what it is she was meaning to say. She wonders if this happens to other would-be poets too. Or if it happens to real poets, as well. She concentrates her attention back on the screen.

Once in a while,
she thinks of herself—like a raggedy puppet
with strung-together limbs that flip-flop
up, down, and sideways.

And although the wooden face wears a painted smile,
tears of worry trickle over its wide chiseled cheeks.
But what if the strings were to fray and rip apart?

Would it tumble into nothingness?
Its life and loves forever lost.
Or would it hold on tight, like the one
lone leaf, as it clings to its bough and
dances to the sounds of the autumn wind?

Argh! she moans and closes her eyes for a moment. Cursing at herself some more, she hits save, turns off her computer and watches, as she always does, for her screen to go black before leaving it.

"Honey, I'm home," she hears Jake yell out his usual, exaggerated singsong greeting from the front hall.

"Perfect timing," she says, going to meet him. "I just turned off my computer."

"Anything new here?" He gives her a quick peck on the cheek.

"No, nothing at all. What about you? Were you able to reach Louis?"

"Yes. He'll call us back first thing tomorrow. You'll come in to work in the morning, okay?"

"Yes. But didn't he say anything about the contract when you spoke to him this afternoon?"

"A little. But can you give me a couple of minutes? I'm desperate to get out of these clothes and put on shorts. I'm boiling hot."

"Hurry up, though. I'm going crazy with all this."

"Short trip," he says, laughing.

"Ha! Ha!"

"Where's your sense of humor?"

"Gone AWOL at the moment."

"Ahh! Too bad," he says, stroking her cheek. "Okay, give me a couple of minutes to change, then I'll go over everything he told me, which, by the way, wasn't really all that much."

He heads up the stairs.

Once again, Hannah is at the kitchen table, looking out at the garden. The trees have grown lush this year. Due to the rainy spring, she imagines. And now they could do with a good pruning. Her roses need snipping too. Tomorrow morning after breakfast, she'll go out to tackle them. She'll also have to remember to remind Jake to call the tree guy. It always makes her nervous when the trees surrounding their house grow too tall and their branches spread low and hang over the roof. She worries they'll split from their trunks, break off, and crash into the house, especially with rainstorms in the fall and snow and ice in winter.

God! She is such a worrywart. But storms have always scared her. As a small child, she remembers, she used to hide under the nearest bed or table when thunderstorms raged. She can see herself, a chubby little four-year-old, bare-chested, with a mop of curly dark hair, blue eyes squinted into slits, and her mouth quivery and curved down to stop the tears. They were on the shore on Long Island one summer. Her parents had shared a rental house on the beach with another family. There was a storm. The adults were laughing. At her? Now, as she thinks back to it, she realizes they weren't laughing at her but laughing at the reason for her tears. Here she was, as Hannah imagines herself, this little girl who had the luxury of being afraid of a thunderstorm when, only a generation before, her family, still living as refugees in London, had to brave the bombs ripping through the neighborhoods of the city, killing, maiming, destroying. That was only after they'd been lucky enough to escape Hitler's Berlin, where they were forced to abandon all their possessions and everything they valued—except, incredibly and luckily, their lives.

"What's for dinner?" Jake says, jarring her out of her daydream as he comes into the kitchen. She turns from the window to find him standing behind her, barefoot and looking more comfortable, though not well-matched, in his black-and-white plaid shorts and navy-blue tee.

"Leftovers from last night's Indian dinner, remember?"

"Right," he says, his voice trailing off in distraction as he combs through the short stack of mail on the kitchen counter. "No mail from the kids today?"

"Not a word, thank goodness. I feel like I've had enough on my plate for one day."

Pushing the mail aside, he puts one hand on her shoulder, the other behind her waist, brings her body in closer to his and whispers in her ear, "Hey, I found something special just for you at the liquor store today. Don't move, I'll be back in a jiff."

"I'm not going anywhere. I'll be right here waiting for you. As always."

She watches him move away from her. At the door, he spins around and smiles with that expression of his, like a naughty little schoolchild harboring a nasty little schoolchild secret. She laughs.

"Stella Rosa Peach non-alcoholic fruit wine," he says, unveiling the bottle from its paper bag as he comes back to the kitchen. He places it on the counter. "What do you think?"

"Looks great."

"Corkscrew?"

Hannah reaches back, grabs it out of the drawer behind her, and puts it down in front of him. She leans sideways against the counter, watching while he uncorks the bottle.

"Wineglasses?"

"Coming right up."

On her tippy toes, she reaches to take them out of the cabinet. After he fills the glasses, he hands her one.

"Let's go sit on the deck for a bit. It's beautiful out there now. Not too hot anymore," he says.

She follows him out through the sliding glass door and onto the deck. Zig and Zag come running, too.

"Okay, now tell me about Louis. I'm dying to hear what he had to say."

She brushes off a couple of dried, stray leaves from the large blue and green striped pillow, then settles into the Adirondack chair.

"Mainly that Artie has no case against us," he says, moving his matching pillow to the floor before sitting down in the wooden chair. "We'll get a copy of the email he's sending to Artie's lawyer later this evening."

"What a relief," she says, closing her eyes to the glare of the setting sun.

"Don't forget, the mediator will need to agree with our lawyer before the whole thing's put to rest."

"I know. When are we meeting with him?"

"When do the kids start school?"

"How many times do I have to tell you? The Wednesday before Labor Day. I think it's August 30th."

"I'll let Louis know. I think it's best for us to meet after Labor Day, after the kids are settled back at home and in school. It will also give you the time to get this complete story ready for him. What do you think?"

"Yes, fine. Whatever it takes."

"Good," he says. "Anyway, how're you doing with it so far?"

"Okay, I guess. Reliving this is . . . how shall I say it?"

"Painful and annoying at the same time?"

"You can say that again," she says and laughs. "But I have a confession to make."

"A confession? About what?"

"I took a bit of time off this afternoon to work on a poem. My head desperately needed a break from them both." She looks over at him and smiles.

"I can't say I blame you. Just don't forget how important it is to get all this down."

"Don't worry, I'll get it finished in time. I promise you," she says.

Chapter Twenty

Louis, their attorney, had sent out a Letter of Intent to Artie and his lawyer on Friday morning. Now it was the following Tuesday and still there was no word from either of them. But thankfully, Hannah thought, not a word from OSHA either.

Artie began trucking down his inventory to our factory at our expense. We had to lease an additional 2200 square feet. Again, at our expense, we hired day laborers to help unload the trucks and put the inventory away. For the business and Artie's employment contracts, we retained the services of both a corporate and an employment attorney, respectively. We also met with an accountant to project the companies' combined income. In the first year alone, we estimated sales could easily surpass three million dollars. Though with all these expenses now, Jake and I couldn't pay ourselves our salaries for the balance of the year.

Hannah and Jake were working like demons to get their Bloom & Co. orders out, as well as working with Artie's people up in Rhode Island to make sure they had everything they needed to produce whatever older orders were still workable, plus any new ones coming in. They were on the phone with his two employees all day long. Hannah couldn't keep from wondering how Artie could have run his business this way. Obviously, these employees were inexperienced. And it felt as if Artie had already transferred his business over to

Hannah and Jake, or more to the point, dropped it like a lost child into their laps.

After Hannah had gone through the schedule of what needed to ship for the day, she came back to her desk. Jake was sitting at his, one hand pressing the phone up against his ear, while the other massaged his temple – a sure sign that something else was up. She turned on her computer and watched the world's most glorious scenery show up on her screen, as if it had decided on its own that she needed a reminder of nature's unsurpassable beauty at the start of each morning. Grabbing the empty water bottle off her desk, she got up and headed for the factory, calling out *Buenos Dias* to each employee she passed.

She loved walking through here. This was the pounding heart of their business. If things ran smoothly in this area, it seemed like all the rest of it fell into place . . . more or less. Those words – more or less – were always at the tip of her tongue. She smiled at herself. Even with the challenges, she loved running the factory – making sure they had the right stock in inventory, scheduling print runs, checking each machine to ensure perfect printing on pens, water bottles, or notebooks, and that the completed orders were then properly packed up for shipping. The other – paying bills, collecting money, eyeing the profit-and-loss statements – filled her with a kind of helpless angst. Here in the factory, though, the only goals were to ensure brilliant printing of each job and on-time shipment. Most days, it went smoothly. Everyone knew their role. Naturally, there were always complications to overcome, like the best way to print a complex or multi-colored piece of artwork. Or certain problems to watch out for, like misread directions on orders, PMS colors overlooked, miscounted product, the last-minute search for inventory they thought was in house but was nowhere to be found, and then missed drop-dead, in-hand dates. Fortunately, these problems were rare.

She filled her bottle from the water dispenser and after a catch-up with Natalia, their factory manager, and a quick walk around checking which orders were on schedule for the day, she circled back to the office.

Jake was off the phone.

—What's going on? She perched herself on the edge of her desk, facing him.

—You don't want to know.

—Try me, she said.

He stood, stretched his arms over his head, and came and parked himself directly in front of her.

—Those people up in Rhode Island have no goddamn idea what they're doing. I just got two calls from distributors, each with a screwed-up order and missed deadline dates. The first, a logo printed in the wrong color and the other, the wrong color item. What the fuck?

He was pacing now, his hands in his pockets, his head down. All his eagerness, his confidence, from the night before evaporated into the air, now heavy with the noises of machinery, high-pitched voices, and the smell of inks seeping into their office through the gaps in the closed door to the factory.

He stopped pacing, turned to face her, and said, —We're going to have to figure out how we can produce all his orders here at our place.

—Along with our own? Oh my God, she said.

—Not only that, but Artie called a few minutes ago to say a truckload of his inventory is on its way down here. God knows what the hell he thinks we're going to do with it all.

After a couple of weeks, though, it became obvious this remote way of conducting business would not work for us. His unsupervised employees were neither printing to our standards nor getting the orders out on time, which further caused problems with customers. We told Artie we needed to bring all the production down to our facility in Stamford. He didn't object. In fact, he didn't even seem to care. It was as though he'd be just as happy to drop the entire business into our lap. His excuse was always that he had other problems to take care of. Our own factory people worked overtime for the best part of the summer to get his orders out. Inventory remained a big problem. And although Artie continued coming to our place for a few hours once a week, it was not nearly helpful enough.

Cool, calm Jake was showing signs of derailment. Hannah, still leaning against her desk, felt her insides freeze.

—Where are we going to put it all?

—Good question. I have a call into the landlord's office to see about leasing more space.

—Oh, my God, she said.

All she could see were their dollar bills floating away, weightless, like dried leaves in a flurry.

—Could you *please* just stop saying that?

Hannah sat down at her desk and stared at the beach scene on her computer screen – the clear, blue, rippling water, pale sand, and palm trees with a hammock strung up between them, all beckoning.

—And we've heard nothing about the Letter of Intent yet? she said, forcing her eyes to focus away from her screen.

—Only what we've already heard – apparently our verbiage was too harsh.

—Too harsh? What's that supposed to mean?

—Your guess is as good as mine, he said.

—Otherwise not a word about the contract itself?

—You got it. And by the way . . .

—What? Hannah said, feeling all her muscles tighten.

—We're on the hook for the trucking.

—But why?

—It's simple. He's out of money, remember? Plus, he needs to get all his stuff out of his factory by the end of the month. Besides, we're going to need a good deal of his inventory, anyway. We're relying on it.

—Yes . . . yes, I know, Hannah said, trying to figure out where he was going with this.

—You see, it's not quite as bad as you think.

He was convincing himself, she decided, as well as her.

Jake's phone rang. Hannah went to the bathroom. When she came back, Jake told her the landlord had space for them in the basement. One problem tackled; one problem solved. Next, they needed to hire day laborers to unload the truck when it arrived and help put all the inventory away.

—I'm off to Home Depot to buy shelving, Jake said, grabbing his keys off his desk.

—When's the shipment due to be here? she asked.

—Tomorrow. Though the trucking company said they could hold the shipment for two days if we needed them to. But you should know that if we postpone the delivery, there will be an added charge for storing it.

—Of course, I know, she said. Though, of course, she really hadn't thought it through.

—So, he said, the faster we can get our act together, the better. I'll be back as soon as I can.

Hannah sank down in her chair again, moved the day's bundle of mail in front of her, and began separating it. She didn't know how they were to pay for all these extra, unexpected expenses. She hoped they'd been correct in their assumption that by incorporating Artie's sales into their company, the combination of the two would mean a growth of fifty percent, which should translate to an increase in their gross profit as well. Jake was right about one thing; they were getting more orders. But to produce them all in their own place, they needed more printers and packers in the factory, inventory pickers in the warehouse, and extra staff in the office. And once Artie came to work full time, there would be his salary to pay for as well. Paying bills would become so much more of a painful juggling act. How would they manage?

They would, a new little voice piped up inside her head.

•　　•　　•

But now, unable to concentrate, even to sit at her desk any longer, here in her little room – room of her own – she stands, picks up the two five-pound weights she keeps on the floor by the window, and lifts them up over her head. As she counts eight pumps, she wonders if the mail carrier has come yet. A walk down the driveway to the mailbox would do her good, she decides; a little dose of fresh air, a short bit of exercise, and she'll be as prepared as possible for another Ella letter.

The mailbox door is closed. She grabs the lever, pulls the door down, and reaches inside for the mail, all the time reminding herself there's only one more week to go. This time, there's just one letter, and it's from Miri. Hannah opens it right away.

The whole letter is written with a green crayon. She has drawn a picture of a 7-Up can, along with the words: *What do you think I would do for a 7-Up? Is getting dehydrated enough?!* Then she tells them about the raffles she has won and that her bunk is sailing over to the village at Raquette Lake for lunch! *How exciting! I'll make you a deal, I'll tell you all about it in 7 more days!!!! Love, Miri p.s. give Z&Z my love.*

Hannah laughs out loud as she makes her way back up to the house. She loves Miri's sense of humor. She has such a great way of making Hannah laugh. Going through the rest of the mail, she's both surprised and relieved she hasn't heard from Ella today.

In the kitchen, she makes herself an espresso and goes back into her little room. It takes her some time to pull her thoughts away from her children and bring them back to work.

If she were there now, she'd be checking in on the factory. It's usual for her to go back there in the late afternoons before leaving for the day, to see if they can use her help. On the factory floor, each job has a defined beginning and end. Once the cartons are stacked neatly onto skids and brought to the dock, where they're picked up by UPS or FedEx, the workday is over. Unlike her perpetual brooding over who needs to get paid, who owes them money, how she will meet payroll. Besides, she feels appreciated even though she isn't as speedy and deft at the packing-up as those she helps. Then there are times when it's a fight against the clock to get the orders out on schedule, and all the employees, including the office staff, pitch in. Hannah thrives on those days – the sudden burst of energy, the panicky directions shouted back-and-forth to one another.

Jake has never particularly cared about working in the factory. He says he has other things to do that are better and more profitable uses of his time. That was once true. But now he has no choice but to help the guys every morning in the shipping area with the incoming shipments and again in the afternoon with the outgoing orders.

•   •   •

—Hannah, you have a call on line one, she'd heard announced over the PA. Standing at her desk, she picked up the phone. It was Lisa.

—I can't talk right now, Hannah said. —Can I call you back when I get home in about an hour or so?

—We can talk later, but I was thinking it'd be great if we could get together for dinner. Maybe help straighten out a couple of things that seem to get stuck between the guys. How about Saturday night? We'd love for you to come out to us on Long Island.

—Great. Hannah's words fired out as she heard Jake's voice in the factory. He was back from Home Depot. —But I really need to run right now. Let me call you when I get home. Okay?

—Sure thing, Lisa said and hung up before Hannah said goodbye.

Still standing, she leaned over her desk to check her email. Nothing.

—Who was on the phone? Jake said as he came into their office.

—Lisa.

—What's she calling you for?

—I'll tell you later. You all set with the shelving?

—Yup, they will arrive first thing tomorrow. And Lisa?

—Only about getting together for dinner on Saturday night. But let me go. We can talk later. There are still loads to pack up. We're most definitely going to need more people.

—I know, he said, That's your next project.

—Ha! Ha! What fun, she said, opening the door to the factory, where the hustle and bustle of it drew her back in.

•   •   •

—Tell me, what's the scoop with Lisa and Artie now? Jake said, coming back into the office from turning off all the lights in the factory and locking the doors. Normally Hannah wasn't here this late, but since both kids had playdates this afternoon, she stayed. With all the employees gone for the day, the place was so calm and silent it felt as if the factory's energy had followed them out the door as well.

—She called to ask about getting together for dinner with them on Saturday night, Hannah said in as off-hand a way as possible.

—How'd that come about? he asked, groaning as he came to sit on the spare chair by her desk.

—Don't know.

—So, she just called to make a date?

—Yes. They'd like us to go out there. To Long Island, I mean. Are you okay with it?

—Doesn't sound like I have a choice, do I?

—You always have a choice, Hannah said. —In any case, I told her I'd get back to her about it. If you don't want to go, we don't have to.

—Well, on the positive side and with a little luck, maybe we'll get to talk about a contract? he said.

—Yes, she said she's hoping for that too.

—And our future together?

—Yes, Jake. That's what Lisa said as well.

—But my guess is we'll only be hearing more of his boring sob stories. He sighed and slumped down in his chair, sliding his feet along the floor and straightening out his legs.

—Oh, for God's sake, stop. What's got into you? You're the one who's always gung-ho and positive about all of this. I think my case of the worrywarts must be wearing off on you.

—You're too funny. No, it's not you. It's him. I can't take him anymore. His demands, his tears, his . . .

—I know, I know. I agree, but at the same time, you have to give the guy a bit of a break. Even if he did bring it all on himself, he's in a yukky place right now.

—Do you know why they want us to get together out there?

—She wants to show me her jewelry.

—Her jewelry?

—Yes. Remember? She designs her own stuff.

—Ah! Got it!

—Are you okay with this now?

—I guess.

—I'm worried I'll be in an awkward spot with her glitter once again, Hannah said.

—What do you mean?

—Will she expect me to buy another piece of her jewelry?

—Probably.

—Supposing I don't like any of it. Or, if what I do like is too expensive.

—Honestly, it'd be the least of our problems right now, he said and stood up.

—Tell me what you're thinking. What's brewing inside that head of yours, Jake? I can feel it.

—Nothing particularly helpful right now. I'm trying very hard not to be pissed at him or his goddamn lawyer. Anyway, are you ready to get the hell out of here?

As he stood up in front of his desk, Hannah heard his fingers on the keyboard and the beep of his computer shutting down.

—I am, she said, turning off her computer, too. —You'll be happy to know a bunch of his orders got shipped out today. Plus, we've invoiced them all. I think the cash flow should be pretty good next month.

—Well, that is good news. With a little luck, we'll get a contract signed before we see them on Saturday.

—Yes, that'd certainly be fantastic, she said, her fingers crossing over each other in hopefulness.

Chapter Twenty-One

Hannah looks up. Jake is standing close to her chair; his arms folded over his chest. She is about to say something to him. Or is there something she wants to ask him? She can't tell. Her mind has suddenly gone as blank as . . . what is it? She can't remember. But wait, there it is. There's the feeling. That familiar fluttering inside her. The watery sensation that knows the precise moment to hijack every part of her, whether it's her mind or her heart. She smiles. "Quick. Come over here," she says to Jake as she presses her right hand flat to her stomach, while pulling him in toward her with her left. "Your newest daughter is weighing in on this as well." And she leans back in her chair, grabs hold of his wrist, opens his hand wide, spreads his fingers and lays them over her belly until, like magic, a broad grin lightens his whole face; and Hannah knows he's felt her too.

Finally, they're on their way. Her girls are coming home from sleep-away camp today. Biting down on her lower lip, her hands find their way to her abdomen once again, spreading them wide to quell the butterflies inside. She keeps glancing over at the clock on the car's dashboard and back to the phone on her lap while also praying for light traffic and no snarls. She and Jake had originally planned to leave their office at around one o'clock, stop in Greenwich for a leisurely lunch – they figured it would be their last one alone for a while – and get to the Cross County Center by three, which is when the camp buses are due to arrive. But predictably, as Hannah can't stop thinking now – with the left-over half of her roast beef sandwich packed inside the paper bag leaning up against her seat on the car's floor and the scenery along the periphery of the Merritt Parkway, speeding past them – Jake wasn't ready to leave when they'd originally agreed to. It was "just one more minute" to begin with. And before she knew it, over sixty of them had gone by.

Jake turns up the volume on the radio. Bob Dylan is singing. The loudness is to mask the quiet in here, Hannah thinks, as she hums along with "Blowin' in the Wind." She's trying to get over feeling mad at Jake for being late. She only hopes they'll make it to Cross County Center before her kids do. She glances over at him. He's concentrating on the road. She looks away; hums, daydreams and keeps her eyes fixed on the passing scenery. And like the sunlight strobing through the car window, insistent memories of that last Saturday night with Artie and Lisa, at their favorite steak place in Queens, keep bursting in and out of her sight, both equally jarring as they are annoying.

•   •   •

Finished with eating and their plates cleared, they decided to share a slice of cheesecake to split four ways. Jake and Artie ordered coffee – espresso for Jake, *café Americano* for Artie. After dessert, Hannah and Lisa left the guys at the table.

In the ladies' room, they stood side by side, each staring straight ahead at the large mirror on the wall above the sinks. Every now and then, they would steal a glance at the other's reflection.

—To set the record straight, Lisa began, her words measured, her voice soft, and although she was speaking directly to Hannah's reflection, something about her seemed far away.

While Hannah waited for Lisa to continue, she found herself struck again by the irregularities in people's facial features – such as one eye being smaller than the other or one eyebrow higher – that she'd only notice when reflected in a mirror.

Still staring straight ahead, Lisa started talking again. —Mark, my cousin, never stole a penny of Artie's money. It was all his, to begin with.

Her eyes dropped from Hannah's reflection to her new large bag, her hand scrounging around inside it.

—He only *lent* it to Artie, she said, pulling out her lipstick. She opened her mouth into an O-shape, painted her lips a bright red, then rubbed them together.

—But Artie was spending way too much, she added, as she plumped up her highlighted hair.

She threw the lipstick back into her bag, stepped back from the mirror, gave herself the once-over, then turned away from the mirror and faced Hannah directly.

·　　·　　·

Thoughts of Lisa suddenly slam shut as she remembers and frets about the time. She leans over toward Jake, checks the clock on the car's dashboard once again, then turns back to the scenery outside her window.

"We're fine for time," Jake says as the Bob Dylan song ends. "Please stop worrying," he adds.

But Hannah can't stop feeling anxious, anyway. What will the kids think if they arrive and don't see their parents? Visions of her two children – like poor orphans, stepping off the bus, their eyes searching for their mother and father amongst all those unfamiliar faces in the waiting crowd of parents – frighten her. She imagines their rising panic, their tears, then their full-blown hysteria. Now she feels her own eyes glazing over. And Jake is driving like a madman. "For God's sake," she says to him. "Slow down. Better to be late than never at all." Ten to three, and thank goodness, here is their exit off the highway. Now it's solely a matter of making all the lights. She holds her breath as he speeds up into the first intersection, the yellow turning red just as they make it through. They've arrived at Cross County Center. And beat the buses. She can breathe again.

Jake drops her off in the circle where the buses are to stop and goes to park the car in the lot across the street. She paces up and down the curved sidewalk, Lisa's words still stubbornly ringing in her ears.

•   •   •

—My cousin, Mark, kept telling him to ease up, but Artie wouldn't listen. He copped an attitude. It was his company, he'd said, and he could do whatever he wanted with it.

Lisa was dabbing a tissue at the corner of her eyes, trying to stop the tears that would cause her eye makeup to run. Hannah remembers how she'd felt an urge to take Lisa into her arms. Give her a hug. But something had stopped her.

—And Mark took whatever cash was in the business, leaving us fucked and stone-cold broke, she said.

•   •   •

Nervous shivers ripple up and down Hannah's bare arms. She takes a deep breath. Why can't she dispel Artie and Lisa from her mind for now and instead picture her two girls, so impatient to be home? Feeling the tightness in her body slowly unwind, she smiles as she surveys the other parents, also pacing the sidewalk. She feels a slight chill, as the sun peeks in and out of a sky filled with racing, gray clouds. But in no time, two sets of young arms will hold her tight, warming her, loving her. Any minute now, she will hear her children's voices, their laughter. And suddenly she can't stand the wait any longer. It feels like they've been gone from her for months, not weeks. Where are the buses? It's past three. Where's Jake?

And then she sees him, snaking around the oncoming cars as he makes his way across the middle of the wide road. It always seems to renew her spirit to watch him from afar. The distinctive walk, the bushy head of thick, brown hair, the baggy jeans, the sandals on his feet. He's a throwback, for sure. She smiles. She does love him. He smiles back. He is so much all hers. Does he look at her in the same way? She sees herself as a vestige, too, of an earlier generation, with her long, curly, frizzy hair, and the ankle-length cotton skirts she wears in the heat of summer. Jake runs the last few steps to avoid a car, and no sooner has he hopped onto the sidewalk than the three camp buses come into view. Noisy excitement rolls through the crowd of parents, almost sounding to Hannah like waves crashing onto a beach. And, in mass, these grownups move toward the curb, pushing, or ignoring those who are in their way. It's as if they feel it their due, their entitlement, to be there, at the front of the line, to show their kids how much more they care for them than those other parents who stand further back. Luckily, Hannah and Jake are at the curb.

The buses pull in. Camp counselors perch next to the drivers at the front of the buses. The kids, directed to get up, strap their backpacks onto their shoulders and look out of the windows for their parents. When they get the all-clear, they come flying off the bus and onto the sidewalk. Some move dreamily through the noisy crowd, seeming to be in no rush to find their mother or father. Still others huddle in groups with their peers, where they tearfully hug each other, over and over, their parents standing by, helpless to do anything other than watch from the perimeter. "See you next summer," are the words Hannah hears all around her.

So absorbed is she by this unfolding scene, she doesn't notice until Jake prods her arm that their own children have gotten off the bus and are making their way to where she and Jake are waiting. Here they are. Tanned and healthy-looking; their hair in tight braids all over their heads. Hannah imagines they'd spent their last night at camp, telling each other stories, while braiding their hair. She's amazed how, in the eight weeks, they've grown up. Look at Miri. She nudges Jake. Her dark eyes seem to take over her face, thinner now, and even more beautiful. And Ella's, like a perfect doll's, still round as ever, though her body has become leaner.

Miri and Ella kiss and hug Hannah and Jake, then run off to a group of kids.

"Wow!" Hannah's stunned, but she smiles anyway as she tries to push away her slight sense of disappointment, like the cloud above her, which blocks the warmth and light of the sun on her skin. "I can't believe it. Ella seems sad to be leaving her camp friends."

"That's good, isn't it?" Jake says, taking out his cellphone to check his email.

"Sure," she says, and sighs as those words, *they are only lent to you,* come rushing back to her.

Hannah watches her two daughters interact with the other campers. More kids come to join their group. In the center there are two counselors. All the girls are talking at the same time. Then they hold hands and sing the camp song. And raise their arms high above their heads and cheer. And afterward, kisses and hugs all around. Even Ella – who complained non-stop and wrote every day to say how she hated camp and all the kids in it – is hugging and kissing everyone around her. *Everyone.*

Chapter Twenty-Two

"I have something very important to tell you both when we get home," Hannah says, twisting her body around to face her two girls in the backseat. Ella is already fast asleep, her head bent to her chest, her body curled and resting against the car door. Miri is busy braiding multi-colored threads of cotton.

She looks up at Hannah. "What is it?" she says.

"It's a secret. I can't tell you now. Ella needs to be awake to hear it as well."

Miri makes an annoyed *tsk* sound in response and goes back to her braiding.

"You'll hear all about it when we get home, after you've both settled in. Okay?"

And when there's no response, Hannah turns to face the front. Jake is unusually quiet. She looks over at him. His eyes stay glued to the road ahead. She wonders what he's thinking. But now's not the time to ask, she decides. Instead, she turns around with a question to ask Miri about camp. But Miri has also fallen asleep. "Welcome home," Hannah says to herself and looks out of the window at the cars weaving in and out of the slow traffic on the road in front of them.

Thankfully, they don't need to stop at the mailbox at the bottom of their driveway. There will be no more of those, *I-hate-camp-I-want-to-come-home*, letters lying in wait for them – those dreaded heart crushers, which always seemed snuck in between the bills and supermarket circulars. What a relief. Tomorrow she'll come back down for the bills.

Zig and Zag greet them at the door. Greet? No. That's an understatement for sure. Hannah doesn't know who's more excited to see whom – the dogs to see the kids or the kids, the dogs. Jumps and licks and tail-wagging follow Miri and Ella as they race up to their bedrooms. Then come the shrieks of happiness at the sight of their own beds in their own rooms, which look exactly as they were, the day they'd left for camp, except for the new teddy bear sitting on each of their pillows that Hannah bought for them. Suddenly, she feels as if these last summer weeks have evaporated, or rather, the days have diminished in her memory—shrunk as if all the air has been squeezed from them.

Jake and Hannah sit across from each other in the family room, waiting for the girls to come back down. She's bursting to tell them her news.

"Feels great to have them home again, doesn't it?" Jake smiles and leans forward in his chair to pick up the newspaper.

"Yes, and now they're here, it's almost as though they were never gone." She smiles, too, and sighs.

"Hmm. I guess so," he says, only half-listening as he scans the day's headlines. But then he looks up at her. "Tell me, I've forgotten, when does school start?"

"The week before Labor Day. Why do you keep asking me?"

"Only trying to gauge when you'll be back to your regular schedule at the office."

"Oh!" And before she can get more of her thoughts on the subject straightened out in her mind, the girls and the dogs come rushing down the stairs in a blustery heap of energy. "Careful," she yells out, always terrified one of them might trip, be pushed accidentally, or miss a step and come tumbling down – her unkind imagination landing them headfirst at the bottom of the stairs.

"Okay mom, what do you want to tell us?" Miri says, snuggling up to Hannah.

Ella is on Jake's lap, leaning her back against his chest. "Yeah," she says, sitting up. "What's the big surprise?"

"Well . . ." Hannah begins. "The big surprise is . . ." She looks over at Jake, not quite sure why she does.

"What your mommy is trying to tell you," he says, folding up the newspaper and putting it back on the coffee table, "is that in a few months you're both going to be the big sisters to a new . . ." He stops talking as if to measure the impact of his words. Since neither gives any sign they understand, he adds, "What I mean to say is, your Mommy's going to have a new baby."

Still, neither girl says a word. Instead, all four eyes, as if on cue, fix their focus onto her belly, and Hannah, feeling as if she needs protection from their penetrating scrutiny, drops her hands, spreading her fingers wide to her middle.

"Wow," Ella says, coming to Hannah. "Can I touch?"

"Sure, but there's nothing to feel at the moment."

"When will we have the baby? Is it going to be a boy or a girl? Where will it sleep? Can it sleep with me?"

"The baby is due to be born at the beginning of February. We'll know if it's a boy or a girl soon. Maybe by the time you go back to school."

"Ugh! School. Don't remind me," Ella says, her face screwed up into a pout.

"Yeah," Miri chimes in. "We're still on vacation. But you never said where the baby will sleep."

"In our room, in a crib next to my bed," Hannah says. "A baby wakes up to be fed at least twice a night . . ."

"Oh," they both say in unison, disappointment in their voices.

"What about names?" Miri is in front of Hannah, staring at her as if she can coach the essence of her unborn sibling to the surface.

"Don't you think we should know if you're going to have a brother or a sister before we choose names?"

"I want a brother," Ella says, her eyes suddenly widening into a mischievous smile. "Then I can see what his pee-pee looks like," she adds, exploding into laughter.

"Ella," Miri shouts in mock horror, but before she can go on, she begins to giggle herself and just as loudly.

"Okay, guys, who's hungry for dinner?" Jake is out of his seat and is obviously impatient and eager to change the subject.

"Me," comes the chorus.

After their promised, welcome-home sushi dinner at Kotobuki, their favorite Japanese restaurant, and their super long showers, punctuated with more happy *oohs* and *aahs*, and their even longer hugs and kisses with Hannah and Jake, Miri and Ella settle into their beds.

Oh, yes, Hannah thinks, as she walks through their rooms, bending to pick up the shorts, tee-shirts, underwear, and socks they've dropped to the floor as they stripped for their showers, her life is coming back to normal. Back to her routine as mother, she says to herself, as she throws their laundry into the hamper; a routine superimposed on her days which reminds her, in a weird sort of way, of those topographical maps of the earth where, each stratum printed on a transparent overlay and stacked one on top of the other, eventually shows her the world map as she might recognize it. Exactly like her days? she asks herself. Yes, she decides. They are the tiers in the topography of her time. And which one of the tiers will she be able to claim for herself alone? She'll figure it out, she tells herself. In one way or another, she always does.

For this very moment, though – as she and Jake close the doors to their children's bedrooms, smiling at each other and glad to have the anxiety of receiving unhappy, tearful letters behind them – she focuses on Zig and Zag, and listens for their tails thumping the carpeted floor, as they lie down on the landing between the children's two rooms; a sure sign they are obviously as delighted, as she and Jake are, to have their charges back again to love and to safeguard.

But as Hannah follows Jake down the stairs, a sudden involuntary shudder charges through her body as the word stone-cold breaks the surface, thaws, and spreads inside all the cracks of her mind.

In the kitchen she stands by the counter, slouching forward, head in her hands, curly hair tied up in an untidy knot at her crown, and one chilled, bare foot resting on top of the other. She watches Jake pour them each a glass of sparkling water, although she surely could do with something stronger; too bad she'd have to wait another five months for that.

"I'm exhausted," Hannah says, stifling a yawn. "There seemed to be no end to this day."

"Hectic, to be sure. It does feel good, though, to have the kids home, to have our family all together again." Jake puts the bottle back in the fridge. "Let's go," he says and, putting his arm around her, guides her to the family room.

"Don't ask why, but it feels good to sit . . . like I haven't been sitting all day." Hannah takes a drink and leans back in her chair, folding up her legs beneath her. "And to have the girls back home. I really missed them so much."

"Me too. And how they've grown," Jake says, his eyes on the TV as he taps the buttons of the remote to flick through the channels in search of an easy show to watch.

Hannah's oblivious to the flitting images on the screen. Instead, her mind replays the moment she first saw her two daughters coming toward them this afternoon in their camp tee-shirts and shorts, Ella's naturally blonde-streaked hair and Miri's darker curls done up into tight braids and their over-filled backpacks hanging low off their shoulders. They looked so surprisingly happy.

"Have you noticed the change in Miri?" Hannah suddenly feels compelled to continue the conversation, to keep Jake talking to her. She doesn't want to lose the moment.

"Impossible to miss," he says. "She's become quite the beautiful young lady."

"Ella has matured, too, don't you think? Gotten a little taller, thinned out a bit." She remembers how surprised she was to see her younger daughter run from her and Jake to join the group of girls singing camp songs – as if she belonged to them, not to her parents, and all those letters sent home were a sham, a joke. Or, as Hannah thinks, her mind, traveling down this bizarre, unreal trajectory, perhaps even written by someone else's child, not theirs.

"Though I sure hope she never loses that beautiful round freckled face of hers," Jake says. He empties the water in his glass and gets up. From the kitchen, she hears him open the fridge, bubbly water pouring into a glass, and the fridge door closing. Zig and Zag pad down the stairs, saunter into the den, and lie down in a sigh of effort beside Hannah's chair.

"So cute," she says to the empty room. The feel of her younger daughter's plump arms tight around her, and her voice, a whisper in her ear is like a mantra, a promise, a reminder that she'll never, ever leave her mother again; the sensation, as strong as if she were still enveloped by her youngest. She closes her eyes for a moment. "She *is* looking great," she says, opening them and looking up at Jake, who is now standing in front of her, pouring more Pellegrino into her glass. "They both do. And despite their letters home, camp seems to have thoroughly agreed with them." She nods her head as if to reaffirm, if only for herself, that she agrees with what she's just said.

"I'm totally with you," he says, sitting back down. "Camp experience certainly seems to have done them the world of good."

Hannah looks over at him. His tone of voice doesn't match his words. Looking away from her, he fiddles with the remote, switching in and out of channels. Nothing is holding his interest for the moment.

"What's going on with you?" she says, leaning forward to pet her lovely, shaggy mutts.

"Nothing really. Why?"

"Hardly a word all the way home. Something's on your mind, I can tell."

"I had a long conversation this morning with Louis," he says, putting the TV on mute.

"I knew it," Hannah says, the words coming out louder than she'd intended and, leaning back in her chair, she crosses her arms over her chest and adds, "Why didn't you say?"

"I didn't want to get into all of it then. I wanted to enjoy the kids' homecoming."

"All of what?" Hannah says, impatient as she watches him take a long drink from his glass of Pellegrino.

"The legal claims that Artie thinks he has against you, me, and our company." He leans forward to put his empty glass back down on the table – the motion, Hannah thinks, purposefully slow. Then he adds, "Louis thinks Artie has no case. He says he's ready to refute every last, goddam shit-hold, Artie has against us." He sighs and smiles.

"Are you serious?"

"Yes."

"But that's all-good news, isn't it?"

"Except the mediator must be in total agreement with us, and this is where you come in."

"I know, I know. But now with the kids home . . ."

"That's why I decided we should meet with Louis once the kids are back in school."

"Which, you think will give me enough time to get the whole thing organized and written."

"I'm sure you'll do it," he says and picks up the TV remote, turns up the volume, and begins surfing through the channels again.

"Stone-cold . . ." Hannah says and looks over at Jake, who's now immersed in the day's broadcast news. Not exactly mind-numbing, she thinks.

"What did you say?" he says, turning toward her.

"Stone-cold broke. It's what Lisa had said."

"When? When did she say that?"

"The night we met for dinner at the steak restaurant out on Long Island. Remember? It was when she and I went to the ladies' room."

"What else did she have to say?"

"You really want to know?" Hannah can hear regret and fatigue seeping in through her words.

"Why wouldn't I?" he says.

"Oh, I don't know. Forget it. I don't even know why I told you what she said."

"You're confusing me. You know that don't you?"

"I don't mean to. I guess I'm simply confused myself. What she said was that her cousin didn't steal the money. It was his to begin with. He'd lent it to Artie. And when Artie was spending the money irrationally – like a drunken sailor, was how she put it – her cousin took back what he could and had all Artie's credit cards stopped, and his bank accounts put on hold."

"But we knew all this," Jake says. "Remember when we went up to Rhode Island with them and he had no money to pay for the gas? And then he cried to us and his supplier about his financial situation – or rather lack of it."

"Except those words, and especially the way they came out of her mouth, shocked me."

She looks away from him and stares out at the night through the darkened window. Leaves rustle on the beech tree by the house, its branches swaying together as if in a dance. The wind has picked up. She sips her sparkling water and wonders once again how to quell these recurring, unnamable feelings still doing somersaults inside her belly, most especially when those three little words – stone-cold broke – perch themselves in the forefront of her mind, worrying and terrifying, like nasty itches needing a constant scratching.

•   •   •

—And if you're talking about my having to let go of my jewelry store, Lisa said to her, as they stood side by side, staring, expressionless, at her own reflection in the mirror. —It was my decision, way before all this stupid shit hit the fan.

Hannah was so puzzled she had turned from the mirror to face Lisa's profile. —But why? she said, and when there was no visible reaction, she squared herself back in front of the mirror again and added, —I thought you were doing so well with it.

Lisa's clearly nonchalant attitude had stunned Hannah. Although, under normal circumstances, it might have been her first impulse to console Lisa to wrap her arms around her in a hug, Hannah had stood frozen instead, facing Lisa in the mirror; her hands, coiled into tight fists, planted at her sides.

—But why? she asked again and once more turned away from looking at Lisa through the mirror to studying her face, instead, which stubbornly remained in profile.

—I don't know. I guess I didn't want to stand behind a counter all day and be a shopgirl. Lisa's face was down, her hair falling over it, as she dug around in her large, new Louis Vuitton bag. She pulled out a comb.

—A shop girl? Hannah repeated, stunned and louder than she intended. —How could you think of yourself like that? You're a jewelry designer, for God's sake.

Lisa combed her hair, leaned forward, freshened her lips again with her bright red gloss.

—Well, anyway, now you know the entire story. But please, don't mention any of this to Artie. He'll kill me if he finds out.

—Of course not, was all Hannah could find to say.

There was something about Lisa, something forbidding in her demeanor that demanded restraint. She was still looking at herself in the mirror.

Once satisfied with her own image, she turned from the mirror to face Hannah. —What about you? she'd said, in a cool, matter-of-fact way. —How're your girls doing?

And suddenly, Hannah had this odd feeling, as if she'd been holding her breath the entire time they were in the ladies' room, because now, as the conversation came back to more familiar ground, she was conscious of breathing in and breathing out in her normal way and smiling at the thought of her own girls.

—They're fine. What about Ethan? How's he liking college?

—I think he's simply happy to be out of the house, and to be honest, I can't say I blame him. Lisa looked at Hannah, as if searching her face for a reaction. —But, in any case, he's doing well, thank you.

—Great, Hannah remembers saying, though her thoughts had already become too fixed on Lisa's words – stone-cold – to believe in her own affirmative ones. Because now she was understanding how those words – stone-cold – applied not only to the financial situation Lisa and Artie had found themselves in.

·   ·   ·

Jake gets up. Heads into the kitchen again and comes back with the bottle of sparkling water. "Want a fill-up?" he says, holding up the dark green bottle.

"Sure," she says and downs whatever is in her glass first. "So, do you think Miri and Ella are happy about the baby?"

He refills her glass. "I'm sure they are. Why do you even ask?"

"Oh, I don't know. I mean . . . yes . . . yes, of course. I think they're super excited . . ."

"I can see them now, fighting over who will hold him, who will feed him but. . ." and he laughs as he sits back in his chair.

"But not who'll be changing the diapers. Whether it'll be *him* or *her*, I can guarantee you that that job will be all mine. No competition there."

Hannah watches Jake reach for the TV's remote. He flicks through the channels, leaving the sound off.

"By the way," he says, putting it back down on the table. "Wasn't there something you wanted to talk to me about?"

"It's nothing. Nothing important. Honestly. It can wait until tomorrow."

"No, let's hear it. I know you, by now. It'll only keep festering inside you."

"It's . . . oh, I don't know . . . I think I'm already feeling overwhelmed. I mean, I just don't know how I'll cope with it all."

He sits up, rests his elbows on his thighs, and with his eyes roaming the carpet beneath his feet, says, "I don't understand . . ."

"Forget it."

"No. I don't want to forget it. Tell me what's going on. Why are you feeling this overwhelmed?"

"Maybe it's the pregnancy making me feel on edge about work . . ."

"The place is crazy; I'll grant you that. But honestly, aren't we used to it? I mean when in all the years of running our company has it ever not been wildly, crazy busy? Tell me what's changed?"

Now she regrets she's started this conversation.

"I don't know. All I know is I feel anxious so much of the time."

"But what about?"

"Artie . . ." And as soon as she's said it, she realizes he's not the entire cause of her anxiety.

"I believe it'll work out; you must see that by now." He leans forward and reaches out to touch her knee.

"I do. But I'm also nervous about my workload. It's already increased by quite a bit. And now with the girls back at home, I wonder how I'll manage it all." She stares at the silent TV, the images seeming to flicker more when there's no sound.

"I think you're getting ahead of yourself here. Yes, there'll be more for you to do at the office, but it'll be a temporary situation. And even you have agreed we need to hire more people. In any case, you'll be leaving work every afternoon to meet the school bus. And soon enough, they'll be needing you less and less . . ."

"Until the baby . . ."

"Well . . ."

"It's true though, isn't it? I'll be a full-time mother once again."

"You're not regretting our decision to keep the baby, are you?" His body shifts slightly away from her. She sees concern – or is it pity, clouding his eyes?

"God no, absolutely not," Hannah says, shaking her head. "I'm so sorry. I didn't mean it like that. No, not at all. It's just the thought of having to put my life on hold again."

"You mean your poetry?" he says, and she wonders why those words still sound so drab and unimportant coming from his lips. He turns his focus on the TV for a moment, then looks back at her.

"Yes, yes, that too . . ." Her voice trails off. And as she listens to herself, she hears the voice of her mother's spoiled child.

"Hannah, I am trying," he says, leaning toward her again. "But I still don't get what's changed so drastically in your life – what's causing you all this extra stress."

"You know what? I don't really know either. Let's forget about it, okay?" She smiles at him, shrugs her shoulders.

"You sure?" Jake leans back in his chair.

"I'm sure. When I figure it out, if I ever do, I'll let you know."

"Promise?"

"Promise." And feeling sudden restlessness overcome her, she throws off the blanket, puts her feet to the carpeted floor. "I'm going up to check on the kids."

As Hannah passes by Jake's chair, he grabs hold of her hand and pulls her into him.

"You know we'll make it work, don't you?" he says. "We've done it before. We'll do it now, and we'll do it all over again, and yet again, in the future. I know, deep down, you believe that as well as I do. You do, don't you?"

Hannah perches on the arm of his chair. She looks at the silent TV screen, then leans over and gives him a kiss. "I do," she says, "because I believe in you."

"No," he says. "It's us, together, we need to believe in."

"Okay, you're right."

"Aren't I always?"

"Absolutely." Hannah gives his arm a tickle, and hopes she sounds convincing enough.

She stands.

"I'll be up in a few minutes." He reaches for the remote and turns up the volume on the TV.

Chapter Twenty-Three

Today Hannah is working from home. Jake dropped Miri and Ella off for play dates at their sister-friends' house. Afraid to waste a single second, she walks past the kitchen sink, filled with the leftover breakfast dishes, and heads for her desk. She wonders how long it will take before this whole Artie and Lisa story will be so deeply buried in her consciousness that it no longer automatically pops into her mind's eye, the moment she enters her room and turns on her computer.

Louis, our attorney, wrote up a contract. It spelled out the amount of inventory we had used and how much we owed for it, as well as our cost for employing his people in the Rhode Island facility, where some of the orders were being produced.

Artie took the summer to close his operation. Originally, he said he would be available to come to work full-time with us on September 1st. Looking forward to having him run our factory and getting the inventory counted and under control, we presented him with an employment contract which his lawyer ignored. Even by the third week of October, when Artie finally came to work with us, he was still refusing to sign a contract. Meanwhile, we continued to pay him his salary and expenses, as if he were already employed by us. And he kept asking for a guarantee of employment and a pension. Neither of which were we willing to offer him. He'd known this from day one of our talks, as well as from the initial interim contract we had drawn up earlier in the summer.

•   •   •

Hannah and Jake were sitting in their den. The TV was on and muted, though they hardly paid any attention to the silent images flashing across the screen. Instead, Artie was their focus of attention – as usual in those days, as he is becoming once again now, in these.

—Yeah, well, Jake had said. —He can always want, can't he? It doesn't necessarily mean he'll get.

—That's one way of putting it, I guess. But couldn't he just as easily pull his business away from us, especially if we haven't come to a mutual agreement?

—As I've said before, what good would it do him? Jake leaned into her, his hand on her arm for emphasis. —Think about it, he went on. —The guy's a fucking loser and he's desperate. By now, he's out of options. Out of time, too, by my reckoning. If he doesn't hurry up and get out of his building before it goes into foreclosure, he'll end up losing everything inside of it as well, like all his inventory, machines, computers, and shelving. The whole darn lot will be sold at auction and the proceeds scooped up by his creditors. He'll wind up with bug-all nothing. Believe me, he knows full well the consequences he's facing. And yes, I'm totally convinced that in the end, these headaches will have been completely worth it.

—But what happens if his demands are so overwhelming we can't come to a frigging settlement? Then what?

Jake grunted. Or was he just clearing his throat? She looked over at him.

—How many times . . .?

—I know, I know, she said, interrupting him as soon as he pulled his hand away from her arm, folded both of his own into a tight knot over his chest, and began jiggling his crossed leg, with an impatience that mimicked the expression on his face.

—But my main point, Hannah continued anyway. —My biggest concern is how we protect ourselves, in case of . . .

—Get a lawyer, which we've done, stick to our guns, which we're going to do. Look, Jake said, putting his hand back on her arm. —He's already too far into this with us to pull out. And to top it all off, we have his sources and his customer base. Do you understand what I'm saying?

She nodded.

—Anyway, look at the bright side of things for a change, Jake said. —Our sales are up and I'm betting they'll continue to go in that direction.

—Okay, I'll agree with your assumption.

—I have set up all the shelves that I bought at Home Depot in the extra basement space we rented, and we hired three men to unload the truck.

—How much did the shelves cost?

—A couple of hundred.

—Not too bad. And the truck? When's that scheduled to be here?

—Tomorrow, first thing,

—Artie said he'll be here to help you.

—Well, that's what he'd originally said. But then when I talked to him again later this afternoon, I couldn't get a straight answer out of him. He kept hedging . . .

—Oh, I bet the fucker doesn't even show up, she said, staring at the weather map as it flashed across the muted screen, showing it to be hot and sunny for the following day.

—I can't say I'd be disappointed if he bailed. To be honest, I've been dreading his coming here. Without him, I'll have the freedom to check out the inventory and arrange it the way I want. But the best part of it will be when I find out exactly what he has, and then what he's missing.

—Just a lot of work for you.

—I don't mind, he said.

—Hopefully, it won't be any more than you can manage.

—Honestly, I'll be fine.

—If you say so, she said.

At about the same time as the last of his inventory came down from Rhode Island, it looked as if the economy was about to take a nosedive. Then another blow to our industry came with the Consumer Product Safety Improvement Act which outlawed the use of phthalates in toys because they have been found to adversely affect health in many ways, including cancer. Since phthalates soften vinyl and other plastics, we could not keep parts of Artie's inventory, especially the beach balls.

Although they weren't given any guarantees as to when the truck would arrive at their place, they had assumed it would be first thing in the morning. But it didn't show up until after lunch and by then, Jake was on the verge of becoming a totally crazed man. The day workers he'd hired had arrived at eight-thirty in the morning. And since there was nothing else for them to do but wait around, they'd spent the entire morning hanging out on the steps to the loading dock, chain-smoking cigarettes and, by the sound of their giggles and raucous laughter, telling each other a slew of dirty jokes. Their presence certainly wasn't helping Jake; rather, they were winding him up still more. And predictably, Artie hadn't shown up either. Had he even called? Hannah didn't want to think about how huge the scramble would be to get all the cartons offloaded onto the dock, brought to the freight elevator, and from there to their new basement space. Never mind Jake's idea of stacking them neatly onto shelves in the specific locations he'd envisioned for them.

Hannah spent most of the morning busying herself with the usual pile of paperwork that had accumulated on her desk, and answering phones, which hadn't stopped ringing since she first got in. Then later in the afternoon, she went down to the dock to see how things were going. She offered to help. He assured her he had it all under control. Besides, he said, wiping sweat off his forehead with the back of his hand, what could she do? Lift the heavy boxes? Definitely not.

So, she came back to her desk and helped with entering the incoming sales orders. Their workload had already more than doubled, though the staff they needed to accommodate the growth had not. How could they have hired more people if this turned out to be a temporary situation? Aggravation and pressure were high all around, especially now with all of Artie's orders being produced in their factory. It was as though everyone in the company had gone into overdrive. If they had all run around like crazy before the takeover, it was nothing compared to how it was now. Every day felt like a race to the finish line, times to go home moving ever later and later into the evening hours.

But despite all this crazy overtime, she could now see how production under one roof had given them a tremendous advantage. Keeping track of all the orders here made their work much simpler, and, she had to admit, they were seeing positive results from the decisions they'd put in place. Not the least of which, was no longer needing to make those dreaded "we-need-more-time" phone calls or answering the calls looking for tracking numbers and having to say, "I'm sorry, but your order has not shipped out yet" and afterward being stuck listening to the angry and abusive language screamed in response. Making a deadline date was the jewel of the industry. Missing a ship date, anathema. Calling to beg for extra time, not as bad, since normally there was a little wiggle room. Luckily for Jake and Hannah, their employees were willing to work those extra hours to get the jobs out the door. Hannah had never felt as indebted to the people who worked for her as she did now.

Finished for the day – the overflow of orders processed, invoices sent out, cash receipts tallied for the bank, bills entered, and the checks printed – Hannah stopped by the loading dock on her way out to see how Jake was doing. It didn't take her long to figure out it was not going too well. The truck had left. And the cartons were stacked up along the entire length and width of the loading dock. Poor Jake, frizzy hair sticking up all over his head and cheeks flushed shiny red, was leaning up against the wall by the door to the building. He looked as though he'd be ready to escape this whole mess, at the slightest provocation. And those three guys he'd hired for the day? They were nowhere to be seen.

—What the . . .? she said, waving her arms around at the sea of boxes surrounding her.

—Nice, huh? He raked his fingers through his hair, at what must have been the thousandth time that day and forced a smile.

—Why couldn't Artie have shown up just this once? I'm sorry, Jake, but I don't get it. I mean, what the fuck's his problem?

—Hey, hey, take it easy. I told you, I'm better off without him here.

—Even so, it would've been the decent thing for him to do. Don't you think? she said, though she knew full well that Jake couldn't understand his apparent disinterest in their business, either. His excuses were always the same – he had too many other problems to take care of.

—I guess he simply doesn't want to work.

—Then, tell me . . . Hannah said, coming to where Jake was standing, the all-too-familiar hysteria about to rise in her voice.

He put his hands deep into the pockets of his jeans. —I don't know why you don't believe me when I tell you . . . I think all these headaches will be worth it in the end, once we've straightened everything out.

—But . . .

—*But*, in fact, we're doing better than okay with production. And you never thought we could do it, right?

—Right. I thought we'd be sunk by now.

—So, I can't be that crazy, can I?

—I guess not, she said, smiling.

—And what do you say? He took his hands out of his pockets and pulled her into him.

—Okay, I agree, you were *right* about . . .

—Right? I was right one hundred percent, he said, tickling her.

—Yes, you were. But then . . . oh, I don't know . . . when I see this. And she turned from him and waved her arms around at all the cartons piled up on the dock. —I'm thrown backward. I'm just . . . altogether not sure . . . about any of it.

—Trust me. We'll be fine. Although I'm sure we'll have the occasional hiccup along the way.

—You and your occasional hiccups. Is that what you call this absurd mess?

He looked around. —Yup, I do, he said. —But let me get back to work now.

—What about those guys you hired? Where are they?

—Gone for the day. Don't worry, though. Hugo promised he'd stay and help me get the cartons inside before he goes home. Tomorrow, when the guys are back, we'll spend the day organizing. He took a deep breath, then added, —It's all fine. Seriously.

—I wish I could believe you, she said, looking more intently at the piles of cartons in the different shapes and sizes surrounding them, all of them stamped with Artie's company name, Playful Promotions, his product codes, and the equivalent in Chinese letter markings.

—I'd feel better if I could stay and help . . .

—You know there's no way you can. Really. Please stop worrying. Besides, he said, looking down at his wrist. —Isn't it time you were leaving? Won't the kids be home soon?

—I still have a few minutes, she said, watching him work his way through the maze of cartons and bend, now and then, to read their markings. —Boy, this is way fucked up, she went on, out of a sudden urge to speak, say something, anything, to fill in the wide gap she was feeling, though what exactly that was, she couldn't be certain. —You're sure you're going to be fine? she asked again.

—I told you, yes. How often must I say it to convince you?

—Okay, okay. I get it, she said and took a deep breath.

—But I'll be home late. Don't wait for me for dinner.

Jake went back to rearranging and re-stacking the cartons. Hannah watched him for a couple more moments. But intrigued by the product codes on the boxes, she wandered in and around the stacks, checking them out. Most contained beach balls. Assorted sizes – six-inch, twelve-inch, sixteen-inch. Assorted colors – red, blue, black, yellow, green, and purple, and each color alternately striped with white. Continuing to move through the maze, she discovered there were cartons filled with kids' jump ropes, others with crayons, and still others with vinyl baseballs. It looked as if they were about to enter the world of Santa giveaways.

She pulled out her phone to look for new messages. Finding nothing she hadn't seen before, she clicked it off and put it back in her bag.

—Since you don't need me, I'm going home now. And she walked over to where he stood.

—That's a great idea, he said, and gave her arm a little squeeze.

—I'm going back to work. If I'm not home by their bedtime, please kiss the girls goodnight for me. Okay?

—Sure, Hannah said, and leaned forward to give him a kiss on the cheek. —But try not to stay here too long.

We were anxious for Artie to sign because, aside from anything else, we wanted to announce to the industry at large that we'd taken over his company and were now producing his orders. We also wanted to begin our advertising campaign.

When we didn't hear back from him about the contract in a timely manner, we wrote to him again, asking him to please sign it. His only response was to say that our verbiage was too harsh. Otherwise, there was no further mention of the contract itself.

•   •   •

Hannah's cell phone rings, startling her. She picks it up without looking to see who's calling.

"Hi, Mom," Ella says, her voice animated. "When are we going shopping for our new school supplies?"

"I was thinking we'd go tomorrow. Why?"

"Carly and her mom went shopping yesterday and . . ."

"You like all her new stuff?"

"Umm . . . yes," Ella says, her hesitancy telling Hannah something's not quite right.

"I can come and get you now. Is that what you'd like?"

"Yes," Ella says and hangs up the phone.

Saving her work on her ARTIE file, she grabs her keys and goes for Ella. She must've had a fight with her friend, which is why, Hannah imagines, she wants to be picked up so much earlier than originally planned. She hopes Miri won't make a fuss, having to leave her friend earlier.

Chapter Twenty-Four

While Miri goes through the various notebooks, pens, pencils, and sets of colored magic markers lining the back-to-school shelves at Target, Ella is inspecting backpacks. Yanking them off the shelves, she lifts them onto her shoulders then runs over to the mirror, stands in front of it and poses, this way and that, to see how she looks. Hannah has promised all new gear for school, payment for her secret indebtedness to her children for giving her the summer. The cart she guards and pushes from area to area is filling up. Never mind, she tells herself with a shake of her head. This shopping spree has always been the best part of starting a new school year. And she loves to watch her girls pick their way through the merchandise. Occasionally, they'll ask for her opinion, but mostly she's left playing a guessing game with herself – what will they decide on in the end? She never wins, though; her kids are way too fickle.

Her cell phone rings. It's her mother.

"Can I call you back in about an hour? I'm out shopping with the girls for school supplies," she says, and then quickly adds, "Everything okay?" having almost forgotten to ask.

"Yes, of course, I'm fine. We can talk later. Have fun."

"Yeah, thanks," she says into the void. As usual, her mother has already hung up.

Hannah wheels the cart over to where Ella is now inspecting pencil cases. The backpack she's chosen is bright pink with pictures of fairies dancing all over it.

"How lovely," Hannah says, gently pulling it off her shoulder and placing it into the cart.

"Isn't it *so* pretty?" Ella says, caressing it, as she might, a sleeping baby.

"You've picked the absolute best, my sweet."

They walk over to Miri, who's cradling an armful of school supplies. Hannah doesn't even check to see what Miri's unloading into the cart.

"Who's hungry for a snack?"

"Me," they both shriek in unison.

"Okay then, let's get checked out of here."

As she drives home, Hannah's concentration drifts in and out of the conversation coming from behind her in the back seat. Excited about their new school purchases, now partially unpacked and spread all around them, they sound like they're playing a game of show-and-tell, as they compare and discuss the various attributes of each of the items they've picked. Hannah's thoughts keep going back to her mother, feeling a little guilty for putting her off. She doesn't normally call during the day, her reasoning is – or perhaps it's just an excuse? – that she doesn't want to disturb her daughter during work hours. Now Hannah wonders why her mother broke her own golden rule. What did she want to tell her? Was it important? Has she decided about her life?

Given what Hannah knows about Leo and Basel and what it's like to uproot and move, she tries to imagine what she herself would do. Part of her thinks she'd jump at the opportunity. Although, the longer she considers the idea of starting her life over – learning a new language, new ways, new friends, leaving old ones, and of course, living without her family – the less she'd feel like taking the plunge for herself. But for her mother? She'd miss too much of the children growing up. And then what about the new baby? Regardless of family, though, she can understand her mother's excitement at the possibility of a new and different life.

Once they're home, and after Miri and Ella have had their snacks and raced each other up the stairs to their rooms with bundles of new stuff in their arms, Hannah goes to her own little room, turns on her computer, and phones her mother. At first, she thinks her mother has gone out. It takes her longer than usual to answer.

"Hi, my darling," she says, a little out of breath. "I'm glad you called me back . . ."

"Why? Is something wrong?"

"Not that I know of. Should there be?"

"No, no. You just sound a little out of breath."

"Probably because I had to run for the phone."

"Oh." Hannah smiles, relieved.

"I only called you," her mother says, "because it feels like a long time since we last spoke."

"I don't think so."

"Perhaps it's my aging days that seem to slide together, rather like windows closing against the outside world, and I don't remember, as well as I used to, what exactly happened when."

"Don't worry. You're not the only one that happens to. For instance, I don't remember if you ever told me, or if I forgot to ask, about your birthday dinner with Leo."

"Ah! Yes. The dinner was marvelous, the food fabulous. French, you know. My favorite. And, of course, Leo is such a gentleman . . ."

"Do I hear a *but* coming?"

"Maybe," she says.

"Is that why you called?"

"Perhaps."

"You can't make up your mind. Am I right?"

"Probably."

"You're confused," Hannah says, hoping she won't get the same noncommittal answer again.

"Yes, confused is exactly the right word."

Now Hannah is stuck. She doesn't know what else to say, how to propel this conversation forward and coax her mother into talking about what's worrying her.

"But you are still planning your trip to Basel to meet his daughters, aren't you?"

"Well, that's the thing, you see. I'm not a hundred percent sure it makes sense."

"Why?" Hannah sits up straighter in her chair and holds the phone as close to her ear as possible to ensure she won't miss a word.

"As much as I love being with him . . . even as much as I think I love him . . . I'm not sure I could manage the move. How do I explain it? The prospect of rearranging my entire life isn't quite as enticing or as exciting as I thought it might be. I think I've crashed back down to earth."

"But you don't have to decide right away, do you?"

"I suppose not," she says, and Hannah hears a long, loud sigh.

"What is it? What's got into you? I thought you were going to decide about living with him after meeting his daughters."

"Honestly? I'm afraid to meet them . . . afraid that by going over there, I will have already committed myself to moving in with him. Do you understand what I'm saying?"

"Yes, but I completely disagree with you. They must know the reason you're going over there is to meet his family before you make up your mind definitively."

"Not so easy. I mean, how will I say, after I've met them, that I won't be coming to live with their father? Doesn't it tell him, in a way, that his daughters turned me off?"

"No. I'm sure you could come up with several reasons."

"Name one I could use," her mother says, a tone of belligerence in her voice.

"You'll miss your own family too much to move so far away from them."

"Now, why does that sound like the perfect excuse?" her mother says, laughing.

"Perhaps, because it's true?"

Or is it only Hannah's wishful thinking? She hears her girls on the stairs. They're arguing.

"I can't do it to him. Besides, what happens if I don't have a good relationship with them? Then what?"

"But you won't be living with them, will you?"

"Of course not."

"Well, maybe, just maybe," Hannah says, "you have this tiny little nugget of doubt about your relationship with Leo, and it's worming its way through your brain."

"Oh, my God! What an awful thought. Worming."

"Well, is there?"

"I suppose it might be something like that, but it's not him."

Ella is yelling out for her.

"Mom," Hannah says. "Let me call you right back. By the sound of it, I'm going to have to play the referee."

Miri and Ella are in the kitchen. Hannah can't tell right away what they're quarrelling about. Is she mistaken about their raised voices? Perhaps shrieking is their new way of communicating. But no, they're in a fight. "What's going on?" she says, coming into the kitchen.

"Ella's being so annoying," Miri says. "She's in my room every few seconds, asking me to trade my pens with her, or my notebooks, or anything else I have."

"Why, Ella? Aren't you happy with what you've chosen?"

"I like Miri's stuff better," she says, her mouth turning down as she crosses her arms over her puffed-out chest.

Hannah inhales, then exhales, and says, "We can exchange whatever you like, as long as you haven't opened up the package it came in."

Miri laughs. Ella bursts into tears. And Hannah knows that everything they bought is unwrapped and, most likely, scattered all over Ella's bedroom floor. "Never mind," she says. "We'll go back to Target and get you what Miri has. Okay?"

Ella nods, sniffles, rubs her nose, and puts her arms around Hannah's middle in a hug.

"This is so not fair," Miri says, marching off. "She's such a spoiled brat."

"Hey, I plan on getting you more things too," Hannah shouts out as she hears Miri's footsteps stomping up the stairs.

"Can we go tomorrow?" Ella says, releasing her arms from around Hannah's middle.

"Yes, we'll go tomorrow. But for right now, I'd really like you to go back up to your room."

"Oh, must I?" Ella says in a whiney voice.

"Here's an idea for you," Hannah says with as much excitement as she can muster. "Why don't you make a list of all those things you want me to buy? This way, when we get to Target tomorrow, you'll know exactly what to look for. What do you think?"

Ella nods and saunters off. And Hannah dials her mother.

"Everything all right?" her mother asks the minute she answers the phone.

"Yes, just the usual. Ella always wants what Miri has. And don't ask me why, but I'm always giving in to her, though I know I really shouldn't. And, of course, Miri gets terribly upset with me because Ella constantly gets her way. And on it goes. Blah di dee, blah di dah."

Hannah knows she won't win an award for being the perfect mother today or perhaps, any day. But she's tired. She needs a break. And if it means another trip to Target tomorrow, that's the price she'll pay for these extra few minutes of quiet now.

"Enlighten me," Hannah says, focusing her thoughts back onto her mother. "What's all this hesitation about?"

"To tell you the truth, I'm not a hundred percent sure," she says, wavering. "You see, I was dusting my bookshelves this morning, and I came across these incredibly old photo albums I'd totally forgotten all about. Need I say more?"

"You stopped dusting."

"Yes. And I got carried away. I ended up spending the whole day looking through each of those albums, some of the photos so old they're sepia colored, and their edges are all curled up."

"But what does any of this have to do with your decision about Basel?"

"Be patient. I'm getting to it."

"Okay, I'll try."

"Anyway, amongst all the old pictures, I found some of my father with his father. My father was in his army uniform. It was during World War I. And that's what reminded me of a story I'd heard. While stationed in Serbia, he'd met an exceptionally beautiful young woman and fallen in love with her."

"How romantic."

"And he asked her to marry him."

"Hmm. . . since she's not my grandmother . . ."

"And, of course, she said yes . . ."

"Why, of course?"

"Because, my darling, your grandfather was the most handsome man you could ever imagine, that's why."

"So, what happened?" Hannah asks, then stands and begins to pace up and down her little room; impatience blooming inside her.

"Just wait," her mother continues. "They set a date, and when my grandfather arrived at the family's home, in a small Serbian village, on the day before the wedding, he asked my father if he was sure he was ready to marry. My father then confessed his confusion and doubts."

"Then why didn't he call the whole thing off?"

"She had seven brothers."

"Seven brothers? Wow."

"Yes, and my father was afraid of what those seven brothers might do to him."

"You mean, like, beat him up?"

"Or worse," she says. "So, like a couple of thieves, the two of them – my grandfather and my father – snuck out of the house in the middle of the night and ran away. Needless to say, no one from our family has ever stepped foot in that country again."

"What a funny story."

"It is, isn't it?"

"But what's the connection?" Hannah says.

"You mean with Leo?"

"Well, yes."

"It made me think how lucky my father was, having my grandfather there to help him find a way out."

"But there's good news about Leo," Hannah says. "He doesn't have seven brothers. Or does he?"

"Ha! Ha! You're too funny, my darling. But seriously . . . you do see the similarity in our dilemmas, don't you?"

"Kind of. But your situation is really quite different. There's no rush on your end. No wedding planned. You're both much older, more mature. You can take your time . . ."

"But I don't want to string him along either."

"Then I'm not sure what else to tell you, Mom. You must realize your hesitation sounds like you're having serious second thoughts about this whole affair."

"Not so much about the affair, as having to move for it. Can you understand that?"

"No question."

"And now when I tell you . . . you'll think I've totally lost it for sure . . . there was something strange and haunting about those old scallop-edged, sepia-colored photos . . . the faces pictured in them, so serious . . . I don't know . . . it was as if, in a way, my future was encrypted in them."

Hannah sits back down at her desk, her dogs nudging each other across her thighs.

"Also, I can't help but wonder what it was, that drew me back to those old photos, in the first place." Urgency is rising in her voice now. "Do you think I'm going crazy?"

"No," Hannah laughs. "I'm sure you're not. After all, this is a life-altering decision you're trying to make."

"Well, yes, that's true," her mother says, as if to confirm the importance of it for herself. "And that's exactly why I need your help. Because, for whatever reason, I can't seem to figure it all out by myself."

"You really want my honest opinion?"

"Absolutely."

Hannah hesitates for a moment, picks up a pen from her desk, and clicks it on and off, then, dropping it back onto the wooden surface, takes a deep breath and says, "If I were you, I wouldn't go."

"You wouldn't?"

"No."

Dead silence.

For a moment, Hannah wonders if her mother has hung up on her. But when she hears her clear her throat and say, "Tell me why," her words sound insistent.

"Honestly, you seem to be having too many second thoughts about leaving New York," Hannah says quickly before she loses her courage. "Perhaps looking through the old photos defined bits about your own life for you, solidified your thoughts, helped you decide."

A deer saunters across the backyard and, as if to listen to Hannah's side of the conversation as well, stops and stares at her, its ears twitching before deciding to move on.

"That's what you think?" her mother says.

"Yes."

"I need time," she says. "But I'll . . ."

". . . definitely be here for your new grandbaby's birth?" Hannah says and laughs.

"Definitely," her mother repeats, resolve in her voice, and she laughs now too.

"Well, at least there's that to look forward to."

"Yes . . ." she says, her voice wavering.

"What is it, Mom?"

"The truth is, moving to a different country has me rattled, unnerved. I honestly don't believe I have the energy, or anything else it'd take, to do it all over again."

"Then explain it to Leo. Tell him you can't make up your mind this quickly. You need more time." She smiles as she hears Jake's insistent voice: *Your mother will never leave her beloved New York City.* How thrilled he'll be to hear he was right once again, as he'll be sure to remind her, he always is. And now Hannah continues, her courage fully engaged, "I'd be thrilled if you stay. Relieved too. I wasn't looking forward to a long-distance relationship with you. But ultimately, of course, you'll make up your own mind."

"What I really want is to stop thinking about it. It's driving me mad. Meanwhile, enough said of me and my life. What about you and yours? How's it going with that other business?"

"It's going. It's crazy busy. And we're extremely happy that Artie, the guy whose business we took over, is finally gone. What a pain he was. Anyway, we're hanging in. The best I can say for now is, so far, so good." Hannah lets out a long, noisy breath in a sigh. Her report to her mother is right, except for the one piece of information – the potential lawsuit – that she doesn't want to let her mother know about yet.

"A relief, I'm sure. And the girls? Are they looking forward to the start of school?"

"You kidding? Even Miri is dreading it, which is totally unusual for her."

"I remember those days," her mother says and laughs. "You know, it all tends to work out in the end. One way or another."

"I suppose," Hannah says, though she's not quite sure she believes it. Rather, it's more like her mom's favorite saying, that it's best to let all those lousy memories lay deep inside their graves. And remembering those words now, she thinks how impossible a feat it must be; perhaps nearly as impossible as her burying the memory of the abandoned newborn.

"So, my darling, when do I see you next?"

"Soon," Hannah says. "I'm overloaded right now, with all the extra work from that other business."

"Call me," her mother says. "And don't work too hard," she adds, and hangs up.

Chapter Twenty-Five

Jolted out of a dream she'll never remember, Hannah's woken up by the radio alarm's usual blaring of the morning's headlines – fears of yet another war in some distant corner of the world, recession, inflation, the Dow up, the Dow down, stabbings, shootings, traffic tie-ups, crashes, collisions – in voices of doom that rudely invade the privacy of their bedroom. She turns around to lie on her back. No matter the day, the news always seems to sound the same. She stares up at the ceiling. Doesn't want to think of all she needs to work on today, and closing her eyes, turns to lie on her side. Ah! Finally, the weather report confirms that, as promised, the sun will be out in its fullest glory today. Suddenly conscious of a slight tickle on her cheek, then a caress to her hair, Hannah opens her eyes again and finds Ella, still in pajamas, kneeling on the floor by the side of her bed. Her cheek is resting on Hannah's pillow and so close to Hannah's face, the tips of their noses touch and Ella's beautiful blue eyes, a shiny blur among the features in her face, are out of focus.

Lifting her head, Ella says, a whine in her voice but a smile of hopefulness on her bright face as she continues to pull her fingers gently through Hannah's hair, "Do I have to go to school today?"

Turning toward her young daughter, Hannah raises herself up on her elbow, leans her head into her hand, and moving closer to level her face with Ella's, she says, "Why? What's going on today that you want to miss?"

"Nothing. I just don't want to go."

"Well . . ." Hannah begins, now stroking Ella's cheek. "It's important you go to school every day. I mean, you don't want to miss anything or fall behind, do you?" But looking at her daughter's face, she realizes her words have little impact. "Listen," she goes on, her tone stricter. "You've no choice. You must go to school. It's the law."

"But I hate it . . ."

"Come," Hannah says and swings her legs over the side of the bed to sit up. "Let's put breakfast in your tummy, get you dressed in one of those pretty new outfits we got for you, fill that beautiful backpack with all the colored magic markers we found at Target, and the notebooks, and . . ."

"*Ugh!* Okay," Ella says and stands. She hovers over Hannah for a moment before turning away and, in slow motion, puts one foot in front of the other, as if balancing high on a tightrope.

"Go on, go get dressed. I'll be in to help you in a minute."

At the door, Ella looks back. "Then will you come down the street after and wait for the school bus with me and Miri?"

"Sure, I will," Hannah says in as reassuring a voice as she can muster this early in the morning.

Hannah nudges Jake to wake him. "It's already past 7:30. I thought you had an appointment at work this morning."

"*Ugh!* I almost forgot," he says. "I have someone coming in to fix one of Artie's pad printers." And he buries his head under the blanket.

Two *ughs!* in one morning before she's even had the chance to wash her face, let alone have her coffee, is not a good portent for the day, she fears. And which one will be the more difficult to navigate in the end? She's not entirely sure.

But when she sees her two dogs waiting for her at the bottom of the stairs, their tails wagging like crazy, she can't help but laugh. "Come on," she says, and they follow her into the kitchen, where she finds Miri sitting at the table, a bowl of cheerios swimming in milk in front of her. Her paperback book, *The Diary of Anne Frank,* leaned up against an empty coffee mug. She's already dressed in her blue jeans and jacket outfit, her curly brown hair brushed and tied up in a ponytail. Even her backpack, bloated with all her notebooks and pens, is standing upright by the door, zipped up and ready to go. No doubt as the day warms, her jacket will end up squished inside her backpack as well.

"Wow," Hannah says to Miri. "You are the most organized person I know."

She looks up at Hannah, her dark eyes disappearing into crescents as she laughs. "I don't know why I woke up so early."

"If you have any questions . . ." Hannah points to Miri's book.

"I'm fine," she says. "It's for school."

Hannah can't help but compare her two daughters, only three years apart, and how different they are.

"At least you won't have to rush for the school bus."

"That's exactly what I figured," Miri says and goes back to her reading.

Hannah fills the dog bowls with food and water, cleans out the espresso machine, adding more water and coffee beans, and turns it on. Once the spluttering stops, she makes a cup for herself.

Ella comes trudging down the stairs, hairbrush in hand. She's barefoot, but otherwise, all dressed – Hannah sighs with relief – in one of her new outfits. The skirt, pink and fluffy like a ballerina's, goes so perfectly with the pink lacey top they found to match. There's something doll-like about Ella, Hannah thinks.

"What would you like for breakfast?" she asks, as she takes the brush out of Ella's hand. Brushing her daughter's blonde-streaked hair, she then parts it down the middle and ties it up into two pigtails right above her ears.

"What's Miri eating?"

"Cheerios."

"Same," Ella says and goes to sit down next to her sister. With an exaggerated sigh, she plants one elbow on the table, holds her head up in her opened hand, sticks her thumb into her mouth, and sucks on it loudly.

"Here's your breakfast. Eat up. You don't have all day. I'm going upstairs to put on some sweats so I can walk you down to the bus. Okay?"

"Okay," they both mumble at the same time. They look at each other and giggle. And just like that, both their moods change. Jinxed is the word she remembers now. How she and Lisa had laughed that day in Rhode Island. What was the word they'd said at the same time? They were sitting across from each other at the table in the conference room. The laughter then, as it does now, broke the tension.

The dogs follow her to the bottom of the stairs.

Jake comes out of the shower as Hannah finishes throwing on her sweatpants and tee shirt.

"Do you think you'll come close to finishing your notes on Artie?" he says.

"Yes, I hope to. But before I can start and because I've had a request – a super polite one, I might add – it'll be after I've walked down to the end of our street to wait with Miri and Ella for their bus to arrive. After which, I promise I'll come running back home, hop in the shower, and immediately get to work. Sound good to you?"

"Sounds perfect to me, so long as it is to you," Jake says, a quizzical look on his face, which tells her he's not quite sure how he's supposed to respond.

And listening to herself, she can tell she's already feeling maxed out. Never mind, she finds herself thinking again. Never mind. She'll calm down once she has the house to herself. She leaves Jake to finish dressing and heads back down to the kitchen.

"How many more minutes before we have to leave?" Miri asks as Hannah refills her coffee cup at the espresso machine before she sits down at the table with her two daughters. The dogs have followed her and now lie down beside her.

"Maybe fifteen," she says, turning around to look at the clock on the wall, its face covered with a white paper plate that Ella decorated at school last year. Jake attached the plate to the top of the clock's face by piercing a hole in the middle of it, making space for the minute and hour hands to poke through. Now, whenever Hannah looks at it, she needs to subtract or add a couple of minutes, one way or the other, because Ella's painted numbers aren't exactly in line with where the clock's quarter-hour markings belong. It doesn't matter. Hannah loves Ella's colorful flowers and rainbows surrounding the numbers anyway, and she can't help but smile as she remembers how proud Ella was when Jake first hung it up in its space on the wall opposite the fridge.

"I'll be right back," Miri says, bringing her empty bowl to the sink.

"Just don't be too long. And what about you, my smiley girl?" Hannah says to Ella.

"Do I . . .?"

"Let's not . . ."

"Wear sneakers or sandals? What looks best with this new outfit?"

"Actually, I think your white hi-tops would look great," Hannah says, thankful that the crisis has been avoided for now. "What do you think?"

"Yeah," Ella says and goes back to eating her Cheerios, not swimming in as much milk as her sister's.

Jake comes down, makes himself an espresso and swallows it in one gulp.

"I'm leaving," he says. "Have a great day Ella and learn as much as you can." He kisses the top of her head, grabs his keys, and leaves.

Hannah hears the car pull out of the driveway and feels a slight sense of relief. She doesn't know why. "Right, let's finish getting you ready for school. Where's your backpack?"

"In my room," Ella says, standing up.

Hannah gets up too and brings the empty cereal bowl to the sink on her way out of the kitchen. As she and Ella climb the stairs, both dogs come rushing up behind them, as if they're afraid they'll miss out on an extremely important family matter. She'll take them down the street with her to wait for the school bus. They'll be happy. Miri and Ella will be happy. And so will she.

She's seen the girls off and is back at home, the house finally tranquil and, thankfully, all to herself. Standing at the window for a moment, she watches Zig and Zag bound across the lawn, a drier, paler green, by now, to lap water at the edge of the pond. Withering yellow, brown, and red leaves begin to fall. They sway and swirl about in the early September breeze. Thick, puffy clouds chase each other across the expanse of a deep blue sky, one moment sheltering the sun, the next moving past it. And as she listens to James Galway play a Mozart flute concerto in her little room, room of her own, the sun alternately lightens, darkens, warms, and cools her. At the end of it all, no matter what the day brings, she always feels lucky to have this space to come back to. And safe as well.

Like the womb, which encases and nourishes her unborn baby girl. Yes, one more girl. And although Jake hasn't said anything to her, Hannah knows he's disappointed. Especially since he makes jokes about the fact that he will soon be the sole male in a family of six females: one wife, three daughters, and two bitches. And that last number, he reminds whoever is listening, can vary with the day of the month, the hour of the day, even the minute of the hour. But Hannah's happy. She won't have to learn a whole new set of dos and don'ts for a boy. She'll know, more-or-less, what to expect from a girl.

Her new habit these days, or rather nights, is that before going to sleep, she looks through a large book of illustrations she keeps by the side of her bed. The illustrations are of fetuses in their varying stages of development. As she looks at the pictures of the unborn development of her baby girl, she's amazed all over again. Growth is so quick, so perfectly intact, and automatic – like the early spring flowers pushing their way up through the cold and hardened ground to bloom at the same time every year, no matter the weather.

But then, she wonders, is it true our children are only lent to us? To guide? To nurture?

Growth. Separation. Always hand in hand. She knows that now. But for the moment, for this short space of time, this baby inside her is all hers. She's free to imagine anything and everything she wants for her, free to pick a history, free to indulge her with a world, a life of this mother's choosing. She's not part of the bargain, not yet. After her birth there will be time, enough. And she'll belong to her own generation, as much as Hannah belongs to hers.

"Hers," she says aloud to an audience of no one, but pictures her voice as if it were a cartoon image, like a zigzag, a lightning bolt, zapping at her pictures, books, knickknacks, desk, monitor, keyboard, and chair. She laughs. "Belonging," she then says, also aloud. As if belonging can ever really be a possession.

She looks up at her screen, rereads the words there. It's slow going. And there are times when she isn't sure what her words truly mean or what they're trying to say. And to whom.

So much to learn.
    & too little time.
        Is fulfillment close?
            Or is it the never-ending
                Process?
   Is there a final realization?
        Or is one realization only the
            Basis for another?
                I wish I knew.

This morning she'd woken up as if she were still in the middle of a dream, where words, like arrows, were battling with each other inside her head. Normally, if she wakes before the alarm goes off, she likes to stay in bed for a little while to let her thoughts wander before the too-chirpy voices on the radio intrude into the quiet of their bedroom. But this morning, Ella was there to stop the stupid chatter, the irritating *what-ifs* spinning around in her head, and the voices coming from the radio, to announce the news of the world and remind her it was time to get her day started.

In the bathroom, standing in front of the mirror, she'd lifted the cotton tee, what she prefers to wear to bed these days, and stared at her swollen breasts. It always surprises her to see how, along with the fetus, her body changes from day to day. Veins, the shape of tree branches in winter, etched thick and thin, in purple and blue, stand out against her pale, taut skin, and remind her . . . but of what? Bringing her hands up to her breasts, she gently tracked the veins with the tips of her fingers. How hard her breasts had become.

The sun, barely peeking above the horizon, slanted in through the blinds hanging over the bathroom window. Hannah squinted against the brightness, blurring the image of herself in the mirror. Again, an odd feeling spread through her. What had she dreamt of last night? Focused on the mirror again, she stared at the rest of her body, the thickened waist, the bulb of her rounded belly. She reminded herself of one of those fertility statues.

Now another picture flashed through her head, a picture she's seen a million times before. She knew she wanted to but couldn't erase the image as it moved along like a film in her mind's eye. Is this what she dreamt of last night? Where had it come from, she wondered, this grainy depiction of masses of naked women, all sizes, ages, and body types, in a line, all waiting? If she had belonged to her grandmother's generation, she probably would have been among them in that line, expecting the warm water to relieve her tired, aching body, never dreaming that the air had been intentionally poisoned to stop her breathing. No enticements of a slim body, a pretty, youthful face to keep her alive.

Why is she thinking of all this now? Was this what she had been dreaming about last night? Or was it those voices on the radio that had interrupted her sleep? Top stories, business news, traffic, and finally, the weather. Slightly cooler than normal for September? Just as well.

Then there was Ella, resting her face on Hannah's pillow, stroking her cheek and whispering love notes into her ear.

Hannah had pulled on her sweats, jammed her feet into her furry slippers, and gone downstairs to make breakfast for her girls.

It is a school day. A workday. Not a day for dreams.

Chapter Twenty-Six

Even though they still lacked a signed contract, Artie and Jake finally reached an informal agreement on Artie's workdays and hours. Before his first official day, Hannah and Jake cleared out a cubicle by the window for him, shined up the desk, wiped down the keyboard, the monitor, the phone, and made sure his workspace was as perfect as possible. Then they left the inventory report – the one he'd created for them – in the middle of his desk, expecting this would be his first line of attack. He agreed they absolutely needed to know what they had in stock, and he promised he would start working on it the minute he settled in at his desk on his very first day of work.

Only, his first official day, already delayed by a month, got put off because of Columbus Day, a national holiday. On Tuesday he showed up around ten, dressed in black sweats, the same dirty worn-out sneakers Hannah remembered from the past times he was here, and the overstuffed briefcase he had slung over his shoulder, causing him to look a little lopsided as he came bustling in.

Now, three weeks later and with barely a nod to Hannah, he gave Hugo the keys to his Suburban and told him to go down to the parking lot with the trolley. There was a carton sitting in the trunk he needed to have brought up. She followed him to the office, but he didn't say hello to Jake, or to anyone else, for that matter. Instead, he made a beeline for his cubicle, dropped his over-stuffed briefcase onto the desk, and picked up the phone.

Hannah went into her and Jake's office.

—Well? she said, standing in front of Jake's desk, her arms folded across her chest. —What do you make of this?

He shrugged.

—Something must've happened on his way here.

—You think?

Unconvinced, she went back out to the factory to help with unpacking a rush order of notebooks.

After about half an hour, Artie appeared at her side with a stack of papers.

—I've been going over the inventory report, he said, as he shuffled through the pages, which, she noticed, had lots of inked-out lines.

—When do you and Jake want to go over this with me?

—If you're ready, then anytime is good for me, she said, surprised he had come to her about this instead of Jake.

—Perfect, he said and walked away. Hannah saw Hugo go into the office with the trolley and the carton Artie had asked him to bring up. After he'd deposited the carton on Artie's desk, he left.

After Artie began working with us, it became clear that he had no genuine experience in the production side of the business. He performed badly and was also a toxic influence on the company environment. Not one of our employees liked him. He would have countless, useless meetings with the factory people, sometimes even behind closed doors. He never got a handle on his inventory. In fact, he could never provide us with proof that he owned the inventory he had shipped down to us. According to his tax return, the bank had already seized the inventory to foreclose on a loan secured by it. We kept asking him for a count. But all we got were incomplete and incorrect reports, time after time. As a result, our problems with inventory continued.

As Rosa was setting up the pad printer for the notebooks, Hannah unpacked them, laying each one on a large red plastic tray, the kind originally used for transporting prepackaged loaves of bread to supermarkets. As Hannah would often do while in the factory, she looked around her factory floor. How lucky she was to have all this, she thought. No matter what happened with Artie and his company, she would still be lucky. She promised herself to try especially hard to remember this. Looking over at Rosa now, deep concentration showing on her face as she set up the machine, Hannah remembers the day Rosa had walked into their factory and, in broken English, asked for work. From the start, there was something special about her that Hannah liked, or more to the point, knew she'd be grateful for. Rosa was always willing to do whatever it took to get the job done. Over time, Hannah learned from her other employees how Rosa had escaped from Honduras. It was in the open bed of a truck. To stay perfectly still, as her driver had ordered her to do, she lay flat on her back, completely covered from head to toe with a large, heavy rubber mat. As the truck drove, the bed heated, burning the backs of her legs. Every so often, Rosa would come to work wearing a skirt short enough to expose the large and painful-looking scars deeply etched onto the backs of her legs.

•   •   •

For Hannah, those scars remind her of the deep sacrifices many people go through to come to a country like this, expecting, perhaps not the proverbial streets paved with gold, but surely a better, a freer way of life. Not so different, she thinks now, to the stories she's been told about her own family, those closest to her; the luckier Jews, she calls them, the ones who made it out in time, who gave life to Hannah and who then gave life to her own children. But there were those members of her family who'd lived in Cracow, Poland, and were rounded up one night, forced onto a truck, and herded to Auschwitz where, stripped naked, they'd stood in long lines, half frozen and looking forward to that promised, warm shower; exactly as Hannah had dreamt it. But what they couldn't have ever imagined, not for a single second, was that the spigots never showered them with warm water, only deadly poisonous gas instead.

Hannah looks out at her garden; at the rabbits, the squirrels, the birds chirping as they fly from one tree to the next and feels. . . yes, that luck has always been on her side.

·   ·   ·

At one point in the spring, we were debating whether to pay Artie to stay at home. We dreaded his scheduled workdays at the office. He was unduly unpleasant (there's a word for this), a toxic influence on our company environment, and not liked by any of our employees. He also told lies about certain employees, saying they did or didn't do what he had asked them to. Our employees had originally gone to him for their questions about his inventory, but after giving them wrong information too many times, they figured they couldn't count on him anymore. Artie hand-wrote inventory schedules, with dates and quantities in and out, and kept them in three-ring binders. One of our employees kept these books. If there was a mistake on an item in the book, he'd yell at her and make her cry. A lot of the beginning entries he'd made were incorrect.

·   ·   ·

Finished unpacking and returning to her office, Hannah saw that the conference room door was closed. Through the glass panel in the door, she saw Natalia and Artie sitting side by side at the table. He'd shut the door, which made Hannah nervous. It was weird and unnecessary, she thought, and stood, where he couldn't see her, to watch them. A three-ring binder filled with a stack of papers, which looked like Artie's inventory report, was sitting on the table between them. Natalia looked uncomfortable. Artie appeared annoyed about something. If their meeting didn't end in the next ten minutes, Hannah decided she'd go in. Disturb them. She checked the time on her watch, then went back to her desk.

—How's it going? Jake asked her, as she sat down and stared, unthinking, at the list of new emails on her screen.

—Okay, she said, not sure whether to tell him anything. She looked at her watch, got up. —I'll be right back, she added.

—What's the matter?

—Nothing, she said, and walked out of their office.

She stood outside the conference room for a moment, looking in through the glass in the door. Natalia was crying. As soon as Hannah opened the door, Natalia got up and ran past her.

—What the hell's going on? she asked Artie.

—The other day, I told Natalia I needed her to double-check items on this report . . .

—You, what?

He stood in front of Hannah; arms folded across his chest. With a look of such disdain on his face, she could almost hear the nasty words rattling around inside his head.

—Correct me if I'm wrong, she said, doing her best to keep authority in her voice and hold his attention. —I was under the distinct impression you were going to be taking care of inventory yourself and besides, whenever you've asked me who you can take to help you, I've said to take Hugo.

—Yes, but he's always busy with other things.

—Then you wait for him to be available. You can't come here and do whatever you please. That's not the deal. And in case you haven't noticed, she said, her voice becoming more emotional than she'd wanted. —Natalia runs production. She has neither the time nor the experience to take care of inventory.

—She offered to help.

—So, why was she crying?

—You'll have to ask her, he said, and turning away, grabbed his binder off the table, slipped past her, and left the room.

Great, she thought, beginning to feel the heat of her own tears behind her eyes.

—What's going on? Jake looked up as she walked back into their office.

—You don't want to know, she said, plonking down on her chair.

—Of course, I do. Tell me.

—Artie made Natalia cry.

—Do you know what they were doing?

—Supposedly working on the inventory report.

—Why Natalia?

—Exactly my question. I specifically told him to go to Hugo if he needed help with anything. Why he involved Natalia is beyond me. Anyway, I told him off. He wasn't happy with me either.

—Why? What did you say?

—That he had no business going to Natalia.

—He'll get over it.

—I guess so. But I should go back out there to make sure she's okay. God, I don't know what to say to her.

—I think showing her your support will do the trick. Tell her you never asked him to work with her, and you honestly don't know why he did.

—That's what I'll do. As long as she doesn't quit. And what about Artie? Will you talk to him?

—Yes, he said.

—Wish me luck. I hope she doesn't think I put him up to it.

—She won't, he said, and after giving her a quick smile, went back to looking at his screen.

But still the biggest blow for us was the fact that Artie had almost no experience with the printing side of the business. He spent three days trying to get a multi-color job printed onto one bottle. He obviously had no idea what he was doing. And on top of it all, he took days off from work, which we felt obligated to pay him for. Ultimately, his lack of interest surprised us, especially regarding sales and the care of the business in general. Most of the time, he would bury himself in his cubicle, ostensibly to work on inventory numbers. We thought he most probably spent a good deal of the time e-mailing and talking to his attorney in Florida.

•   •   •

Hannah closes her file on ARTIE, opens the file with her poems, and notices the time on her computer. It's late. Miri and Ella will be home from school in a few minutes. Then this world of words will close, and her other world will open and belong to them, along with her thoughts, her words, her love, her all. But for this very short moment, her words will still belong to her, to her very own self.

Chapter Twenty-Seven

Hannah can hear her girls' voices before they even make it to the front door. They're arguing. Her body tightens. She'll have to play the referee. A job she hates. Nobody wins. She runs to the door, flings it open, and there in front of her stand her two daughters, backpacks at their feet, socks scrunched down around their ankles, open jackets off their shoulders, hair half in and half out of ponytail holders. They look exhausted.

"We're starving," Miri says, pushing her way through the door past Hannah.

"And thirsty," Ella says, following her sister into the house.

"What about saying hello? Or giving me a little kiss on the cheek. Or a 'how was your day, Mom?' No, my mistake. I realize that'd be too much to ask." Hannah closes the door behind them and follows her girls to the kitchen. Backpacks abandoned to the floor, they're already checking out the pantry to see what there is for them to eat and drink.

"How was school?" she asks. "Anything new?"

"Nah," they say in unison – with their mouths already full – as if they have rehearsed the scene ahead of time.

"Homework?"

"Yeah," Ella says, a frown of frustration crossing her face. "I have a lot."

"Well then, let's get started." Hannah picks up Ella's pink fairies backpack off the floor and pulls out her crumpled workbooks. "What about you, Miri?" she asks.

"I need to call Nana."

"Why?"

"It's for school. About the Holocaust," she says.

Hannah can feel her insides sink as the images, twisting in and out of her mind this morning, come rushing back to her now. "Okay," she says. "Go and fetch the phone. I'll tell you her number and you can dial."

"I think I'm the only one in my class who has a relative . . ." Miri says, coming back to Hannah with the phone.

"Ready?"

Miri nods. Hannah calls out each of the numbers slowly. She watches her daughter's small fingers press the lighted buttons on the phone's dial pad and then turn away from her.

And Hannah brings her attention back to Ella. The workbooks she's taken out of Ella's backpack haven't moved an inch since she placed them on the table. Ella, with her thumb in her mouth, her head barely held up in one hand, looks about as ready for homework as Hannah is to cook dinner.

"Come on, let's see what you need to do." Hannah picks up the workbooks. "Where's your homework assignment?"

"I'm too tired." She half-closes her eyes.

"I know you are. But the sooner we get through this, the sooner you can eat your dinner and go to bed."

"When's Daddy coming home?"

"Late. He's got tons of work to do."

"He's always got tons of work to do," Ella says, her mouth setting in a pout.

Hannah sighs. "Yes, and like you, he needs to get it done," and skimming through the paperwork, her eyes blur as she looks more closely at the different pages. "How about you take a quick nap first?"

"No." Ella shakes her head so vehemently, more of her blonde hair loosens from the ponytail holders. "How 'bout a cookie first?"

Hannah laughs. "Will it keep you awake long enough to tackle your homework?"

"Uh-huh," she says, nodding her head, a coy smile now peeping through the strands of loosened hair masking her pouty face.

"Okay." Hannah shrugs her shoulders. There are times when giving in is the easiest thing to do; fighting a tired child never gets her anywhere.

Ella is off her chair in a flash, as if afraid her mother might change her mind before she even makes it to the pantry. Meanwhile, Miri is listening intently to her grandmother on the phone. Now and then, she nods or shakes her head, says yes or mutters no. Otherwise, Hannah can't figure out which of the stories her mother is telling her daughter; or what her daughter's reaction will be to what she's hearing.

"I'm giving the dogs their *bikkis* too, okay?" Ella shouts out from the kitchen.

"Sure," Hannah calls back. And the dogs, enlivened by hearing the word *bikki*, codename for treat, scurry into the kitchen, their tails swishing, their tongues salivating in expectation.

"Come on, Ella," Hannah says. "Let's not make more of a production of this than is necessary."

What a sight, Hannah thinks, as she watches her daughter saunter back to the table, a chocolate chip cookie clutched in each hand, and the dogs at her heels. Sighing in exasperation, she plonks herself down on her chair. The dogs settle themselves below her on the floor, happily chomping away at their treats. Hannah opens the math booklet and looks for the right page. Hopefully, Ella's ready to tackle her homework now.

With the phone still in her ear, Miri is coming toward Hannah. She says goodbye to her grandmother and hands the phone back to Hannah.

"Did you get all your questions answered?" she asks.

"Yeah, more or less," Miri says, walking away.

"Mom?" Hannah says into the phone, though unsure she hasn't already hung up.

"I tried, but it's difficult," her mother says. "She's still very young. I'm just not sure what I can tell her. I mean, what she will understand . . ."

"Understand . . .? Who the hell understands any of it, anyway?"

"*Ach*! What is age appropriate, then? I don't want to scare the living daylights out of her either."

"So, what story did you tell her?"

"I told Miri about an extremely fastidious man, a father– a neat freak is how I explained it to her – who told his wife that they should leave their apartment perfectly tidy and clean. Try to think of it, he'd said to her, as if we were going away on a vacation and will be returning home again in two or three weeks. So, she made believe. And deep inside his heart, he secretly harbored that same tiny glimmer of hope and make-belief; surely, they would be back home again one day. Together, they tidied, they cleaned. And afterward, he brought down their suitcases from the top of the wardrobes and the bottom of the cupboards, where they'd been stored, and they started packing. First their clothes. One suitcase for him, another for her. Then came their shoes. When they'd filled the suitcase with as many pairs as would fit, he locked the latches, and as he turned the case up on its side, the shoes slid and clonked as they rushed down to the bottom. He put his hand through the leather-padded handle to lift it. He couldn't. The suitcase was unbearably heavy. He had to lay it back down and open it up. Shoe trees, his wife said. We need to pull all the shoe trees out of the shoes and leave them here."

"Did you explain to Miri what shoe trees are used for?" Hannah asks, as she tries to remember if she's heard this story before.

"Naturally. I explained what they looked like, what they were made of, and what exactly they were used for. Her only question, afterwards, was why we called them shoe trees."

"That's my super logical girl for you. So, what did you say?"

"Nothing. I had no answer for her. Absolutely none. But I must say, the thought of using shoe trees nowadays is such a strange concept, don't you think?"

"We're in a disposable society," Hannah says, watching Ella struggle with her homework. The bits of rubber from her over-used eraser, like leftover sprinkles of soot, dot the table and cover her math and spelling workbooks. Guttural sounds of frustration sneak out between the exaggerated loud sighs that escape through her pouting lips.

"Anyway," her mother continues, consumed now with the re-telling of her story. "They took the shoe trees out of the shoes and put them into a separate suitcase, which, of course, they had planned to leave behind, stored away in a closet. Then, deciding against using a separate suitcase for their shoes, they wrapped each pair up in newspaper and slipped them into the spaces between their neatly folded clothes . . ."

"And Miri listened to all of this?" Hannah moves her chair closer to Ella, rubs her back, kisses her head, and mouths to her, "I'll help you in a minute, okay?"

Ella squirms in her chair and nods.

"Yes, and why not?" her mother says with a slight hint of indignance.

"It's a little long winded is all. But go on."

"You think it's too much?"

"No, no. Please, go on."

Ella slides off her chair and comes to sit on Hannah's lap. She dangles her legs wide over Hannah's and thrusts her head back against Hannah's chest. Hannah rests her free hand on Ella's belly.

"Next thing they did was gather up all their photo albums," her mother charges on. "And the loose pictures – such a jumble of them, stored in no special order, inside a cabinet, at the bottom of their bookshelves in the living room. And from the walls, they unhooked their favorite framed photographs and poems; all the ones they'd written in rhyme for each other's birthdays, anniversaries, and special occasions. With care, they freed the mementos from their glass enclosures, layered them between sheets of wax paper, and put them down into the next suitcase. Impossible to leave any of these behind, they'd agreed. These, the hard copies of their memories, the chronicles of a time in their lives, when days were filled with happiness, optimism, and wellbeing; their imaginations then, too innocent, too trusting, too settled in, to foretell, and to know all the horrors they would have to witness, and escape from, in their future.

"After they had lined up the packed suitcases by the front door, they went to bed, for the last time, in their apartment. The next morning, they made their beds, checked to make sure the rest of their apartment was as it should be and left for the station, their suitcases piled in the cab behind them. The train brought them from Berlin to Bremerhaven. From Bremerhaven, they sailed to the port of Southampton, and from there they traveled by rail to London. When they arrived at their destination, dog-tired, but relieved beyond any measure to be safely out of Nazi Germany, they unpacked their suitcases. He unpacked his suits; she, her dresses. They figured they didn't need to unpack the last suitcase with all their photos. Except, she said to him, there was one photo of the whole family she adored and wanted to put on the nightstand by her bed.

"She clicked open the suitcase. And shrieked. To her horror, all she saw when she pushed back the lid was a jumble of old shoe trees. They had left every single one of their beautiful photos, poems, and memorabilia behind, in their Berlin apartment."

"Oh, my God!" Hannah says, sudden nausea sweeping through her. I can't imagine, she thinks, how it would feel to lose . . . *everything*. Trying to change her position in her chair, she becomes conscious of Ella's stillness and her sprawled body's weight. She's fallen fast asleep, her thumb planted inside her mouth, her cheeks going in and out as she sucks, her index finger curled and stroking the bridge of her freckled nose. "How unbelievable, how truly awful," she says into the phone and bends to kiss the top of Ella's head.

"Yes, but in the scheme of things . . ."

"Tell me," Hannah interrupts, "How did Miri react? What did she say?"

"Nothing too much. Only asked why they couldn't have gone back for their forgotten suitcase."

"Hmm . . . Did you explain how it would've been impossible?"

"As best I could. I told her that, at that time in Germany, the Nazis forced Jews from their homes. They could've never gone back, even if they hadn't left Berlin yet; it was forbidden. But then I explained to her how those who could leave, even the way they did, were, in fact, the lucky ones."

"Did you tell her why?"

"I only said that, like now, some people had the wherewithal to go away, while others didn't."

"She accepted your explanation?"

"I think so."

"She didn't ask about the fate of those forced to stay?"

"No. She just said she had to begin her homework. That's when she passed over the phone to you."

"Well, I'll find out what she thinks when I read her report. She's been reading *Anne Frank*. By the way, where did this story come from?"

"My aunt and uncle."

"And this is an actual story, not a made-up one?" The second the words pass through her lips, Hannah wishes she could swallow them back.

"Of course it is. What do you think? That I can make up such stories?" Her mother's voice rises, no small hint of exasperation there.

"I'm sorry. The story . . . it's so incredibly sad."

"Yes, it is. But you must remember that they *were,* in fact, the lucky ones, as were my parents and me."

"I know. Listen, I hate to do this, but I've got to go. Poor Ella's out cold on my lap. She was going crazy with her homework and needs my help badly."

"I understand."

"Thanks for telling Miri your story."

"An ironic one, for sure. But I enjoyed telling it, or rather, the opportunity to tell it. Unfortunately, there are many more of those stories."

"I'll call you tomorrow, okay?"

"Sure. I hope the kids appreciate what a wonderful mom you are."

"Don't know about that." Hannah laughs and tickles Ella awake. "Until tomorrow then."

She hangs up the phone. Ella's awake and whimpering. Miri's up in her room.

"How about a bath?" she says to Ella. "You'll feel so much better afterward. It'll give you back all the energy you'll need to tackle your homework. Come, let's go."

Ella slides off Hannah's lap as if in slow motion, her thumb still gripped inside her mouth. Hand in hand, they climb the stairs.

As Hannah starts the bath, Miri comes into the bathroom and taps her on the shoulder.

"Mom," she says, her voice loud over the running water. "You know the story Nana told me?"

"Yes, she told it to me too."

"I have a question . . ."

Oh-oh, here it comes, Hannah thinks.

"Could it happen to you?" Miri asks.

"What do you mean?" Hannah hedges, expecting the worst.

"Well, could you make that kind of mistake?"

"Mistake?"

"Yes, like picking up the wrong suitcase."

"Well, I suppose if I were in a terrible hurry and nervous about the new place I was going to, I might make the same mistake. Why?"

"No reason. Just thinking."

"Thinking?"

"It's nothing."

"Will you need my help writing your report?"

"I'm okay," she says and goes back to her room.

Hannah turns off the faucets, checks that the temperature is exactly right, and calls for Ella.

"She's conked out on her bed," Miri yells from her room.

"Oh, boy!" Hannah mutters.

There, still fully dressed, legs and arms spread wide, her sweet child is lying on top of her bed, her soft, pink belly peeking out from where her too tight Cookie Monster tee-shirt has ridden up, her blonde hair, now completely loosened from their ponytail holders, feathering her tear-stained face.

To wake her or not? She complained she had too much homework. Well, it will have to wait until tomorrow, Hannah decides, as she covers her child, kisses her cheek, turns off her light, and tiptoes out of the room.

She pokes her head around Miri's open door. She's at her desk. Concentrating. With one leg curled beneath her bottom, the other swinging back and forth, she is busy writing in her notebook.

"I'm going down to start the mac 'n' cheese," Hannah says. "Looks like it'll just be you and me for dinner tonight."

"Why? Where's Dad?" Miri glances up at Hannah for a moment.

"Remember? He's at work. He'll be home late," she says. "You'll let me know, won't you, if you need my help with that story Nana told you?"

"Sure."

And barely acknowledging Hannah's presence at her door, Miri concentrates on her homework – the Holocaust Project.

Chapter Twenty-Eight

After she and Miri have finished dinner and cleared the kitchen, Hannah returns to her study, her little room off the kitchen. She turns on her computer. But almost instantly, feels a heavy yawn push up from some place deep inside her, forcing her mouth to open wide and her eyes to narrow and tear as her screen saver, a new one – the latest photo of the four of them taken a couple of weeks ago outside the Museum of Natural History – appears on the monitor in front of her. She didn't realize how tired she was. How much effort, how much concentration will it take for her to think up which keys to press on her keyboard to make the right words appear on her screen? Especially now, at the end of her day. She opens the file she has last been working on. There are her four poems. She sent them off to a contest but hasn't heard back yet. She sighs. Up to now, she hasn't done all that well with them. Depressing to think about. She looks at the screen. Fiddles with a word here, a phrase there. But realizes her mind isn't on her poetry; it's on Miri. There's something odd about her daughter's silent reaction to her mother's story. Why won't she talk to Hannah? Tell her what she's thinking? And then, she wonders if there's more to this story than her mother told? Knowing her mother, Hannah figures there most probably is.

She's also curious to know what they've been teaching Miri at school. For most of the kids in her class, if not for all, the Holocaust is only another ancient history lesson: An important one. And one Hannah hopes they will learn and never forget. For Miri, though, it's different. Different because she knows she has family who lived through those years and escaped the worst just in time. At all their family gatherings, she's listened to the stories her grandmothers have repeatedly told of their bucolic childhoods in Germany before Hitler's rise to power. And then how those days suddenly ended, as if an axe had come down and chopped them off, discarding every moment of their life, as they'd known it. Yes, they must have influenced her.

Hannah wishes she knew how to coax Miri's thoughts and worries out of her. She's quite different from Ella. More secretive. Or maybe she's learned how to hold the cards close to her chest. Ella, on the other hand, wastes no time letting Hannah know exactly what she's thinking, or how she's feeling, at any given moment.

She hears the front door open, Jake's singsong, "Honey, I'm home." Then his footsteps on the stairs. He's going up to kiss Miri and Ella goodnight. She saves her file for the couple of words she's changed and turns off her computer. Why does her writing always feel as though she's keeping a secret, or is she, like Miri – or Miri like her – simply holding her hand close to her chest?

She comes back into the kitchen at the same moment as Jake does. Here's the other reason she can't concentrate on her writing, she reminds herself, the business is sucking the energy out of her. There's nothing she can do about it. She needs to work, even if it weren't at their own company. And the thing is, she has more flexibility working for herself and Jake than she would, working for anyone else. But when will she ever be free? Free to discover who she really is. And what she can accomplish for herself in her life. Why does this always have to be so complicated?

"Hungry?" she asks him as he saunters into the kitchen, dressed in his sweats and slippers, his evening uniform for TV watching. "There's leftover mac 'n' cheese I can heat up."

"No, I'm good, thanks. Hugo ran to the supermarket and got us roast beef sandwiches."

"Then you've eaten enough?"

"Yes. And tomorrow's a big day. We expect the freight company to deliver all Artie's multi-color pad printers. I'm over the moon excited, even at the thought of having to reorganize the factory all over again. But I must say, right now, I'm beyond dead beat."

"I don't doubt it. I wonder if there's a good movie to watch on TV."

"I'll see what I can find."

"By the way," Hannah says, as she rinses off the dishes in the sink and loads them into the dishwasher. "Was Ella still fast asleep when you were up there?"

"Yup, out cold. And Miri's busy, busy. What's she working on so intently?"

"Isn't she ready for bed yet? It's late."

"She's in her pajamas, if that's what you mean by ready for bed."

"No, not exactly. She needs to be *in* bed."

"In that case, I'm not sure she's altogether ready."

"Shit," she says between closed lips.

"What's the matter?"

"To be honest, I'm a little worried. I know she's trying to make sense of my mother's story . . ."

"Now that's almost always an impossible feat . . ."

"Ha! Ha! You're too funny."

"What story has your mother told her?"

"Well, they're doing a lesson on the Holocaust – not exactly sure which aspect of it – but anyway, her homework assignment is to write an essay on a topic that relates to what she's learning. So, she called my mother, who gave her an earful and told her the story about her aunt and uncle who'd grabbed the wrong suitcase as they'd left their apartment in Berlin – the one packed with shoe trees instead of the one with all their photos and memorabilia."

"*Oy*," he says.

"*Oy* is right."

"And what was her reaction? Did she understand it?"

"That's the thing. I'm not sure. The only question she asked my mother was why they couldn't have gone back to their apartment for the right suitcase; to which, my mother said, it was too late. They were not allowed back, and, in any case, by the time they realized their mistake, they were already out of the country."

She closes the dishwasher, sets it in motion.

"Then she asked if it could happen to me," she says, looking up at Jake.

"And you said?"

"If I were in a state, nervous and terrified, the way they were, it could definitely happen to me."

Jake smiles. He pulls her into him. She knows what he's thinking; it would take a lot less to put her in that state.

"What are you grinning about?" she says, pulling away from him and tapping his chest with her index finger. "In all seriousness, though, how do I explain any of this to Miri? How do I tell her that even amid the worst of it, they didn't, couldn't, understand what was happening to them?"

"I don't have an answer for you. And to be honest, my mind is in such a complete state of mush right now, I don't think I'm good for anything but my chair and the TV. Shall we?"

"Go ahead. I'll be in, in a minute."

Jake kisses the top of her head, then turns from her. "But tell me," he says, turning back around, as though the conversation they were having earlier has just sunk into his muddled brain. "Why are they teaching this to eleven-year-olds? Isn't she too young?"

But he doesn't wait for her answer, and she isn't sure she knows what it would be, anyway. What she knows for sure is that he's reclaimed his easy chair in the family room, lifted his slippered feet to the hassock, turned on the TV, and, depending on his level of concentration or impatience – obvious to her by how long he'll stay with one channel before moving onto the next – is looking for a show interesting enough to keep watching.

"Well, if they're studying the Holocaust in school, what are we to do, ban her from the class?" she says, once in the family room and settled under her fluffy blanket on her usual spot on the couch with her legs crossed Indian style beneath her. "Maybe I should find out exactly which aspect of it they're learning about. Although, who knows what difference it'd make?"

"Yes, you could," he says absent-mindedly.

Still clicking through the channels, he stops at CNN, but once the commercials come on, he switches to Shark Tank. Hannah enjoys watching the faces of the people who stand before the Sharks, their pitch perfectly well-rehearsed, obviously upbeat and filled with optimism. Hannah finds herself looking for signs of disappointment, hurt, or insult when their ideas, products, or company valuations are knocked down or, worse yet, derided. Mostly though, as each Shark ends any interest in their project with the dreaded words "I'm out," the contestants will smile, then thank each one for their time and generosity. Hannah can't imagine she'd be able to keep smiling through what she would view as a terrible letdown or more precisely, abject failure. But each time the contestants walk away with nothing, she reminds herself that these people have not lost, but have won – won by being brave, by putting themselves out there, by auditioning to be on the show in the first place, and ultimately, by gaining the credence and the growth through this exposure. How can she practice this bravery, emulate this way of life for herself?

"I'm going up to check on the kids," she says and stands.

"Will you be back down to watch TV with me?"

"Probably not. I'm ready for bed. I'll read for a bit. I must say, having to relive all this Artie crap has me exhausted, both mentally and physically."

"I know what you mean. I'll be up in a bit. It's been a long day."

"I really hope this whole thing won't be too much for us."

"Don't worry. We'll be fine. I promise you."

Hannah folds up the blanket – sitting for more than five or ten minutes always chills her, no matter the temperature in the house – and lays it over the back of the couch.

Upstairs, she peeks into Ella's room. Just a glimpse of her sleeping child – her comforter, thrown off her too warm body, piled at the foot of her bed – brings Hannah tiptoeing all the way into the room. With her legs and arms spread out, she's still dressed in her pink Dora tee shirt and blue jeans. Hannah bends down to kiss her daughter's cheek which, propelled by an inner force, still puffs in and out as she continues to suck away on her thumb. Watching her sleeping child like this makes whatever is inside her chest clench into a tight knot, makes her want to pick Ella up and hug her so, so hard. Naturally, she won't do it. Letting children sleep is always the motto she stands by. She straightens the comforter, covers her up again, and waits for a minute or two to make sure Ella will settle back down and stay asleep, even after she's stirred a bit. Then Hannah turns off the light and tiptoes back out of the room, leaving the door slightly ajar.

Miri's still at her desk. Hannah watches her from the doorway. Such an intense little girl. A deep thinker for her eleven years. Was Hannah the same at that age? Probably still is, at this age. There is no, *probably,* about it. Most definitely she is, for better or for worse.

"You know, it's late. I think you should go to bed now."

"I'm almost done with my report for school."

"There's always tomorrow."

"Yes, but . . ."

"I'm sorry, no more *buts*. Tomorrow is another day, and besides, if you don't get to sleep soon, you'll never wake up in time for school in the morning."

"Okay," she says, closing her notebook and stacking it with her other books into a neat pile on her desk. Curious to know what Miri has made of her mother's story, Hannah's tempted to sneak a peek while she waits for Miri to come back from the bathroom. "Don't forget to brush your teeth," she calls out. Moving away from Miri's desk and her own temptation, she goes to sit on the bed instead.

"Goodnight, my love," Hannah says as Miri crawls under the covers. Hannah brings them up to Miri's chin and kisses both her cheeks. "I'll help you with it tomorrow, I promise."

"But I told you, I don't need help."

"Well then, what about we only discuss Nana's story? How about that?"

"Sure," Miri says, and she closes her eyes.

"Sweet dreams."

Hannah turns off the light as she leaves the room, making sure the door stays ajar.

Chapter Twenty-Nine

During the whole time Artie worked for us, he would never negotiate an employment agreement. Instead, he insisted we extend him certain guarantees of employment, knowing full well, we were in no position to offer him any. On July 26th, he came into our office at around eight in the morning, which was extremely unusual for him. He rarely came in before 9:30 or 10:00. It was also on one of his two unscheduled weekly workdays. According to one of our employees, who had come in early that day, he left the office after about twenty minutes, carrying a carton filled with papers. Obviously, he didn't want to be seen by us. We later discovered Artie had stolen proprietary customer information, which he admitted to having. The next morning, we received an email, a fax, and the dreaded letter via FedEx from Artie's new attorney. In the first paragraph, the letter said we were not to speak with either Artie or Lisa. In the second paragraph, it also said that Artie would be back to work the following morning. Then came the list of his twenty-four complaints. After contacting our employment lawyer, we responded to Artie's new attorney to say that Artie was no longer welcome at our company.

Hannah arranges with Sophia to meet Miri and Ella this afternoon at the bottom of their street, where the school bus drops them off. At breakfast, she preps her girls. She tells them she's not sure their mom and dad will be home in time for dinner. Secretly, she wishes they won't be. Wishes they'll have the best reason in the world not to be home early but to celebrate, instead, over a fancy dinner in the city;

she doesn't care where they'd go. If only she could have a glass or two of wine, but that part of the celebration will have to wait until after the baby is born.

They catch the 9:50 morning train into Manhattan to meet Louis at his office – immediately across the street from Grand Central on Vanderbilt Avenue – to go over their notes to make sure they have all their important details in line, before taking the elevator up the three flights, for their meeting at the mediator's office.

There, the only furniture in the conference room is an enormous, polished wood table with six chairs on either side, positioned to face each other, and one at each end. The mediator is already sitting in place at the head of the table and to his right is Artie's lawyer, then Artie, and next to him, Lisa. Across the table from them and to the left of the mediator, sit Louis, Jake, and Hannah, all in a row. Keeping her eyes glued to the mediator and to each of the lawyers as they speak, Hannah dares not even glance directly across the table, too afraid to imagine how Lisa must be feeling.

Since Louis, their lawyer, hand-delivered Hannah's Pre-Mediation Statement and Jake's records (including printed notes and emails) to the mediator the day before yesterday, he said the meeting shouldn't last too long.

As the mediator knocks out each of Artie's lawyer's twenty-four complaints, Hannah scratches them off her imaginary score board. The final determination is that Artie will be awarded $27,000 by Bloom & Co. With the decision reached, Artie pushes his chair back and stands. His lawyer and Lisa get up as well. But as they're about to walk out of the conference room, Artie stops and turns to face Jake. Leaning across the shiny, wood table, he slams his fist into it and then pointing a shaky finger at Jake, he shouts, "You, you fuck..." Before he can finish though, his lawyer is at his side. He puts his arm around Artie's shoulder and guides him out of the conference room; Artie's all too familiar scowl scrunching up his face, the picture of a defeated man. Lisa follows them, but as she gets to the door, she turns around to stare straight at Hannah for a few seconds. Hannah knows there must be a message in her look. Is it blame? Regret? Or sorrow for the loss of a friendship between them that Hannah suspected, from the beginning, could never have furthered into anything more intimate. Hannah doesn't want to know what the message might be, so she lets it go from her thoughts, at least for now.

Louis suggests they go for a drink to celebrate. They walk out of the building, feeling much lighter than they had when they'd walked in. At a bar in Grand Central, Hannah orders a virgin Bloody Mary and both Louis and Jake order beers. They drink to their success. She likes Louis a lot and likes him even more when he tells them his wife is an artist. And when he orders another round of drinks, she decides he must be enjoying their company too. When they're ready to leave, both she and Jake are too exhausted for Hannah's wished-for celebratory dinner. Home sounds so much better.

"And that's that, as the saying goes," she whispers to Jake as they sit side by side on the train on their way home. "It's over."

"Yes," he says. "It's really over."

"On to the next. You didn't hear from OSHA, did you?"

"No. I've been so busy making sure we had all our paperwork straight for today's meeting. I forgot all about them."

"One thing's for sure," Hannah says. "They won't forget about us. Hopefully, Ms. Sandra Brown didn't find too much wrong."

"She'll have found enough to make her time worthwhile. Of that, you can be assured."

"As long as the penalties don't put us in the poorhouse."

"I seriously doubt it," Jake says, and on hearing the conductor call out for tickets, he pulls theirs out of his pocket and holds them up. "Besides," he continues, once the conductor has taken the tickets. "As far as I remember, they offer a monthly payment option."

"That'll help," she says.

"Oh, come on, cheer up," he says and nudges her arm. "Didn't we have a *win-win* today? You know we'll always have challenges. I mean, haven't we had them all along? Nothing comes from nothing."

"Is that your favorite expression these days?"

"But I think it's so true."

Yes, she repeats to herself, nothing comes from nothing and, turning to stare out at the night, at the lit-up streets and windows in the buildings they pass, she wonders why she's feeling this down. She ought to be ecstatic. But now she can't get Artie out of her head. Perhaps his problem has always been expecting everything from nothing, not only with her and Jake, but with his own company as well. He assumed he could depend on other people's efforts to make his world work for him.

She sighs, and as she's about to tell Jake what she's been thinking, she hears her phone ding. She expects the message to be from one of her girls or Sophia. But when she opens the text, she's suddenly conscious of the muscles in her body tightening up, her heart racing like crazy, and her fingers trembling as they work to enlarge the message – the message from Lisa.

This is most probably the last text in the world you'd expect to be getting right now, especially from me. But sitting across from you this afternoon, at that enormously wide table, and knowing how you were purposefully trying your best to avoid eye contact with me made everything feel so much more incredibly hurtful. That's all. I just wanted you to know it.

Hannah closes the text and puts her phone back into her bag.

"Who's that from?" Jake asks.

"No one. It's only an ad," she says, not in the mood to talk about this now. Maybe she'll be able to sort it out for herself – the Lisa thing, the whole enigmatic Lisa thing. Or maybe it's just one of those things best left behind and forgotten. *Buried*, as her mother would say.

The conductor announces Stamford is the next stop. Hannah nudges Jake. They go to stand by the door as the train slows into the station.

In the car, they barely say a word to each other.

The minute they come through the door at home, Sophia excitedly tells Hannah to follow her into the kitchen. Hannah's imagination gets ahead of herself, as usual. "What's wrong?" she says, rubbing her arms up and down, expecting the worst. Except everything in the kitchen is tidy and quiet, and even the dinner dishes are washed and put away.

Sophia turns around and grins at Hannah. "Nothing's wrong," she says and, seeing the puzzled, worried look on Hannah's face, laughs. "Really, nothing's wrong at all. I promise you." She stops at the espresso machine and, with a flourish of her arm, exclaims, "Ta dah!" and points her finger at the countertop. There, between the espresso machine and Hannah's vase of yellow roses, is Miri's homework assignment on the Holocaust. It was Miri's version of the story her grandmother told her. At the top of the page is a gold star and right beneath it, a smiley face. Printed in red ink right next to the smiley face is an extra-large capital A, along with not just one, but *two* big plus signs. "Wow," is all Hannah can say, picking up her daughter's handwritten three-page story, its title now *The Wrong Suitcase*.

"She must've been over the moon," Hannah says, glancing down at the pages.

"You can say that again. She wanted to call you, but I didn't think . . . I mean . . . I knew you were in town on business."

"Yes," Hannah says and automatically adds, "you were right." But as she comes to rethink it, she decides, no, it isn't what she would've wanted. She would have preferred the interruption – preferred to have heard from Miri the second she got home from school, to have heard her excited voice through the phone, and to have been able to tell her, right then and there, how incredibly proud and happy she is for her brilliant, young chronicler.

After Sophia has gone home and Hannah is out of her city clothes and into her sweats, she brings Miri's pages into the den to read them. Jake sits in his chair, and even though his face is hidden behind *The Times*, she can hear him tut-tutting in disgust every other minute or so. Hannah wonders what he's reading about that's making him so annoyed. But right now, she's more curious about the handwritten pages in her lap.

The story, as she reads it, is told in more-or-less the same way Hannah remembers hearing it from her mother. But then, as she comes to the last paragraph, she's stunned. Where did Miri hear this? Surely, she didn't come up with all this on her own.

"Jake," she says. "You have to listen to this."

"Why? What is it?" he says, bringing the paper down to his lap.

"Miri's homework assignment on the Holocaust. Remember it? Well, here is the last paragraph."

Hannah brings Miri's last page forward, looks at her daughter's handwriting, neat and plain on the page, and clears her throat.

"Perhaps," she reads, "it was just as well they accidentally left all their photos and memorabilia behind. The reason I think this is that on especially difficult days in their new life, they would have felt even sadder, coming back to the pages of an old photo album, and remembering the people, the places, their older way of life, and how it was all so quickly and brutally snatched away from them. But since they didn't have those happy, smiling faces in the old photos to look at, perhaps they could – not ever forget – but let themselves be open more freely to their new world, and put away their frightening past, just as they had neatly packed all their old photographs and memorabilia in the suitcase they'd accidentally left behind."

Hannah looks up at Jake. "Well?" she says.

"Your mother must have dictated that to her. I can't imagine she could have thought . . ."

"Doesn't really sound like my mother, either."

"Then you'll have to ask Miri."

"It's no wonder she got the A-plus-plus. But I'll find out more tomorrow. Are you ready for bed yet?"

"Yes, I must say I'm dead beat. It's been one hell of a day. Did I tell you that all we need to do, is pay the freight bill, and Artie's silk screen machines will be all ours as well?"

"You really must be exhausted. This must be the third time today you've told me this."

"Sorry, I don't mean to bore you. But didn't I tell you, from the get-go, that this whole thing would work out for us in the end?"

"You did. You were right."

"What was that?" he says, cupping his hand around one ear while letting his grin go all the way from one to the other.

"You were *right*. You're *always* right," she says, getting up. "And on that note, I'm going up to bed. Goodnight."

Chapter Thirty

Hannah leaves her car in a standing-only spot and runs up the ramp to the platform just as the eastbound train from New York rattles into the station, and grinds to a squeaky halt in front of her. The doors slide open, the people inside pour out and, crowding past her, rush away. Chilly in the gray, late October air, she crosses her arms tightly over her chest and hops from one foot to the other to keep warm. The longer she stands there, the more the familiar flicker of doubt, like a fly's insistent buzz, flits through her mind as she wonders if this was the right train, or even the right day.

But there she is! Her mother. A splash of brightness amongst the boring grays, blacks, and browns of the business suits coming off the train. Hannah walks toward her, keeping her gaze glued to her mother's worried-looking face – to the green eyes, outlined in deep brown, the purple-shadowed lids, the mascaraed lashes – as if Hannah's gaze alone can send her a telepathic message – *Here I am*. Then comes the sudden moment of recognition when the worried frown on her mother's forehead smooths out and her steps become a little surer and faster. And before Hannah knows it, her mother's arms are wrapped around her in a hug, her lips brushing up against her cheek in a kiss.

"How are you feeling?" These, her first words, sound slightly panicked to Hannah. Is she expecting to hear unwelcome news?

"Fine," Hannah says, hearing a slight tick of annoyance or impatience in her own voice, as she takes in her mother's usual cursory glance at her for signs of paleness, tiredness, unhappiness, and now, the added glimpse at her growing bust and belly. Satisfied there's nothing too wrong to detect, other than perhaps looking a little pale, Hannah feels her mother's arm slip through hers as they move away from the bustle of the station platform and walk down the ramp to where Hannah has parked her car on the street.

"Lunch at the usual?" Hannah turns the key in the ignition, then glances over at her mother to make sure she's buckled up. There's always that odd feeling of added responsibility when she's the one driving.

"Lovely," her mother says, and, arranging herself in the passenger seat in Hannah's small car, she folds away the newspaper and sunglasses she's been carrying, and drops them into the oversized brown vinyl tote she holds in her lap.

In the restaurant, they sit by the window. The street outside is as flat and gray as the October sky above it, the passing cars the only dots of color and animation on this patch of citified suburbia.

"So, tell me, what's new?" her mother says, an air of expectancy in her voice as she leans forward, puts her elbows on the table and rests her chin on top of her clasped hands. Hannah feels her body stiffen. The right words suddenly elude her. What is there to tell her mother? Still-life images pop in and out of her mind – kids, husband, dogs, their work, her poetry – and, as if she were flipping through the pages of a glossy magazine, they all blur into a fuzzy, multi-colored, oneness.

"Nothing really," she finally says, shaking her head. "Just the usual. You know, kids, Jake, work. Although, I must say, work is way at the top of our list right now. Other than that, though, life is happily uneventful."

"I must say, I'm amazed. I honestly don't know how you do it all."

"It's not like I do everything by myself. The girls are becoming a little more independent, Miri for sure. Seriously Mom, it's all fine."

"And the pregnancy?"

"Yes, of course, I do get tired much more easily these days. But honestly, I can't complain. It's been easy this far."

"Well, that's great news." And her mother lets out a long sigh, as she leans back in her chair. And Hannah wonders what words of disaster, her mother was expecting to hear from her.

"Anyway, yesterday I went for my monthly checkup. And I'm perfectly on track. The heartbeat's good and strong, the baby's growing."

"Marvelous," she says, perhaps a little too loudly, and claps her hands together.

Hannah leans in toward her mother, resting both arms flat on the table in front of her. "So, there's no need for you to keep fretting like this."

"Just wait until your girls are all grown up. You'll see how hard it is to stop worrying about them." She nods her head, points a finger at Hannah, and adds, "just you wait."

"Talk about waiting. Have you come to a final decision about moving to Basel?" Hannah is trying hard to keep a straight face, to keep from giving away the hopeful happiness and relief, she expects to feel.

"I've pretty much decided not to go."

"I figured as much . . ."

"First of all, the city of Basel doesn't hold a candle to Manhattan."

"Yup, I'm sure that's true."

"And second of all, or rather, I should say, first, there's the uncomfortable thought of uprooting myself again, which keeps nagging at my brain and won't let go . . ."

"Then you've really given up on the idea?" Hannah says, trying to keep her voice solemn, her relief hidden.

"Yes," she says, in a drawn out, hesitant way.

"And Leo? Does he know?"

"Yes, he knows."

"Well?"

"He says he understands. And since he comes to New York quite often, we can continue to see each other, just the way we always have."

"That's good, isn't it?"

The server brings them menus.

"Yes. He's such a decent man." Her voice trails off as she rummages around in her large bag for her reading glasses. "But tell me," she says, looking back up again. "What about you? Everything going well? I guess the kids must be happy . . ."

"Happy? You kidding? Not my two. I'm always besieged with constant complaints about school, friends, and homework. Never a dull moment at my house."

"You know, kids will be kids."

"Always, so I'm told . . . no matter how old," Hannah says, and they both laugh.

"And the business? It's going well?"

"Yes, it's all working out. I can't say we haven't had hiccups along the way, but I'm beginning to see daylight. Poor Jake is up to his eyeballs at work . . ."

"And you too, no?"

"Yes, me too. But, at least, the arrival of the school bus ends my days. His don't. In any case, we have no choice now but to keep going with it."

"I wasn't actually talking about the business."

"Oh, then what were you . . .?"

"What I mean is. . . Don't you have enough to do, besides working in the business? How will you be able to take care of Miri and Ella, as well as yourself, and your newborn baby?"

"Well, Mom, in case you haven't noticed, the trend these days is for women to have babies, even if their circumstances aren't perfect. Somehow, we make it work. Has it really changed all that much since your day? Motherhood has always been a challenge, don't you think?" Hannah looks over at her mother and starts to laugh.

"You're too funny. I think your husband's wacky sense of humor is wearing off on you."

Leaning back again, Hannah stretches out her hands and flattens them over her belly. "Could be. But seriously, Mom, you must stop this. You're making me nuts."

"Well, I was thinking that, perhaps, I'd come and help you out from time to time, now that . . ."

"You know you're always welcome to visit. But you mustn't feel it's an obligation. You have your own life."

"True," her mother says, appearing relieved and happy to acknowledge and accept Hannah's assessment, if not exactly in self-pity, then maybe, a little too readily.

Her mother puts on her glasses and looks down at the menu. "Have you decided what you're going to eat?"

"Farmer's omelet, I think."

"Mm. Sounds delicious. I'll get the same."

After the server has taken their orders, Hannah becomes distracted by a sudden commotion at the front of the restaurant. A group of six young mothers and their babies have just come in. After they've lifted their sleepy little ones out of the carriages and strollers, they've parked by the cashier's desk, they're shown to a large round table in the middle of the room. Highchairs are rushed out and once the babies are settled, the mothers arrange themselves at the table. Hannah can't help feeling an unusual tug of nostalgia for those days when she and her friend, Jan, would walk here with their babies. Jan would push her little boy in his stroller. He was just a little older than Miri's three years. And Hannah would push Ella, who was just a few weeks old and usually fast asleep in her carriage. Jake had attached a narrow bench across the bottom edge of the baby carriage for Miri to sit on in case she got tired and needed to rest. But Miri, stubborn little Miri, always preferred to walk, which was fine with Hannah so long as she promised to keep her small fist wrapped around the base of the carriage's shiny chrome handlebar.

"Reminds me . . ." She smiles at the memories playing inside her head as she continues to watch the mothers, now rattling keyrings and toys at their babies to keep them occupied and quiet.

"You'll be back there again before you know it."

"I suppose," Hannah says. "Time's flying by so quickly, I can hardly believe it."

"Wait till you get to my age. You'll see how it flies, at double-double time."

Hannah steals another look at the young mothers, settled now in their seats at the table, their attention on themselves as they chat and laugh with each other. "I guess I haven't been here in a while," she says. "Seeing those women over there is taking me back." And she turns to face her mother. "Did I ever tell you the story about the most embarrassing thing that ever happened to me?"

Her mother shakes her head. "I don't think so."

"The three of us were out shopping in a children's clothing store. Ella, who was only four or five months old, sat like a happy clam in her stroller. Miri, meanwhile, had wandered away. As she always did. From the moment she could take steps on her own, she'd be off and running. The grand explorer, I used to call her. Anyhow, when she'd disappeared from my side, I left all the clothes I'd picked out for them on the counter and went to look for her. Moments later, a sales lady came up to me, my curly-haired toddler in tow. After she was assured that Miri was mine, she continued to tell me how Miri had climbed up on the low dais where the baby equipment stood on display, found the potty, pulled down her pants, and peed in it."

"Oh my God, how funny," her mother says, laughing.

"Not then, it wasn't."

"So, what did you do?"

"Other than feeling totally mortified and offering to clean up the potty? Nothing. The sales lady told me not to worry; she'd already taken care of it. I remember we both laughed and then told each other one or two more embarrassing kid stories."

"At least Miri had the right idea," her mother says and takes a drink of water. "Too bad she picked the wrong place."

"After that day, I never saw another potty on display there. Apparently, Miri wasn't the only kid to have made good use of it."

"Oh, my God! How hilarious."

"Yes, especially since at home she always had to be bribed to sit on the toilet, never mind to pee or to poop."

Their omelets arrive.

"I must say I'm ravenous," Hannah says, picking up her knife and fork.

"I'm always ravenous these days," her mother says. "Which is my problem."

"You don't have to worry."

"Ha! That's what you think. If I only look at food, it seems to magically appear on my hips."

They laugh for a moment and then eat their lunch in silence. Hannah, still preoccupied with those old days, searches for the strands of memory which will take her back to Miri and Ella's baby years. What kind of mother had she been to them? What kind will she be to this new baby? Different. Of that, she is quite sure. Circumstances, as well as she, herself, have changed.

She glances up at her mother for a moment, and her mother, feeling Hannah's sudden scrutiny, looks back up and smiles. She is sure her mother never thinks, let alone worries about the impact she might've had on Hannah, as a kid. Was this kind of worrying a new-fangled concept? she wonders. The result of a life that is too easily lived? Survival taken for granted?

"Did you have enough to eat?" her mother asks, as Hannah puts her knife and fork together on her empty plate.

"Yes, thank you," Hannah says.

Is this what mothers are wired to worry about most of all? That they have given their children enough food to eat? In too many places around the world, she knows those worries are all too real, leaving no room in a mother's brain for any other thoughts, existential or otherwise. Survival, purely just a matter of hard work and luck, always takes precedence. Was that in the mind of the young woman who wrapped up her naked newborn in newspaper and abandoned it in a Seagram's liquor box in a corner of Grand Central Station?

The server comes to their table to clear the dishes.

"I think I'd like a coffee," her mother says to the server. "What about you?" she asks Hannah.

"Yes, I'll have one too."

"By the way," her mother says. "Whatever happened with the guy whose company you took over?"

Hannah smiles. The server is back with their coffees. Then glad for the excuse not to have to answer her mother right away, she lifts her cup and takes a few short sips of her too-hot black coffee. "Thank goodness, the worst of it is over," she finally says. "The mediation went well. We came out okay."

But the picture in her mind of Artie, his lawyer, and then Lisa, the last one to go through the door as they were leaving the mediator's conference room, is one that's stubbornly staying with her. It was genuine sorrow, after all, Hannah had come to believe she'd seen in Lisa's face, as she'd turned back – sorrow that she and Hannah would never have the friendship Lisa was sure they'd be able to rekindle, once they'd settled all the business issues.

"It must be quite a relief," her mother says, and now Hannah can't help wondering if perhaps she's being too harsh on her mother. She knows she worries about her well-being because she's her mother and, naturally, is concerned.

After lunch, they stroll up and down the street, looking in at the dress shop windows. Hannah can't think about new clothes. It'll be months before she's able to even look at what she has in her closet, never mind what she'll be able to fit into. She sighs, flattens her hand against her growing belly, and suddenly conscious of the passing time, looks down at her watch.

"Do we need to go?" her mother says.

"I don't want to be late."

"We're always so short of time, aren't we?"

Yes, always. Ever since Hannah can remember.

•   •   •

"Have you thought of names?" her mother says, once they are back in the car and on their way to picking up Miri and Ella from school. The fall leaves swirl about in the steely air and brush up against the windshield, as if giant multi-colored snowflakes.

"Ella has taken on that job. Every day she comes home from school with a new name. She's so cute, but unbelievably fickle. What she loved yesterday, she'll hate tomorrow."

"It's great she's so involved. What about Miri?"

"A different story. She's a little more reserved about the whole thing. She has questions."

"Questions?"

"Yes, like what happens if no one hears the baby cry in the middle of the night, or if she gets a cold and her nose is so stuffed up, she can't breathe, or if the baby will learn to love her unconditionally, or if she, herself, will love the baby automatically because she is her sister? Stuff like that. I think she's wondering, maybe also worrying, how her life will forever change."

"Can you blame her?"

"No, not really," Hannah says, trying not to read into her mother's words. "She's graduated from being my baby grand explorer to my wisest philosopher and now to my most brilliant chronicler."

"Oh my God, yes. I thought the way she had written *The Lost Suitcase* story was amazing and so clever. I couldn't believe it."

The rain starts as Hannah pulls into the school parking lot. The kids haven't been dismissed yet. A sigh of relief. They get out of the car and run to the door just as the first of the children, scruffy and full of energy, come rushing out.

Here come her two. Eyes bright, cheeks red. Smiles. Kisses. Hugs.

"Can we go to the mall?" Miri and Ella pipe up at the same time as they settle into the back seat of the car.

"By all means," Hannah's mother says, and out of the corner of her eye, she sees her mother turn to her for confirmation. "Are you looking for anything in particular?" she asks, twisting slightly in her seat.

Hannah can't help smiling. It's her mother's standard question. In the rearview mirror, she catches the look Miri and Ella give to each other, then sees their shoulders rise in a shrug.

"Not really," Ella says. "But anything you want to buy us would be fine."

"Ella!" Hannah says in unison with Miri. "How could you?"

"It's okay," her mother says, laughing. "I can buy you each a little something, but I'm afraid that's about it. Nana is rather broke these days."

Hannah wonders if her mother took her financial situation into consideration when she decided not to go and live in Basel. How will she manage? Will Leo help her out anyway? And then, will she accept his help if he does? Or is she too proud? Hannah will have to ask her about it. But not today. She'll have to remember to have that conversation with her, the next time they meet for lunch.

"Nana," Ella pipes up from the back seat, "do you know we're going to have a little baby sister in a few weeks?"

"Yes, I know," her mother says, and pressing her hand to her neck, as if it pains her, she turns around as far as she can, to face Ella, sitting directly behind her. "But it'll be a few months, not a few weeks. It's now October and the baby won't be born until late January or early February."

"Whatever," Ella says with a shrug.

"It'll be a new year, Ella," Miri says. "We'll have a new baby for a new year."

"Wow, Miri, you're a poet and didn't know it," Hannah says.

They all laugh.

"So, tell me," her mother says, facing forward again. "How did you enjoy camp in the end?"

A groan in stereo emanates from the back seat.

"That good, huh?"

"Actually," Miri says, "it turned out to be okay."

"Speak for yourself."

Ella's grown-up words catch Hannah off guard. She's compelled to turn around to have a look at her daughters. Ella is facing her older sister, an expression of such loathing on her face, anyone might think poor Miri has committed the worst possible treason against her.

"You didn't have a good time at all?" her mother says.

"Oh, come on, Ella." Miri pokes her sister's arm with her finger. "We had fun."

"Only a tiny bit," Ella concedes with a punch back to Miri.

"Ow!" Miri rubs her arm. "Why'd you do that?"

"Come on, girls. Let's not fight," her mother says.

Hannah glances back again at her two daughters in the rearview mirror. Ella now stares out of the window, pouting, her lower lip protruding from her sweet, round baby face.

"It really wasn't that bad," Miri says, sounding like the adult, trying to reassure Hannah, although Hannah isn't exactly sure who needs the reassurance more.

"Speak for yourself," Ella says again, but more to the scenery outside her window than to her sister.

Hannah's mother tries to cheer up Ella. Hannah knows it's a useless proposition. But she can't understand what's suddenly got under Ella's skin. Has she heard from a kid at camp?

"What about school?" her mother is asking now, as Hannah drives into the mall parking lot and luckily finds a spot right away.

"Ugh!" they say in unison.

"Okay, guys," Hannah says, turning off the engine. "We're here. Do you know what stores you want to go to?"

"Ylang-Ylang," they both shout.

"I never thought it was going to be this easy," Hannah says to her mother as they get out of the car.

"What kind of store . . .?"

"Don't worry. They sell all kinds of costume jewelry. Quite beautiful. And not expensive."

The mall's crowded with fall-time shoppers. Mothers, anxious expressions on their faces, herd their sulking children from shop to shop. Groups of teenagers amble by, as though on the lookout for something to do. If Hannah shows any expression on her face, she hopes it's neither angst nor pleasure, only patience. In the store, she hangs back while her mother and her children discuss the virtue of a particular necklace, bracelet, or ring. It always amazes her how well they get on with each other. And how seriously her mother takes them, as well as their individual whims and fancies.

The three of them move back and forth alongside the glass display cases. Such seriousness. She loves the look of intensity on her children's faces. They take their time first picking this, or deciding on that, until finally, they find the absolute right one. Everyone smiles, happy with their choices. Even Ella.

Afterward, they go up to the food court, where Hannah buys burgers and fries for Miri and Ella, a special treat, and coffee for herself and her mother.

·   ·   ·

By the time they bring her mother back to the station, the sun has gone down. Hannah parks the car. They walk up the ramp and stand with her mother on the drafty westbound platform.

Hannah watches Miri and Ella hug their grandmother, their fingers splayed across her back with their new, sparkly, colored crystal rings throwing off spears of brilliance, as they reflect the station's bright lights.

"I had a wonderful day." Her mother turns to face Hannah as the train roars into the station. "I'm glad I came. We should do this more often."

"Yes, we should." Hannah leans over to kiss her cheek.

Her mother then turns away from her, steps onto the train, and finds a seat by the window. She smiles and waves at them. Miri and Ella blow kisses. Hannah waves and smiles back.

As the train pulls out of the station and she grabs each girl by the hand to make their way back to the car, Hannah's thoughts inadvertently slide sideways to her mother's decision not to move away. How odd that she hasn't thought to say, true or not, that Hannah and her children are the primary reasons she's decided not to leave. How will her mother continue to cope without a live-in man by her side? But then, just before she has the chance to fully plan her next thought, her unborn child flutters inside her belly. Is she weighing in on Hannah's conversation with herself? She stops walking, pulls her two girls into her.

"Feel," she says, planting each one's hand on her abdomen. "Can you feel your sister move around inside me, like one of those fish swimming around in our pond?"

"Yeah," they say together and giggle, as if they're being tickled.

"Did you guys have enough to eat?" Hannah asks her girls as they continue their walk back to the car.

"Yes," they both say.

Satisfied, she takes up where she left off in the conversation she's been having with herself. Who, she wonders – as she unlocks the car doors and watches her girls slide into the back seat, while on the verge of fighting over whose sparkly ring glitters the most – will be the loser if her mother doesn't try to come out and visit them more often? It's a toss-up. Yes, just like a toss of the dice, she thinks, and feels a giggle bubbling up inside her, as she realizes how silly she is but, also, how incredibly lucky.

Acknowledgements

I am honored to be a part of Black Rose Writing's family of authors. Thank you, Reagan Rothe, for accepting this, my second novel, and to David King, who has designed such a fabulous cover.

To my editor, Pamela Taylor, who has proofed my manuscripts. I am grateful.

To that time in my life when those fluffy dreams of becoming a writer were encouraged by those who not only taught but also inspired in me that special drive to keep writing. Thank you to Jeff Skinner, Dick Allen, Joan Silber, Myra Goldberg, and Suzanne Hoover.

A special thank you to my readers—Meryl Ain, Ellie Aronowitz, Peter Herz, Marie Hughes, Jules Litwin, Carla Nelson, Cindy Pinkus, Nikki Rivas, Evelyn Wajcer, Michael Witkes—I so appreciate your helpful thoughts, comments, and reviews.

But most of all, I am incredibly grateful for my family—my husband Peter, my daughters and sons-in-law, Jordie and Rory Freedman, Nikki and Paco Rivas, and their children, Sammy, Devin, Lucy, Harley, and Maeve—who have never lost faith in me and my endeavors, and whose love I cherish more than any of my words could tell.

To all of you who have read and reviewed my debut novel, *Circumference of Silence*, your words of encouragement have touched me beyond my wildest dreams. I can only keep saying: thank you, thank you, thank you!

And finally, I believe that the very heart of my writing is, in some way, owed to those generations of my family who came before me.

Jacquie Herz

About the Author

Jacquie Herz, born in London to immigrant parents who had escaped the Holocaust, cannot remember a time in her life, even as a young child, when writing was not a major part of it. A member of the Women's Fiction Writers Association, her award-winning first novel, *Circumference of Silence*, was published in 2021. Retired from her duties as co-founder and president of a manufacturing company in Stamford, Connecticut, Jacquie and her husband, Peter, now live on the ocean in Lauderdale-by-the-Sea, Florida.

Note from Jacquie Herz

Word-of-mouth is crucial for any author to succeed. If you enjoyed *Hannah Bloom: Dream Juggler*, please leave a review online—anywhere you are able. Even if it's just a sentence or two. It would make all the difference and would be very much appreciated.

Thanks!
Jacquie Herz

We hope you enjoyed reading this title from:

www.blackrosewriting.com

Subscribe to our mailing list – *The Rosevine* – and receive **FREE** books, daily
deals, and stay current with news about upcoming
releases and our hottest authors.
Scan the QR code below to sign up.

Already a subscriber? Please accept a sincere thank you for being a fan of
Black Rose Writing authors.

View other Black Rose Writing titles at
www.blackrosewriting.com/books and use promo code
PRINT to receive a **20% discount** when purchasing.

9 781685 136802